Pa

Brooklyn Ver Beek

With Love,

Part One

A world broken; destroyed from riots, virus, and simple greed. That was my childhood. But of course, through my early years, I did not notice it yet, although it was definitely there.

Instead, I turned to my family as a light in the darkness. My siblings, Finn and Sammy, were my whole world. We did everything together; got up the same time every morning, played together hours on end, and all dreamed big. Our family lived with the impoverished, in a small metal trailer centered in a luscious field of tall grass and a few trees to climb on.

There was our cozy living room; old beaten yellow and green furniture, an old CD player with our stacks of music passed down through our generations. Sammy and I spent our time listening to all three-hundred-eighty-five songs while coloring pictures on scrap paper or the backs of old tax forms with crayons.

Our adjoined dining room, which was literally a table with bar stools and a bowl that sometimes contained apples or a couple oranges. The kitchen, where Mother taught me to bake homemade bread and occasionally cookies. The bedroom that my siblings and I shared; a wooden rickety bunk bed for Finn and I, and a small cot for Sammy. I remembered the mornings where Finn would fall out of the top bunk because he'd roll around too much, Dad had to put in a mismatch railing made of scrap metal. Dad and I would never stop making jokes about Finn falling.

Dad was hilarious, Mother was kind, Finn was tough, and Sammy was so shy and sweet, no one could imagine her doing anything bad. And me... I watched it all fall apart...

Our parents were killed, both murdered on different occasions. I won't get into that...not now...

Finn and Sammy and I turned to stealing, for food and clothes at first. As time went on, and our faith faded, we began doing it for fun. Stealing became more extreme; grand theft auto and bank robbing becoming the top two things we flourished on. Finally, it led to multiple murders; all government-loyal men and women. Once we were all caught, the three of us were placed in multiple facilities- being transferred several times for attempted escape. We were finally placed at America's finest master facility for America's most threatening juveniles.

That was all the past, the present is coming... if you think you can handle it, keep going. I know I'm ready, are you?

"Now calling Patient 606, Victoria Hartley, into the room..."

Entering the office, I approached Doctor Kinderman, who was drumming her fingers on her desk, "Hello, Victoria." She offered a forced smile.

She hated us. All of us.

I did not reply, I only plopped down into the plush blue chair. Doctor Kinderman picked up her clipboard and scanned the sheet of paper. Funny; I had not seen a clipboard in years, but everyone was very old fashioned here.

"As I see from this document, you have been placed here for..." her smile vanished,

"Well since you seem independent, why don't *you* tell *us* why you're here?"

Us?

My eyes fell on the cameras tucked into the corners of the room. That should have been obvious. My whole life is like a movie. I'm constantly being watched like a bug under a microscope, everywhere I go. In a sudden burst of inspiration, I shot a coy glare right back at Kinderman.

"My name is Victoria Hartley, I'm sixteen years old, from Dover-Foxcroft, Maine. And I am here for many reasons..."

The response rolls effortlessly off my tongue, rehearsed many times.

"I robbed 50 Grand from a bank in Florida, bought a car, and drove it into a monument. the car blew up, setting the monument on fire. I even shot two of your government soldiers in the act when they tried to snag me."

A smile tugged at the corner of my lip,

"I killed 'em both."

Doctor Kinderman cocked an eyebrow.

"And you're proud of that— why?"

I leaned forward,

"I've always had beef with people like you… Y'all are kinda the reason for my dad's death. Y'know, just kinda."

"Well I'm very sorry for your loss, but Victoria, I see in the form you've been in six different facilities. You do realize that you'll be spending the rest of your life here. As you may know already, it is considered a mental death sentence…"

"Yeah, I got that," I snapped, sitting back.

Doctor Kinderman set her clipboard down and gave me her full attention.

"Then I hope you are prepared for a lifelong journey of interrogations and misery."

"My God, you make it sound like I have a choice!" I choked a laugh.

"Your attitude is impulsive and is not welcome." Kinderman sighed.

"Alright thanks, *Mom*," I snorted.

This woman thought she was the perfect person to make my life a living hell. Well by no means would I give her that satisfaction. Kinderman now glanced at the guard outside the door.

"Bring the next fugitive in," she demanded.

When I stood up, Kinderman gave me an irritated look.

"Sit down, Victoria."

She got out a new document.

"Calling Patient 607, Finn Hartley, to the room."

My brother, Finn, entered the room with his hands shoved in his pockets.

"Why do you always gotta announce people in the room, Kinderman? I ain't no president of the United States." His volume filled the office.

"I mean, not that we've had one for, like, a century."

"Half a century, due to population decrease and the ensuing chaos."

Kinderman corrected him,

"Every president that has tried to take over has been assassinated from riots, gun violence, even killed in their sleep. Those are very valid reasons not to have one any longer."

Finn put his feet up on Kinderman's desk once he sat down. Kinderman opened her desk drawer and took out a shock pen.

She carelessly poked him with it, sending a jolt of electricity through his nerves.

He yelped and put his feet back down.

"You could have just asked me to move..." he nearly shouted.

"Yes, and I'm sure you would have listened." Kinderman rolled her eyes.

She held up her clipboard and said aloud,

"Now, Finn, tell me why you are here."

"You got a document, why don't you just read it?" Finn waved his hands in the air.

I punched him in the shoulder.

"Why don't you shut your mouth and just tell her?" I growled.

"Fine..." Finn mumbled, still clutching his aching arm.

"My name is Finn Hartley. I am fourteen, and I stole cars."

Kinderman averted her eyes down to her clipboard.

"Go into detail, Mr. Hartley."

Finn rolled his eyes, tapping his foot on the floor somewhat aggressively

"I walked into a car lot at eleven p.m. I tased the car lot owner and stole the three most expensive cars in the lot. I drove them to Rockland, Maine. and traded them in for $700,000."

"And?" Kinderman was becoming very annoyed.

So was Finn, unfortunately.

"I bought a firearm robbed a bank in Brunswick and stole another $700,000."

I glanced at my brother. He was money-hungry and loved to get into trouble. Just like I did. There were many outlaws in the world now. All hungry for something in life. Any outlaw caught would be thrown in a facility like Black Gates, which was where we were at. There were only a few neighborhoods in each state, and they were only for rich people.

Their neighborhoods always had electric fences 60 feet-high so people like us could not get in. I've always wanted to see a mansion. I heard they were glorious. All my life we lived in a trailer; a small metal trailer. We would travel all around, for we were as poor as mice. Welcome to year 2222, folks. Most everybody was poor.

In society now, you were either poor, rich, an outlaw, or part of the government. You had to choose. And obviously, there wasn't much of a contest. Finn glanced back at me and we both turned to Kinderman, who was writing once more.

"Well, it sounds like you two got into your own shares of trouble." She took out one more sheet and flashed her eyes towards the guard again,

"Bring in the last patient."

The guard dipped his head, opening the door and beckoning the last fugitive into the room. Kinderman announced them coolly,

"Calling Patient 608, Sammy Hartley, to the room."

Our sister walked in then, quietly. She was always quiet. Sammy sat down in her chair, facing the doctor with her wide, doe eyes. Kinderman studied the paper.

"Well, Sammy, can you tell us why you're here?"

Sammy glanced down, twiddling her thumbs.

"I'm Sammy Hartley, I'm…..... eleven… and I came because I…because

I..."

She jumped when the clock dinged 11 a.m. I cringed. Sammy was so meek; It was hard to image her committing even a single crime.

"It started when I accidentally shot a man… I was aiming for the man who killed my dad... his name was Joseph Stonewall. But someone just walked in front of him! Right when I pulled the trigger. It turned out he had been a father to a nineteen-year-old son… Benny, who's still alive and would most likely give anything to see me dead." Her eyes filled with tears as Kinderman asked:

"Did the man that killed your father know you were going to shoot him?"

"No, I hid behind a truck. With a gun..."

Kinderman jotted an extra note on her paper and asked her final question:

"How old were you when that happened?"

Sammy bit her lip.

"I was… uh.... eight."

Kinderman did her best to appear professional after this statement but failed.

"Well, the government has concluded that the three of you will spend the rest of your lives at Black Gates. You have transferred from six different facilities; this one will be your final and permanent stay. And you three will behave. You have made mischief in all your other facilities. This will be your last chance."

Her gaze darkened.

"If you three cause trouble here… you will be put to death."

Our eyes held hers firmly, bravely, but deep down, we were scared.

"How will we die?" Finn asked with a wavery grin.

Kinderman shook her head.

"That all depends."

"On what?" I spoke up.

This woman would not be the cause of my death.

"You three are dismissed. You will be sharing a room for now. Henry will take you to your room."

It was strange to me that Kinderman was allowing us to stay in the same room together after the havoc we all caused; the thought lingered on my mind. I sent a sharp glare in Kinderman's direction as we stood up to leave.

"Come on," Henry grunted.

He took us to our room.

—

Just knowing that feeling like the world came crashing down on me and I can't pick up the piece's sucks. Finn laid in his bed, staring at the ceiling. Sammy sat in her bed, twiddling her thumbs like she does when a bout of anxiety comes on. I did my best to remember my parents and calm my panicked nerves.

We lived in Dover-Foxcroft, Maine, in a small metal trailer, nice and cozy but not large. My dad, Dean Hartley, had been a really blessed guy. His features were handsome, his demeanor kind. His eyes were a soft blue. They reminded me of dark ice.

I also remembered my mother, Nora Hartley. She always wore her brown hair in a messy braid going down to her hips. She liked to wrap herself in a brown scarf to protect her pale face from the smog all the pollution gave to the world. Especially the area we grew up in.

Some of her teeth were crooked, but her smile made up for it. It was a beautiful, glowing smile that lit up her entire face. Her eyes were chocolate brown, and combined, her features could reel in any man she wanted. She was a very shy lady. Mother had been shot when I was seven. Outlaws shot her, followed by stealing the food she had tried to bring back.

Whenever I looked at Finn, I saw dad. His hair was a light brown, wavy and soft. Dad's hair was like that when we were all younger, except his was blond. His eyes were like mother's, a chocolate brown. Except the way the world wanted his attention was if he was dead or alive, you could say. Finn had a tall stature, also like dad, but his smile was all mother.

Sammy's hair was blonde like dad's. But it was short, almost shoulder length.

She wore black, thick framed glasses that made her rosy red nose look tinier than it already was. Her eyes were like dad's too. Such a pretty blue, almost like a blue jay. I always loved her long eyelashes, and how when she closed them, they stuck out like long blades of soft grass coming from her eyelids.

And me? Dad used to say I looked just like mother. My hair was a wavy brown, long too, but not down to my hips. My lips were thick like hers. I, too, had chocolate eyes, but my eyelashes were short like Dad and Finn's. My smile reflected mother well too.

Lord, thinking of them always had me circling back to one topic: their deaths.

Mother's was tragic, but not as tragic as dad's, oh no.

He had told us to stay put. That was his number-one order. Whenever he told my siblings and I to stay put, we would do so. The world was nothing but danger to us. Dad went into the grocery store, even though we had no money, and snuck through one of the windows. Which was, of course, against the law.

Sammy, being only four years old at the time, and Finn, being only seven, had to cover their mouths so they wouldn't whimper when they heard gunshots from inside the store.

I was nine at the time, and had learned to hold my tongue. I hid behind the wall at the back of the store, waiting for my dad to come back out the window with some food.

He was a no-show. We waited and waited until a body was dragged out by a man we would soon know as Joseph Stonewall, I remember the look the killer wore on his face that day; triumph. I remember recognizing the body of my blood-drenched father lain across the gravel. Following out his last orders, we stayed put. The name Joseph Stonewall would be a sinister name that haunted my being when his companions congratulated him for killing my dad. They spoke his name aloud, so we could hear the name of the killer.

Luckily, the paramedics took Dad away before Sammy had to see the bloody mess his head was. That was back when we still had paramedics. We buried him in one of our favorite parks. Finn broke down despite himself, but Sammy just stood there, confused at why her daddy was underground. I was the one who had to plant the shovel into the dirt.

"Victoria?" Finn spoke up.

I turned to him,

"Yeah?"

Finn folded his hands.

"Are we gonna end like this?" He asked me.

I raised my eyebrows and Sammy looked up with wide eyes. She began shaking her head nervously,

"You mean we're gonna get--"

"Sammy, get a grip." I ordered,

"Finn, right now we need to worry about ourselves and what will happen to us. This is our seventh time being in a facility. Honestly, do you really think our lives are gonna get any better?

"You think this is the final improvement? That our lives just go downhill from here?" Finn was one step away from shouting in annoyance.

I shook my head.

"No, I don't Finn, our whole life has been one big heist, remember?"

"Yeah but at first it was for survival... now it's..." Sammy glanced downward,

"For fun... I guess..."

Finn stood up.

"This has never been fun." He growled,

"I remember dad telling us about when people would have time to watch a tv, play video games, go to sports events… They would also *play* outside."

I scoffed,

"Outside ain't for playing. It's crawling with government soldiers."

"Yeah well it used to be for playing!" Finn exclaimed,

"I wish we could be a part of that! I want to be able to enjoy Christmas like we used to, I don't want to have to sit by a fire outside in the blowing cold, hungry and terrified of starvation!"

Sammy smiled a little,

"I've always wanted to sled again like we did …"

I was becoming frustrated,

"When are you two going to wake up?! We are trapped here! This is the best facility in the U.S., that's why we've been transferred here. We are with some of the worst outlaws in the world!"

"That excites me greatly," Finn grinned,

"maybe I can get an autograph."

"Are you kidding me right now?" I whispered bitterly.

"What is your deal? Aren't you the one that set a monument on fire, hotshot?" Finn challenged me.

"Oh! Hi, welcome to Rockland Car Garage! I'm-" I paused my sentence and pretended to be jolted by a taser to imitate my brother's latest crime.

"Very nice." Finn replied with a smile,

I pretended to take a bow and we all chuckled quietly until there was bang on our door.

"Shut up!" A guard snapped.

We kept our laughing at a quieter level, and eventually got to sleep. Eventually.

—

Two months. We have been rotting in Black Gate's graveyard for two months now. The food was terrible, the beds were terrible, and so were the uniforms. The uniforms, which were gray dresses for the girls and gray shirts with pants for boys, looked ugly as sin. They smelled of sour milk too.

"Alright, on the ground, gimme thirty! Let's go!" Jimmy hollered.

Jimmy was the man who made sure kids like us got our exercise. His voice bellowed constantly when he talked, and his huge chest reminded me of an overgrown cartoon character. Everyone groaned except for my siblings and I, getting onto the ground. Our hands sunk into the mud.

"Come on! Keep it coming!" Jimmy hollered in Finn's ear.

"Wanna join me, Jimmy?" Finn hollered back.

Finn got a nice kick in the stomach a couple seconds later. I winced while I watched the whole scene and did my twelfth push-up. Sammy was counting hers under her breath. She was on push-up number nine. Finn began doing his, clenching his teeth from the ache that now settled in his gut. Jimmy moved onto roaring at another kid.

"This has to end..." Finn muttered under his breath.

I kept my eyes on the mud as it began covering my hands.

"I am not gonna keep telling you... this is it... this is our end."

I had basically accepted the fact that we would be stuck here by now. Sammy did too. Finn was set on leaving.

"Yeah, well, I'm not gonna put up with Jimmy anymore."

"You've put up with him for the past two months, why does the rest of your life make a difference?" I asked dryly, finishing my work out and standing up.

Finn and Sammy also stood up.

"Two months is enough for me. Forget this, Victoria, I'm going to eventually leave this place. If you wanna come with me, that's your choice, but right now I know you and Sammy are too scared."

Sammy became downright offended, but I was too pissed off to feel the same.

"Finn Hartley, if you dare step one foot out of this building, I'll skin you. Koppisch?"

"How are you going to skin me if I'll already be gone?" Finn frowned.

"*What do you three knuckleheads think you're doing*?!?!" Jimmy yelled at us,

"Get your scrawny hides back in the mud and do crunches, Y'all are far behind, get to it!"

I crossed my arms,

"Why do you talk to us with such ignorant manor? It's rude." I said with a small smile.

Jimmy pointed a finger at my chest.

"Rude? You're one to talk, little missy!"

I raised my eyebrows as he now pointed to the ground.

"Crunches, go!"

I joined my brother and sister on the ground and bore the cold mud seeping into my clothes.

—

I remember having a personal life. I could hide things from people if I wanted to. No one could demand me to tell them everything I've done. I could keep to myself.

Now it was the opposite.

I stared at my plate of rice, beans, and broccoli. Sammy ate quietly while Finn chowed down.

"Nothing like good ol' beans and rice to make your day better after tracking in the mud!" Finn said heartily. "I swear, Jimmy's gonna get a piece of my mind tomorrow." He added, gulping down his small glass of milk,

"Just get over it, Finn." I told him.

Sammy set her fork down.
"Victoria... when can we leave? I mean... this place ain't the worst and all... but I'd rather be home..."

Before I could say anything, Finn interrupted; "Yeah well, if you hadn't checked that lost dream off your checklist, we are home, at least according to sissy over here." He gestured to me.

"Who are you calling a sissy?" I mocked, standing up.

Finn also stood up.

"Face it, Victoria, you want to leave. I know you do. We all do! So why don't we do something about it?" He said in a low tone, but his anger was like the growl of a lion.

"Finn, keep it down!" I ordered under my breath.

"Hey! Sit down and eat!" One of the guards yelled at us.

Finn and I returned to our seats. Sammy chewed her broccoli and didn't say a word. Finn stared sadly at the three of us.

"Look at us," he whispered.

"We're in hell! No pun intended with the name of this place."

I pushed my tray aside. This was no gates of Hell. This if anything, was the rapture. You know, the thing that happens to all the people in between life and death. Christians believed in that concept. If God existed, then he put us here. He put us here at Black Gates. In my mind I would silently pray, to whom I do not know, that we would get out. But that was only a fantasy. It would take a miracle to get out of here. I may have known God and believed in him, but miracles are surely hard to believe in.

"It's almost like you forgot that we were put in Black Gates for a reason,"

I leaned back in my chair,

"It's not the same anymore. Since the virus of 2143, many people died and our economy failed, resulting in businesses failing. Riots broke out, police were defunded, and others lost their lives for lack of protection. The world had been in chaos for a long time. Banks did what they could, some people used freelance gigs for actual jobs to support families. The government finally rose from the ashes, ended the chaos when people like us began to take over. Now all of this happens to us..."

Finn stared at me with wide eyes, Sammy did too.

"I didn't ask for a history lesson, Victoria." Finn chuckled a little. I gave a small smile,

"Finn, you think I don't care about leaving--"

"I never said that," Finn pointed out.

"But you thought it," I breathed,

"And it's not true. I would gladly do *anything* to get out of here."

Finn cocked an eyebrow.

"*Anything?*"

—

"Patient 606, Victoria Hartley, entering the room." Kinderman announced.

I walked in, fed up with this woman already.

"What's up, Tyrant Kinderman?"

"No, your attitude isn't necessary." Doctor Kinderman corrected me.

She picked up her clipboard, which must be her best friend because they are inseparable. She looked me in the eye.

"How have you been doing these past two and a half months now?"

I gave her a withering gaze.

"Fine..."

Kinderman tilted her head.

"How stupid do you think I am?" She asked lightly.

I furrowed my eyebrows.

"Do you really wanna know?"

She grimaced but said nothing. Her phone's ringing broke the silence.

"One minute." She said to me.

Oh, the urge of wanting to stand up and leave. But I didn't. Kinderman picked up her phone irritated mannered.

"Hello?"

There was a long pause as she listened to the voice coming through the phone. Why hadn't she asked me to leave the room? She drummed her fingers on her desk.

"Yes, well the electric fence should be able to boot back up in two days."

I froze.

The electric fence stopped working? Part of me wondered how, but I didn't care. All that matters is that this fence was out right now for the next two days, and this was our chance. I suspiciously wondered why in the world she allowed me to hear this. Was it a trap?

Kinderman continued her conversation, oblivious to my epiphany.

"Well, then we'll double security...yes...yes, the Howlers will do for this."

The hairs on my neck stood up. Oh lord...Howlers...

Howlers were creatures that were like giant wolves created by the government. They were half robotic, but only on the inside. They have the heart of a real wolf and the fur and body to keep it alive, but the bones are all robotic. I had never seen one in real life. Dad had seen one. He told me plenty of tales and said they are terrifying to look at.

The government allows these beasts to kill anyone that tries to escape facilities. Runaways usually don't survive Howlers. No man or woman would ever want to meet their maker from one of them. Let alone a child.

Kinderman hung up the phone, pinching the bridge of her nose.

"I'm so sorry, where were we? Ah, yes, how are you doing?"

I was barely able to conceal the mischief in my eyes,

"I think I want to go back to my room now…" I whispered.

-"Patient 606, you're on kitchen duty!" Jimmy yelled.

Jimmy never looked at me, but continued to order me around,

"Stop your work out and go to the kitchen immediately!"

Finn and Sammy gave me knowing looks. They knew we were going to get out of here. A plan had been constructed in furtive, and we got lucky.

I walked back inside and down a dozen halls until I made it to the cafeteria where the kitchen was.

There was no one in there, surprisingly, so I suppose I could get to work. I saw the stew cooking on the stove in a huge pot. I knew the guards and Dr. Kinderman ate the same food the prisoners did since food was not as plentiful these days.

I added salt and pepper to the mixture of stew and scooped it into bowls for lunch. After the prisoners' bowls, I got to the dirty work. I scooped the guards' bowls, then Kinderman's bowl.

Only they would be getting a little more spice than just salt and pepper. I walked over to one of the cupboards. I was on kitchen duty multiple times already, so I knew where almost everything was. I guess I was "trusted" here, so they allowed me in the kitchen. I went to the cupboard, trying to open it. Locked. Great.

I needed the key. An idea hit me, and I grinned darkly to myself. Jerry. Jerry the janitor. He had the key to every cupboard and every room in Black Gates. I just had to find him. A lie was needed first. After a few moments of thinking, I had the perfect, if not somewhat malicious, idea.

I stalked from the kitchen quietly, rolling pin and dishrag in hand.

I hid behind every statue, every corner and every sign to avoid the guards. I finally spotted Jerry trying to screw on a lightbulb. The fat, clumsy, old man never knew what he was doing.

"Hey, Jerry." I tried to sound as polite as I could.

Being polite was not a mastered skill of mine. However, he didn't seem to notice, and smiled down at me.

"Hello there, Victoria! What can I do for you?"

I almost felt bad. Almost. I jerked my thumb towards the hall.

"I need one of the closets unlocked so I can get to a mop. Someone made a big mess in the kitchen again." I lied.

"Oh, not again..." Jerry groaned, walking with me down the hall.

I kept the rolling pin hidden under my skirt and inside my leggings. The skirt was thick enough for the rolling pin not to be noticeable. It took two minutes to make it to the hall that I "needed" to go to. Jerry brought me to the closet door and pulled out his series of keys on a chain.

I slowly reached under my leggings to grab the rolling pin while he focused on finding the right key to the closet. I really didn't know if the closet was locked or not, but whatever. Before Jerry could exclaim that he had found the key, I whacked him on the back of the head with the rolling pin.

He was out and on the ground within two seconds. I quickly took the key that flew from his hand, but luckily did not make much noise due to the floor being carpet. It came off the chain and separated from the others. Stupid chain. Stupid Black Gates. This place was so old fashioned. In some places back in 2039, everything was based on technology. Now people scavenged for food and became primitive in 2222, and no one focused on making them. It was every man for himself. I unlocked the closet as quickly as I could.

Jerry's eyelids were still open and rolled back in his head to reveal bloodshot whites.

I had to get him in the closet before I was spotted. I slipped out the rag from my dress to bind his mouth shut. I then found some rope in the closet, tying his hands together, and securing it to one of the shelf legs.

I hurriedly shut the door after that. Holy crap I had not done that in ages! I ran down the hall and still attempted to avoid guards. Once I made it back to the kitchen with the keys and rolling pin both hidden, I shut the kitchen door just to be safe. No one was in there still, which was good.

I put the rolling pin back in the drawer and searched for the right key to the cupboard that I needed to unlock.

The cupboard was labeled C14.

The keys were labeled as well, which was handy. I found the key that had C14 engraved into it. Grinning, I unlocked the cupboard to reveal its contents.

Rat poison.

I knew it was there because I saw one of the guards taking it out from this very cupboard due to a rat infestation in the basement. I separated the guards bowls from those belonging to the prisoners. Praying no one would walk in on me, I decided to pour the toxic substance in a bowl, then storing it back in its place. I relocked the cupboard and hid the keys inside a jar of baking soda.

I sprinkled rat poison on each of the guards' bowls of stew. I saved Kinderman's for last.

Stirring the stew, I set the bowls aside as I heard the prisoners coming in for lunch. Finn and Sammy sat down within my line of vision. I grabbed the poison-free bowls and set them on trays for the prisoners to grab. I gave my siblings a nod and brought the poison spiced stew to one of the rooms where the guards usually ate. They grinned when they saw the food and accepted it without a thank you, but I didn't care. They would not need to thank me after this meal.

I then brought Kinderman her dish. She let me in her office and had the same reaction as the guards when she saw how enticing it looked.

"Thank you." She dipped her spoon into the broth and ate it slowly.

I gave her a small smile and left.

———

Finn and Sammy followed me down the hall after the prisoners ate their lunch. A lone guard leaned against the wall, sweating from the side effects of the rat poison.

"Hey..." he pointed at us but closed his eyes, too weak to run after us.

Most of the guards were out of our way now. But that was when we saw Jimmy. I almost wanted to cover my face with embarrassment. Finn gave me an awestruck look.

"You forgot about Jimmy...?" He threw his head back.

"What was I supposed to do?" I asked him defensively.

"You could've knocked him out like you did with Jerry!" He whispered sharply at me.

"I still can't believe you did that..." Sammy sighed, shaking her head.

Jimmy's eyes bulged out of his head when he saw us.

"Hey, what are you doing here? You're supposed to be in your rooms!"

Before I could protest, Finn took a step forward.

"No, Jimmy." He growled.

Jimmy gave him the deadliest look I had ever seen.

"What was that?" He asked lightly, advancing swiftly towards him.

The two faced each other. But rather than man to boy, it was man to man.
Finn crossed his arms.

"I'm done listening to you. How could you work for this government,
Jimmy? You used to be one of us."

Jimmy's gaze darkened further.

"I chose to be here with this government, Finn. I am done runnin'. I
might as well be the person that makes others run. And I know you know
me, Finn. You don't think I didn't recognize you?"

I glanced from Finn to Jimmy. They knew each other?

Finn threw his hands up.

"If you wanna make us run, why don't you come and get us?"

Jimmy kept his hard gaze.
"I'm not gonna do that, Finn Hartley. I'm gonna do this."

With that, Jimmy took out his pen and shocked my brother. He held the
pen against his skin even after Finn collapsed, jolting like a scared bunny.

I screamed, lunging on Jimmy's shoulders, until he swung me around,
slamming me onto the floor. Sammy nailed him in the crotch.

He groaned a little and then hooked her in the jaw. She yelped, falling
over.

I jumped to my feet, my fist greeting his face. He fell back but was on his
feet again in seconds, blood trickling from his nose as he tried to swing at
me, but I ducked and grabbed him around the waist, shoving him against
the wall. I jammed my knee into his gut. He groaned, trying to shove me
off but I punched him repeatedly in the stomach as though he was a
punching bag.

Sammy got back up, lightly pushing me aside and she roundhouse kicked
him in the head. Jimmy fell to the ground, unconscious.

"Nice one, Sammy!" I gasped and hurried to Finn.

He jolted a little but was mostly out.

"I better help Finn, you go hide Jimmy." I told Sammy.

She nodded and lugged Jimmy from the room.

I clutched my brother's face.

"Come on, Finn!" I exclaimed under my breath.

He lay there, not breathing. I got that feeling like the world was gonna crush me. What was that feeling called? Oh yeah… panic.

"Finn," I whispered.

I cradled his head and tears came to my eyes.

"Come on!"

I gently laid his head back down on the floor.
I gave thirty chest compressions to the best of my ability and then plugged his nose and did mouth to mouth.

It took three tries, but then Finn came back to the world.

He gasped and took a few breaths.

"Where-?" He was gasping for air,

"Where is Jimmy? I'm gonna kill him!"

"Sammy and I took care of it." I told him,

"Now come on! We gotta find Sammy and then we're out of here!"

"What is she doing?" Finn asked me.

"Hiding Jimmy's body. Come on!" I ordered, taking his arm and bringing him with me.

I did not know exactly where Sammy went, but I knew she hurried left so that's the way Finn and I headed.

"Wait, so Jimmy's dead?" Finn had a hint of hope riddled in his voice.

"No! Just...unconscious." I answered.

It was then that we stopped. Sammy stood before us, but she was frozen. A spell of fear had been casted in her eyes.

"Sammy?" I whispered.

She put a finger to her lips. Finn looked scared but said nothing.

The two of us crept towards her. She frantically shook her head.

"Don't move..." she breathed.

Her eyes darted to the right. I could not see what was going on, but I heard a grumble from something. Something inhuman. Finn did not listen and continued to creep forward. I followed suit. Sammy closed her eyes, a tear or two escaping them.

When I could see what was going on, I wished I was blind. Before my eyes were six Howlers. They were devouring one of the poisoned guards who had already been killed.

I quickly turned away. If we didn't move or make any noise, they wouldn't hear us. They were too busy eating. I waved my hand at Sammy, motioning for her to come to me.

Sammy backed away slowly, step by step. Someone released the Howlers on us. I did not know who. But part of me had a good idea. Sammy seemed to be looking behind me. Finn and I turned around.

We froze at the sight of Kinderman limping towards us. She almost looked like a zombie, cradling her side and clutching a gun. That's when we knew, she released the Howlers. She knew she would not be able to kill us, but the Howler's would.

Kinderman opened her mouth to speak, but fell dead before words could escape her lips.

When she fell to the ground, her gun went off. We all screamed in fright and the Howlers raised their heads, growling when they saw us.

Finn and I slowly backed away. My eyes were wide.

"Sammy... Finn..." I whispered.

Just as I whispered the names of my siblings, one of the Howlers walked in front of the pack. I didn't realize how many there were. They emerged from rooms, other halls, and the cafeteria. The Howler that walked in front of the others was the most terrifying beast we had ever seen. It had only half a face, the other half was its skull. You could see its gums along with teeth, and the veins from its flesh. An eyeball was missing. It looked like it had been burned bad. He must be the alpha. He let out a howl.

"*Run!*" I yelled.

We all dashed down the hall, the Howlers chasing us. By God, I would not die like this. Finn ran down one hall, Sammy ran down the other, and I kept running forward. The pack appeared to have split up. The alpha and a couple others chased me. I snatched a small statue from a pedestal and threw it back at the running Howlers. It hit one and the Howler cried out, stopping and rubbing its snout against the floor.

The alpha followed by one other Howler chased me, right on my heels, nipping at my dress. I had to get to the doors. I ran past guard after guard, all of them dead.

It was almost like the feeling I used to have when I played tag as a kid. The chaser would be so close to catching me, but I would keep running, forbidding myself to fall on the cement, or worse, get caught.

These Howlers were my pursuers and I was running from them. This was just a game of tag. I continued to run until the door came into my sight.

This runner wouldn't be caught.

That was when the alpha got ahold of my skirt and ripped a chunk out of it with his fangs. He and the other Howler continued chasing me, with no sign of exhaustion. I summoned one last burst of speed.

Please close, please close.

My wish came true, because the doors closed right before the Howlers could follow me. I fell to the ground, the grass cold and wet. The Howlers were howling and trying to bang down the doors, but they couldn't crack them.

I held my side, groaning and feeling the cold air nip at my bare skin. It would be dark soon. Did we really lose so much time?

I froze.

Finn and Sammy!

"Oh my God..." I whispered,

Hauling my exhausted body upwards, I searched outside through the haze of the sunset.

I jogged around the building, stopping when I saw a guard run outside.

"Hank!" He yelled into his intro pad,

"Hank I need-"

A Howler mauled him. Some of the Howlers were outside now; my heart raced while I frantically searched for my siblings.

"Finn! Sammy!"

I couldn't see them. Panic settled in my gut. I hated that feeling. What if they were inside yet? Inside with all those Howlers?

"*Sammy! Finn!*" I screamed.

"What?" I spun around, and Finn and Sammy stood there. Finn's arms were crossed.

"Are you gonna keep screaming, or can we go?"

I breathed a sigh of relief, mouth curving into a shaky smile. So much for panic. I could hear the Howler's howling from not so far away. I turned back to the only companions I had.

"Let's get outta here."

Part Two

It had been a week of hardly anything to eat. We all knew stopping was not an option and had to keep moving anyway.

Finn huffed,

"Victoria, I can't do this anymore. We need a car, not to mention food. We can't just keep going like this."

"I agree..." Sammy echoed.

I turned to them, not feeling like talking. They had a good point. We did need a car and some food. I could drive okay, I had trouble turning and drove extremely fast, but that would be good for the situation we were in.

"You're right." I sighed,

"But I feel too weak to even walk. How will we rob a store? Or a car lot for that matter?"

"Well, first things first...we need food." Sammy mumbled,

I thought hard. Stores were run by impoverished people. If they caught us stealing, they would turn us in, and we would be taken to another facility.

I could not help feeling like not everyone died back at Black Gates. If some people had not died, then they would be on the hunt for us.

We could not afford that.

Sammy seemed to be observing something.

"What are you looking at?" I asked her curiously.

Sammy pointed east.

"I see a building out there." she said quietly.

Finn and I looked to see where she was pointing. Sure enough, there was a building. Perhaps they had food or something to sleep in. I was determined to see what was over there.

"Come on," I ordered as we began jogging towards the building.

It took about five minutes to get through the tall, yellow grass and thick mud.

We made it, but we had to be stealthy. I read the dusty old sign that had white, faded letters.

'Welcome to the Pine Shawl Inn...'

I read the phrase spray-painted beneath:

'Outlaws Only!'

I grinned. Perfect. Finn and Sammy seemed pleased too, for the most part. We may have once been poor, but we were outlaws now. No matter what. Our criminal record was to show for that. Finn and Sammy were about to walk for the door, but I grabbed their arms.

"Wait!" I exclaimed.

They were both pissed.

"What now, Victoria?" Finn groaned.

"We need to disguise ourselves!" I gestured wildly to my Black Gates uniform.

"Look, I know outlaws are hunted by government officials all over. But we're the *Hartley's*. They'll see us as gov magnets and never let us in! Especially if word got out that we just got out of *Black Gates*."

We all looked at our cheap excuse for clothes.

"Well what should we do?" Finn sighed.

I thought for a moment before an idea came to my mind. I reached down into the mud and smeared it on my dress. Then I tore my skirt, revealing pale skin on my thigh. Finn and Sammy grinned when they realized what I was doing and copied me.

Finn ripped his shirt and caked it with mud, along with his socks. Sammy threw her shoes out into the field.

I rubbed dust and dirt on my socks until they were almost black. Sammy ruffled her hair and stuck some pieces of grass in it. I did the same and smeared dirt on my cheeks.

If we got our clothing filthy enough, we might pass for three helpless outlaws long enough to get a meal or two in this joint.

This had to work. We all looked at ourselves, almost laughing at how funny we looked.

"Let's go," I whispered.

We ran up the porch steps and knocked.

I turned back to my siblings.

"Try to look pitiful," I ordered.

They both nodded and gave the most depressing and imploring looks possible. I did my best to give one too. I had never been much of a beggar. I was a thief. But in this case, I would have to play the part.

The door opened, and we were greeted by an elderly lady. She smiled curiously at us.

"Well, well. What have we here?" She observed.

I stepped forward, raising my hands as if pleading for coins.

"Ma'am. We are terribly sorry for disturbing you. We haven't had food in a week... no rest, no way to get clean. Could you-?"

The woman seemed exasperated.

"Oh, cut the crap, would ya?" She exclaimed,

"You're not the first phony beggar that has shown up on my doorstep this week! Come in, for God's sake!"

Finn huffed, walking inside before Sammy and me.

"So much for pretending." He griped.

I smiled a little, mostly because it was awkward at how she caught us.

"Thanks." I said.

Sammy gave a small nod and followed Finn indoors.

When we stepped inside, the first thing we saw was a spiral stairway at the corner of the room, and in the center were a dozen wooden tables and chairs. The place was very rustic, indeed. Many people were inside having food and conversations that were totally unknown to me. Some glanced up at us but did not say anything.

For some reason when I entered here, I felt a sense of welcome. Not sure why. Maybe because these people were all outlaws too. They had guns in their hands and knives, but I was sure they weren't planning on using them.

Because I knew these people like the back of my hand. They were one of us. Not against us. We were all a team, whether we were familiar with one another or not. It was us versus the government. The rich people never interfered with us or them. Another memory would contradict my way of thinking, however. Outlaws were responsible for my mother's murder. In all honesty, whether it came to survival or not, I did not know what idea I could withhold over another.

These people were who I was. They were outlaws. Come to think of it, "outlaws" isn't even the word to describe us. I guess we all use the phrase "outlaws" because that's what the people of the government refer us to. We weren't really outlaws. We were just people who weren't rich or working for government-ran businesses like poor people do to earn side cash.

People like us usually stole from stores, so they could have food for their families, or for themselves so they wouldn't starve. The government didn't see that. They saw it as stealing from stores and it was a crime.

Sometimes we would steal a car, so we could get to a place quicker.

If we had a gun, it was usually for protection. I mean, sure there are some people out there that are downright insane and use guns to murder people, but not everyone. We aren't all psychopaths. Unfortunately, the government thinks we are.

I understand if some people don't understand where I'm coming from. A lot of them don't.

I looked at the groups of people sitting at the tables. The old woman who let us in tapped on my shoulder and I turned to her.

"You alright?" She asked me gently.

"Yeah, I'm fine," I replied quickly.

Finn and Sammy both looked at me with furrowed brows but decided to not question me.

The old woman jerked her head towards the stairs.

"This way." She guided us up the steps and down one of the halls.

Through the halls, she led us through the hallway to the right. The walls were a creamy white; small portraits hung on them, giving a homey feeling to the place. We followed her to the end of the hall where she opened a door to reveal a small bedroom.

"I hope only two twin beds are fine." She said kindly.

"That is fine." I responded.

She folded her hands over her apron. I could study her well in the sunlight from the window.

She wore a blue shirt and jeans. Her hair was winter gray and went down to her shoulders.

"You can call me Ms. Trotter," she introduced herself with a warm and welcoming smile,

"Now what can I call you three?"

I decided to speak for my siblings,

"I'm Victoria Hartley, and this is Finn and Sammy. We are siblings."

"How nice! I will run a few baths and you three can get washed up. I will have some fresh pairs of clothes laying out for the three of you. You can also have some dinner." She told us.

I liked this woman a lot. I knew she was trustworthy. At least I think she is. I just told her our real names. I knew that she knew better not to ask us where we were from. People like us have trust issues for good reason: the government.

Finn offered a meek smile. Almost a fake one. I wanted to glare at him but decided against it. Why was he fake smiling?

I gave the old woman a real smile as did Sammy.

"Thank you," Sammy said.

She nodded and left us alone. I faced my brother,

"Finn are you okay?"

Finn stared at the door.

"I'm fine."

He gave me a questioning look,

"How about you? Why were you dazing off downstairs?"

I smiled and shrugged,

"It feels nice, I suppose. Just to have people that are like you all together in one building."

Finn glanced downward. I became annoyed, but Sammy spoke before I could.

"Why are you acting like that?" She asked him.

He looked back at the door.

"You forget that it was outlaws that killed Mom. I get it that this is a place to get food and shelter...I don't know, I feel like you shouldn't have given Ms. Trotter our names, Victoria." He almost whispered.

I felt confused,

"Why?"

"Because I have never heard of an Inn for outlaws. Most places like stores, hotels, and all other places are run by people that value the government. Not by outlaws." Finn tried to explain.

"What are you saying?" I sighed.

Finn closed his eyes,

"How do you think spiders catch their prey?"

As strange as the question was, I answered;

"They lure it into their web and then they kill it, why?"

"That's what she's doing." Finn insisted,

"She is loyal to the government; she wrote that sign out there and lured all these outlaws in!" He whispered in horror.

"Finn..." I said calmly, laying my hands on his shoulders,

"People would not be so stupid as to come here, if they didn't trust her." I said.

Finn raised his eyebrows.

"Those are the exact same thoughts of a spider's prey."

I nervously looked towards the door. I knew she was out there. Sammy sat on the bed, discouraged.

"I wish outlaws did not have to enter stores or anywhere else being afraid if someone would recognize us and turn us in..."

"It's just the way things are Sammy. Poor people work in jobs monitored by the government for pay, the rich sit back with their inherited money or money they were able to salvage during the downfall of our world, and we just do all we can to break the rules." I explained this to her countless times.

Patient 606 35

Sammy's eyes watered. There were times when she would have breakdowns like this, and we would have to be patient with her and calm her down.

"I never understood why mom was killed by her own kind." She whispered.

I sighed; this was another answer I had to explain a thousand times to her.

"We had money at the time, before Dad lost his job in the mines, and some bad men killed her to take the food she had in her bag."

Sammy exhaled slowly.

"But why?"

Finn stood up.

"Welcome to 2222. My advice to you? Get over it." He said shortly.

"I never asked for your advice..." Sammy muttered.

Someone knocked on our door and we spun around. It was Ms. Trotter.

"I have your baths now," she said in a hushed voice.

"Finn, your bath is downstairs, and you girls can go in the bathroom with the two baths down the hall."

"Thank you." I said gratefully.

My siblings walked ahead of me, not saying anything.

I stopped Ms. Trotter before following them,

"I just wanted to say thank you for welcoming us here." I said,

"I had never felt safe with anyone since my parents."

Ms. Trotter gave me a soft smile.

"Your welcome, honey."

I folded my hands and then went with my sister to the bathroom.

Ms. Trotter had clothes out on our beds for us. They were not pretty, but they were much better than Black Gates uniforms.

I wore a red shirt with white polka dots and blue jeans. My hair was now no longer wavy, it was curled, and I wore bright red lip stick and mascara. Ms. Trotter insisted that I give makeup a try.

Finn was covered by a long sleeve, blue and white plaid shirt and khaki pants. His hair had some hairspray in it to slick it to the side. He looked like a prep boy.

Sammy looked very nice in her white short sleeve shirt and black skirt. Her glasses were cleaned and shined in the light. She received gold hoops from Ms. Trotter.

We looked better than ever and it felt great. Now the best part: food. Ms. Trotter brought us downstairs where all the tables were.

People continued to talk without noticing us.

"Now, I'll get you kids some dinner," Ms. Trotter said as she brought us to a table and pulled up three chairs.

The tables were like tree stumps made with polished wood along with oak stools. We sat down and waited.

"This place is nice." I murmured.

Finn leaned forward.

"This place is a bust. Gone to the dogs."

Sammy rolled her eyes.

"Why are you in such a bad mood?"

"You know why," Finn snapped.

I shook my head.

"Still thinking Ms. Trotter works for the government?" I sighed,

"Well, I am thinking against it."

Finn side smiled,

"Maybe this'll be like one of those horror movies where you don't believe me about something and I turn out being right and we end up screwed," he suggested.

"You haven't watched a horror movie before, we barely had even seen any movies in general. We can't afford to go to the theater." I said.

"Nah, I saw one horror movie." Finn argued.

"What did you see?" Sammy peeped.

"*A Quiet Place.*" Finn answered.

"Oh my God, that movie is soooo old." I groaned,

"That was made in, like, the early 2000's."

"I know." Finn chuckled,

"The classics are the best. Even if they're from two-hundred-something years ago."

We all smiled, but then I thought of a question that had been preying on my mind for a while.

"Hey Finn?" I spoke up quietly.

"Yeah?"

I had to know this.

"How did you know Jimmy was one of us?"

Finn played coy,

"Jimmy?"

"Yes, dummy. Jimmy from Black Gates." I said.

Finn glanced side to side.

"I saw him on the streets one day." He answered.

"You see all kinds of people on the streets..." Sammy pointed out,

"Did he stand out to you?"

"Yeah," Finn answered,

"I was walking one day with a couple pals and I saw him with a gang, hanging in an alley. They were smoking weed and drinking whiskey, they also sat with a bag of something...money, I'm guessing."

His eyes averted downward.

"That's when they were caught by government soldiers; they..."

He had to take a breath, as if he did not want to say what happened.

"They came out with guns and shouted something at them. All I know is that they were being arrested. Jimmy seemed the smallest out of the gang at the time. They pulled guns on the police."

I bit my nails, already knowing the ultimatum.

"The cops killed all the people in his gang. But because Jimmy didn't have a gun, they took him because they automatically assumed he stole the money and the drugs with them. So, they took him into their custody."

Finn shook his head.

"I saw the whole thing."

I suddenly felt sorry for someone, which rarely happened. Jimmy didn't deserve to experience what he did. But it does not matter anymore. He was as hard as stone, and it was too late to help him.

Ms. Trotter came to our table with plates of piping hot food.

Fried chicken, sweet potatoes, peas, and stewed apples. My mouth watered. I could have sworn Finn drooled, and Sammy immediately picked up her fork and dug into her food as soon as her plate was set before her.

"Thanks." I said quietly.

"Your welcome." Ms. Trotter smiled.

After she left, Finn chowed down on his chicken.

"I may have some prejudices against that woman, but God. This food turns this world of hell into heaven."

I chuckled and ate a spoonful of peas.

"I wonder where they got this food."

"This woman obviously has money. She was probably able to buy it from one of the stores." Finn pointed out.

"What store? There can't be any stores around here, this is basically country. Pine Shawl Inn was the only place around for miles." I said.

Finn only shrugged, and Sammy picked up a glass of milk. Milk had been given to us too? I must have not noticed.

"Can we all just shut up and eat our wonderful food that has been given to us by a gracious lady?" Sammy almost snapped.

Finn and I looked at her as though she had lobsters crawling from her ears.

"Geez, hangry much?" Finn mumbled.

Sammy said nothing but devoured her stewed apples like it was nobody's business.

That's when we were interrupted by a fellow with big ears, a big nose, and a bald head. Many glared at him as he passed by.

"Hello there," he greeted us,

"New here?"

We looked up at him, almost like a glare, because we were not in the mood for talking to anyone.

"You could say that." Finn spoke up, looking back at his food and eating.

The man chuckled a bit and then pulled up a stool to sit by us. I glanced at my siblings. Finn pretended not to notice. Sammy was staring at him, wide eyed, too.
The man grinned at us.

"Where did y'all come from? What's your business here at Pine Shawl Inn?"

"We don't give out personal information." Finn said right away,

"Besides, it ain't nobody's business."

The man tried not to frown, so he kept his smile.

"Well if you can't tell me where you're from, can't you tell me what your names are at least?"

Is this man stupid or something?

"How dopey are you? I just said we don't give out personal information!" Finn exclaimed angrily.

He was just acting that way towards this man because we hadn't eaten in ages and when we finally get food, someone interrupts us from eating in peace.

"Well I'm sorry." The man said politely.

I studied him closely. He didn't seem like one of us. He wasn't wild and cursing constantly. He was very friendly. It was no good to be friendly out here. Ms. Trotter got away with her kindness because she is one hundred percent one of us. In this man's case, I was not sure.

Sammy tried to stop staring at this man, but she couldn't help it. I could see it in her eyes. She almost seemed afraid of him. I wanted to ask her what was wrong, but I wouldn't ask in front of the man.

He would not leave us be.

"If you won't tell me your names, I guess I will have to tell y'all a little bit about me."

Oh boy.

"I am here looking for someone. She goes by the name of Sammy Hartley." He said aloud.

Some people glanced at our table but continued to talk. I felt the hairs on my neck stand straight up. Finn tried to stay calm. Sammy did too, she was clearly failing.

"What do you want with Sammy Hartley...?" I asked curiously.

The man drummed his fingers on the table.

"She killed my dad a while back..." he answered,

"I heard she was apparently trying to kill the man that shot her father...but my daddy walked in the way."

"Could you see her?" Finn asked, as if not knowing the story.

"Nah. I was getting some watermelon, so I actually didn't see it until my dad was on the ground...and the man the girl supposedly aimed for ran off. I didn't see the girl either. It took a lot of research and visiting facilities. It was then that I found out she was admitted into Black Gates. I was on my way there until I found out what happened over there. Terrible tragedy."

A million questions ran through my mind. I had to take it step by step. But I also had to pretend that I didn't know who Sammy Hartley was, even though she was my own sister.

"How did you supposedly research where this Sammy Hartley was?" I asked.

"Newspapers, visiting facilities, asking other folks...stuff like that." He answered,

"Same thing with the whole Black Gates massacre too. It's spreading around the US."

He leaned forward, a wicked gleam in his eye.

"And I heard that there's gonna be a reward on their hides."

I forbid myself to shiver.

"A reward? Really?" I pretended to be fascinated,

"How much do they offer?"

The man thought a moment.

"Right now, it's twenty thousand dollars per kid." He answered,

"But I'm sure the reward size will expand. Those kids will sure be hard to find. They are smart little buggers."

Finn and Sammy and I chuckled. Deep down, we were terrified. A reward? That was not good. People were dirt poor these days and would do anything for that kind of money. Money like that could cover taxes and food for a long time. The man suddenly studied Sammy.

"Say..." he observed, eyes squinted,

"You look like Sammy Hartley...almost..."

Sammy turned white and looked like she was going to pass out. The man studied her a few moments more before bursting out laughing.

"That's funny. People can seriously look alike! If I were you, I'd get some highlights or something. If people think you're Sammy Hartley, ohhh boy. You're in for it deep."

He stood up, about to take his leave.

"Wait!" I stopped him.

He turned back to me and I cleared my throat.

"If you don't mind my asking, what's your name...?"

The man crossed his arms,

"If you won't tell me your guys' names, why should I tell you mine?"

I sighed, closing my eyes.

"If I tell you my name, will you tell me yours?"

The man chuckled again.

"Why, I think that'd be fair." He agreed.

I prayed this name came out of my mouth right.

"My name is Pepper Black," I falsely introduced myself.

My siblings almost cocked their eyebrows at me but stopped themselves. The man held out his hand.

"My name is Benny Whitehead."

I smiled feebly.

"Nice to meet you."

"You too." Benny replied.

With that, he left.

After he was gone, Sammy's eyes watered, and she hid her face.

"Sammy." I laid a hand on her shoulder.

She would not raise her head but held her hand up, body signaling me not to touch her. I removed my hand and quietly continued to eat my food. Benny was lucky none of these outlaws killed him already. Finn sucked in his cheeks.

"Well..." he grumbled,

"There goes my appetite."

As he said that, Ms. Trotter came over with three thickly cut slices of chocolate cake.

Finn's eyes became wide as he took his slice.

"I take that back."

Ms. Trotter glanced at Sammy.

"Is she alright?" She asked concernedly.

I gave her a nod and Ms. Trotter took her leave.

——

Sammy was quiet the rest of the night. She didn't even make a grunt of satisfaction when our bodies hit our soft beds. Even though Sammy and I were sharing a bed, she hardly took up any space.

She faced the wall and said nothing. I watched her carefully but did not address her.

Finn was too full of chocolate cake and fried chicken to notice.

"Night," he groaned, getting into bed.

"Good night," I replied.

I stared at the ceiling, almost like I did back at Black Gates. I did that every night, wondering when my life would end.

There were only three things that I was sure of;

1. Get out of here in the morning
2. Disguise ourselves
3. Get a car

Knowing Finn, he would want some money along the way. We could not go hungry again like we did before.

We wouldn't be able to handle that again. As I thought of these things, I slowly drifted off to sleep.

'Stay put.' Dad ordered,

'I'll come back with some food.'

I stood with my brother and sister.

'Can you bring us jellybeans?' Sammy asked excitedly

Our dad chuckled, picking her up and setting her on his knee.

'Of course, sweet thing.'

'What about pizza? We haven't had pizza in a good while, dad.' Finn
suggested with a grin.

Dad ruffled his hair.

'Sure thing, bud.'

He looked at me.

'And is there anything you want, little lady?'

I gave a smile and tapped my chin.

'Pancakes.' I finally decided.

My siblings scrunched their noses, thinking I made a funny decision. Dad
touched my cheek briefly with his pointer finger.

'Pancakes it is.' He declared.

He kissed each of our foreheads, turning to the back window and
climbing in. We sat by some bushes and waited, hoping not to be spotted.

Sometime after mother died, dad lost his job working in the coal mines.
He had to sell off our trailer to someone else for some money. But that
money did not last long. We spent it all on some warm winter clothes and
no longer had any money left for food.

Now we were penniless.

Our dad could sneak anything. He could do anything. No man could tell him otherwise. Our dad was not a lowlife or a thug. He was providing for his family.

We waited for a few minutes more.

'I can't wait to have jellybeans!' Sammy exclaimed in her pipsqueak voice.

I shushed her gently, holding her sweet face in my bandaged hands.

'You have to keep quiet, Sammy.' I whispered.

'I can't wait to have jellybeans!' Sammy whispered excitedly.

She clapped her bandaged hands together. We wore bandages to keep our hands warm. We could only buy coats and hats for winter clothes. The rest is what we needed for food.

'I wonder where dad is,' Finn said in a hushed voice.

'Maybe he couldn't find the pizza.' I replied quietly.

It was then that we heard gunshots in the store. It wasn't uncommon to hear those lately. We just waited for dad.

I saw some people running away over the hills, but none of them were my father. We just stared at the back window that he had gone through.

No one came out.

We waited one minute.

No one came out.

Two minutes.

Sammy was gonna cry.

'Daddy?' She squeaked, standing up and waddling over to the window, trying to climb up.

She couldn't reach, so she cried while trying to jump.

'Daddy!' She called in a sob.

Finn ran up to the window.

'Dad!' He hollered,

'Dad! Come out!'

I stood back, frozen with shock, anger, and sadness. Sammy climbed on Finn's knee and he picked her up to look.

'Daddy!' She cried, tapping on the window.

I ran over to them, grabbing them both by their arms and running with them to the front of the store.

Two men dragged our dad's body out onto the parking lot. I covered Sammy's mouth and held her tight, so she wouldn't scream.

'You really got em, didn't ye, Joseph?' One man with a Scottish accent said.

Joseph grinned.

'Yeah I did! We don't want no outlaws around here!'

My eyes burned with tears. The Scottish man patted Joseph on the back.

'Ye did real good, lad.'

'Let this be a lesson!' Joseph shouted to all around,

'To anyone that messes with the government! They will end up like this outlaw here!'

My dad was not an outlaw. He was a good man, trying to get food for his family.

'I am Joseph Stonewall and I am loyal to the government!' He yelled.

"Victoria!" Finn whispered harshly.

I sat up, drenched in sweat. Sammy and Finn stood by my bedside. I stared at them, dumbfounded.

"Huh?"

"You were talking in your sleep...." Sammy said.

I dabbed my head with my new pajamas given to me by Ms. Trotter.

"I had a dream..." I replied quietly.

"About Joseph Stonewall... and Dad."

Sammy closed her eyes and Finn waved his hands in the air.

"Oh, so now you get all meaningful about our parents because of some dream you had?" He asked me rudely.

"No, Finn. It is because of Joseph Stonewall! Sammy, you tried to shoot him, right? But that other guy walked in the way, and that guy turned out to be Benny's dad, right?"

"Yes, Victoria...we've been through this a million times." She sighed in an annoyed way.

"Well it's time for a million and one!" I announced, a little too loud.

"Keep your voice down!" Finn ordered under his breath.

Sammy inhaled sharply as Finn and I approached one another, arguing.

"Why should I?" I questioned him,
"You're always loud and rude, why can't I be loud for once?"

Finn was ready to lose his temper.

"Rude? You wanna talk about being rude? It's rude how you don't listen to me, no matter how suspicious I am of Trotter! I have a bad vibe with her, Victoria!" He said defensively.

"Oh my God, Finn! Are you mental? Do we need to abandon you and let the gov's throw you in Black Gates again?" I asked.

Finn clenched his fists.

"You mean what's left of it? Because of your bright idea to put rat poison in the stew? Now people may be onto us, Victoria! Especially Trotter because you had to be so *stupid* as to give her our names!"

"I put rat poison in the stew back at Black Gates because you wanted to get out, didn't you? Well, didn't you?" I half shouted.

"Yes!" Finn hit the wall with his palm,

"I did! Because you let them take us, Victoria! You put your hands in the air that night when we tried to escape the facility of Rockland! It was you! It was all you! We followed you! Give us credit for that!"

I scoffed,

"Yeah, I give you credit for being just as stupid as I am."

Before anything else could be said, we realized Sammy had left out the door. We both exchanged glances and raced out into the hall and saw Sammy swiftly walking for the stairs.

"Sammy, where are you going?" I demanded in a whisper.

A tear rolled down our sister's cheek.

"I'm going to tell Benny the truth." She whispered.

My and Finn's eyes watered with horror as we dashed forward to her, but she sped up and hurried down the stairs.

"Sammy!" I said sharply.

"Sammy, get back up here!" Finn echoed.

We followed her into the area where a few men still sat eating. Benny was among them.

I wanted to scream for her to stop, but it was too late.

"I need to talk to you in private." Sammy said to Benny.

Benny patted his knees.

"Why, sure!"

Sammy shot me and Finn a dark glance as she walked with him into the kitchen. Finn and I followed them. No one was in there, luckily. Sammy and Benny knew we followed them. Finn and I sat at the counter. Sammy stood before Benny.

"I gotta tell you something...and it ain't gonna be easy..."

Benny waited patiently. Sammy closed her eyes, barely able to look at him.

"Look, this is gonna be hard to say..." she mumbled, then looking him straight in the eye.

She opened her mouth to talk, but all that came out was a shaky breath.

I watched her, my lips parted. Finn tightened his mouth and his eyes were wide, not knowing what was going to happen. I wanted to yell for her to shut her mouth, but I couldn't. Sammy was different from Finn and me. She most likely didn't want to be an outlaw. She was happier when we were kind, simple poor people. But that was years and years ago and she has probably accepted her life now.

I realized that if she told Benny the truth, we would most likely be thrown into another facility and put to death. Or, Benny would shoot all three of us on the spot. I stood there like a statue, listening to Sammy utter the words:

"I killed your father..."

Benny's face went from a friendly smile, to a look of dismay.

"What?" He barely spoke the words,

"You're Sammy Hartley?"

I closed my eyes, taking Finn's hand and squeezing it. Sammy gave a nod.

"Yes."

Benny looked sick to his stomach.

"How? Why?" He was horrified.

Sammy twiddled her thumbs.

"It was never my intention... listen, our father died a few years ago...killed by a man named Joseph Stonewall... I saw him one day and I hid behind a truck to shoot him with a firearm."

Sammy took a shaky breath again,

"But instead your dad walked in the way...and I shot him instead. Joseph ran away, and so did I. I watched your dad's funeral from one of the rooftops of a trailer and I saw you." She told Benny.

Benny looked like he wanted to understand but couldn't bring himself to it.

"I..." He could barely sputter words out from shock,

"I gave up everything, just to find the person that killed the only thing that mattered to me..."

Sammy's eyes filled with tears.

I bit my lip and now Finn was the one to squeeze my hand.

Sammy tried to give a feeble smile.

"Looks like we both have a mission..." she said.

Benny shrugged in sadness and sat down on one of the stools. Sammy pursed her lips,

"If you want to turn me in for the reward, I won't stop you...I'll go with you right now. Just please," Tears escaped her wide blue eyes, "Don't do anything to my brother and sister. They didn't do anything to your dad...it was only me...but I want you to know that I'm sorry, okay?"

Benny was so silent, you'd think he was dead.

"I'm not going to turn you in." He grumbled.

Sammy was awestricken, but then guessed the next possible thing he may do,

"Then shoot me." She told him,

"Get your justice satisfied and shoot me."

"No." Benny clenched his fists in and out,

"But I want you and your brother and sister out of my sight."

Sammy couldn't believe she was getting off that easy.

"Um, yes...of course...we will leave first thing tomorrow after we get some breakfast."

Benny closed his eyes.

"She knows it's you guys..." he said under his breath.

The hairs on my neck stood up, like when I saw the Howlers back at Black Gates.

Sammy's eyes were wide.

"What?"

Benny shook his head in a depressed manner.

"Ms. Trotter knew it was you from the minute your names were listed."

Finn shot me a glare and let go of my hand. He was right. Benny cried now,

"She told me it was you three that were the Hartley's. I didn't believe her because you three seemed so young and innocent when I came up to you and talked to you."

So that was why he talked to us! He was coming to see if we looked and acted like the Hartley's! Then again, he hardly knew us. He wasn't even an outlaw. He was just a poor person that lost his dad and came here, looking like an outlaw. I understood now.

"Trotter is gonna turn you three in." He said to us.

"Why isn't she gonna turn all the other outlaws in?" Finn almost hollered in rage,

"Why only us?"

"Trotter trades outlaws in for food and supplies from the government. How she gets away with it, I don't know. Most of these outlaws here have only stolen food or minor items. But because you three demolished one of the best facilities in the world, they're offering twenty grand for each of you! Trotter knows that's a lot of dough, and it can get her a mess of things!" Benny explained.

"She told me that after she also told me you were the Hartley's!"

Sammy was very confused.

"Why are you telling us all of this?"

Benny gave her a bitter look.

"Because unlike you, I am willing to help people and I care about them."

That stung Sammy, I could tell.

"Okay, I deserved that." She mumbled.

"If I were you, I'd leave tonight." Benny advised us,

"To be safe."

"You're right, but we have a bit of a problem... we don't want to go hungry again, at least not for a while." I said.

Benny thought a minute.

"You can take some food from the pantry. Trotter's got loads of stuff. Try not to take too much, or you'll also be wanted for stealing."

We all nodded. Benny stood up. Sammy touched his arm.

"Thank you..." She whispered.

Benny would hate her forever. All three of us. But he was a good person, we knew that.

"Get outta here." Was all he said and then left.

I was pissed at Sammy, she put all three of us in danger and could have gotten us killed.

Finn walked over to the walk-in pantry.

"Let's get some food!" He whispered excitedly and gave a small, crazed laugh.

Finn may have loved money, but he loved food just as much.

We stole a bag to put all our necessities in, along with our clothes that Trotter had given us. We had food to last us about two weeks. Hopefully, she wouldn't notice. We dashed away from the inn quietly, without a sound.

"Now, we just need to get a car!" Finn exclaimed into the night.

I stayed quiet while I carried the bag, and so did Sammy. That was our last day ever at an inn. I can promise myself that.

Part Three

There was a lot of shouting, along with vile cursing coming from inside the bank. I waited with Sammy behind a garbage bin.

"So, can we talk now, or not?" Sammy asked me.

"Nope," I answered quickly, not in the mood to listen to her.

I hadn't spoken to her since she almost got herself killed the other night and could have blown our cover. Admittedly, I had too. Ms. Trotter wanted to turn us in, and I had given her our names. Like an idiot.

Finn ran back with two sacks of money. Sammy and I jumped to our feet, eyes bulging.

"Finn!" I exclaimed.

"Yeah?" Finn huffed as he set down the sacks.

"What took you so long?!" Sammy demanded.

"Yeah, and how did you get that much money?!" I crossed my arms.

"Well..." Finn glanced side to side;

"It's a long story."

—

Finn entered the bank with a hood over his head. His hands remained in his pockets. An aged man sat at the desk and raised his eyebrows at Finn's appearance.

"C-can I help you?" He asked awkwardly.

"Yes." Finn tried sounding as polite as he could,

"I need some cash taken out for Walter Green, please."

"Certainly."

The clerk bent down under the desk to take out a key and look for a name. Banks were a lot different nowadays. The clerk needed to know your name and see it in a file to know if you were ever with their bank or not. He raised the file in front of his face to look for "Walter Green's" name. His eyebrows furrowed when he realized there was no such person as Walter Green.

"Wait a minute..." he murmured.

He hurriedly set the file down but froze when he saw that Finn had a gun in his hand.

Finn pointed it at him, looking as though he was disinterested in shooting him, but it was Finn. You never know with Finn. The clerk was simply annoyed.

"You've got to be kid- "

"Well I'm not, sir," Finn told him lightly,

"Give me all the money in your bank, unless you want a bullet in your skull."

As serious as Finn was trying to be, he wanted to grin because it had been ages since he'd done this. He wasn't just going to take the money, he wanted to make a scene this time.

The clerk tightened his lips,

"I'm so sick of people like you..." he grumbled.

"Hold on."

He got under his desk to get the right key, but he was really going to pull a gun right back at Finn. Finn knew that trick already. By the time the clerk arose with his firearm, Finn was gone.

"Huh?"

Just then, the clerk felt something pressed to his head. Finn had his arm wrapped around the man's neck and his face was close to his ear.

"Gimme. The. Money." Finn ordered.

The clerk slowly shook his head.

"No."

It was Finn's turn to tighten his lips. He grabbed the clerk by the back of his neck and slammed him against the table.

"Fine, old man." Finn took out a rope that had been hidden in his sweatshirt. Don't ask how he hid it there...

"What in the world?" The elderly man observed from behind,

"What else do you have in there? A cannonball?"

"Yup," Finn answered sarcastically.

He sat the clerk in his wheelie chair and tied him to it, giving him a boastful smile while the clerk returned it with a dirty look.

"You can't just tie me to a chair and take all my money!" He exclaimed.

Finn looked at him, dumbfounded.

"What's it look like I'm doing?"

The clerk grumbled to himself while Finn held onto the lock.

"What's the combination?" He asked, as if he would get an answer.

The clerk scoffed as if Finn were the dumbest kid in the world,

"I'm obviously not telling you!"

Finn was discouraged,

"Come on, now, you're ruining my fun. I'm having a good ol' time here, and you're being a negative Nellie. Now please, give me the combination so I can rob your bank."

The clerk cackled,

"You'll have a jolly good time in a facility, young man."

Finn moved past the man and kicked down the lock on the safe. It opened. This was probably the world's easiest bank to rob.

"What the-?!" The clerk tried to wheel himself forward, but Finn shoved his chair back.

Finn's eyes lit up when he saw the gobs of money. It made him hungry for the dough. He pulled a burlap sack from his deep sweatshirt pockets and loaded the sack with money. He wasn't sure how much he took, but that didn't matter. It was money. One of the things that mattered most to Finn.

He smiled at the clerk.

"Have a nice day."

Then Finn left with the money while the clerk hollered at the top of his lungs.

—

After Finn told his sisters the story, they rolled their eyes.

"As if that wasn't the most predictable Finn story ever..." I sighed.

"Hey, I'm the polar opposite of predictable, thank you." Finn replied,

"Now we better get outta here, before he breaks free...if he breaks free, I mean."

I huffed.

"Okay, now what? We got money, now what do we do?"

Finn smiled slowly.

"Now we have to do what we should have done long ago...disguise ourselves."

We hustled about all day. That was when we luckily came across an old clothes store. I tried to read the dusty sign; I think it said something like Maple's.

"Let's give this a try," I suggested.

My siblings were agreeable as we walked inside. The doors still worked because the automatic sensor opened them when the three of us walked up. When Finn and Sammy and I looked around the large room, we saw there were limited options.

People must have come here to take clothes. No one worked here, at least not that we've seen.

"I guess we'll split up to look for clothes. It saves time," Finn sighed.

He hated shopping. It meant he had to spend his money on something other than cars or weapons. In this case, we would not need to spend any. Since we will be disguised, we would get to buy a car like a normal human being. I searched the store with little interest for the things that I saw.

It seemed all the clothes that were my size looked slutty. I frowned at all the outfits. It felt like forever before I could even find something that looked half decent.

Until I saw it; the perfect tank top and a jean jacket. The tank top was a bright pink and the jean jacket had silver chains aligning the pockets, boasting large silver buttons that gleamed dully beneath the flickering fluorescent lights. I took both items and then searched for some pants. All I could find was a pair of jean shorts. They would do.

I also found a pair of white tennis shoes. They looked very boring, but I guess I had no choice. My outfit was mismatched, but at least it wasn't like Black Gates uniforms.

"Victoria!"

I turned to see Sammy run to me with a look of excitement. As much as I did not want to talk to her, a gave her an annoyed look and responded,

"What?"

Sammy had a wide smile.

"Hair dye." She said, holding up a random bottle.

I grinned. Of course! Hair dye! Disguising was not just about the clothes, it was the hair too! We could not be recognized whatsoever.

We both hurried to the hair dye and studied the limited options. There was either pink, black, or green. We both frowned. I glanced at the color in Sammy's hand.

"What color is that one?" I asked.

Sammy read the bottle, her frown deepening.

"Orange."

I quietly groaned. We slowly looked at the black hair dye. The only natural color out of all the color options. The two of us glanced from each other to the bottle repeatedly.

We both reached out and grabbed the bottle at the same time.

"Give it!" I hollered.

"No, I call it!" Sammy protested.

We yanked it back and forth until Sammy stomped on my foot.

"*Ow God d-*!"

I saw the bottle enclosed in her hand. She gave a triumphant smile.

"It looks like you're gonna have to pick between orange, green, or pink."

I rolled my eyes.

"Come on Sammy, we both know I'd look better in black," I pointed out.

"Nah, I'd look better!" Sammy argued,

"Quite honestly, if you dye only some strands of your hair pink to give yourself highlights, perhaps you would actually look okay."

I thought a moment.

"I guess. But I can't look like that with my hair this long. It should be shorter to look good."

Sammy nodded.

"Okay, if that's what you want. I'll go find some scissors and tinfoil if they have any."

I decided to go to one of the changing rooms to get into my new clothes. By the time I was dressed, I studied myself in the mirror.

"I look like a slut in denim," I murmured under my breath, walking back out.

I ran into Sammy, who had the supplies to get my hair ready. She smiled when she saw me. I chuckled.

"I look awful, don't I?"

Sammy shrugged.

"I don't know, you still look pretty."

I smiled at her and that was when I remembered; she was eleven years old and probably terrified of the Howlers finding us.

I had been hard on her. She was just trying to do the right thing.

"Hey I'm sorry." I sighed.

Sammy tilted her head and I continued,

"I'm sorry for being harsh with you, I know you were just trying to make things better."

Sammy seemed happy that I understood where she was coming from.

"It's okay, sis. Now, sit down so I can get your hair ready."

While she began snipping the scissors in my hair, Finn walked over. We both froze at the sight of him. He looked like a supermodel. He was clothed in a white T-shirt and a black leather jacket.

His khaki pants had a few stains on it but the nice black shoes he wore compensated. I laughed.

"Finn, you look great!" I exclaimed.

"Thank you, thank you very much." Finn replied in a low voice tugging on his leather jacket collar.

We looked at his hair. Sure, he wore different clothes, but his hair looked normal. His hair would probably be the most noticeable thing about him. It was so thick and pretty, it would blow our cover.

Sammy seemed to be thinking the same thing.

"Finn..." I said nervously, knowing he would absolutely freak at what I was about to say,

"We gotta fix your hair..."

Finn raised his eyebrows.

"Fix it- how?"

I folded my hands while Sammy continued to cut my hair.

"Well...we gotta cut it."

I saw my brother shudder as if his world just ended.

"Like a....b-b-b-buzzcut?"

I closed my eyes, tightening my lips.

"Like a buzz cut, yes."

"You can't cut my hair! Are you out of your pea sized mind?! My hair is the reason I get babes!"

"You've never had a girlfriend, Finn...only...well...I'll just say, other girls." I shook my head.

Finn's look was dirtier than dust.

"Fine, but I won't let you cut my hair." He insisted.

"Oh yes, we are." Sammy snapped,

"Sit your scrawny hide in that chair or else I'll tie you down."

I gave her a look of shock.

"Sammy, you're like a fireball!"

Finn uttered things to himself in anger and sat down on a bench. Sammy continued to fiddle with my hair.

After about two hours, all our hair and outfits were done. I stood there with my pink tank top, blue jean jacket, jean shorts, white tennis shoes, and brown hair with pink highlights.

Finn now had a buzz cut with his leather jacket and khakis. Sammy wore a black, long sleeve shirt and black pants with black boots she found in the returned section in the changing room. Her hair was also black with a blonde streak because she missed a spot somehow.

"We look great!" I exclaimed.

Finn rubbed his hands together.

"I hate my hair- but I'm excited to get me- I mean *us*- a car!"

"We gotta get fake names," I said aloud.

Grinning, Finn responded,

"That's my specialty."

We slept in a field the night before, trying to keep each other warm. I used the sack with the food and small amount of supplies from Trotter as my pillow. We huddled together to stay warm.

In the morning, we ate some pancakes and cold sausages from the sack. We were now running very low on food.

Luckily, there was a car lot not too far away from Maple's. Maybe it had food there.

We entered the small car lot. There were a few people there trying to buy cars. A man walked up to us. Finn had hidden quite a bit of cash in his coat pocket. Not many people used credit cards anymore. The man grinned at us.

"Hi I'm Kyle. How can I help you?"

A nice guy like Kyle seemed perfectly fit for the government. He looked like a total nerd. His hair was a red and he had huge glasses that gave him bug eyes.

His appearance matched that of a total kiss-up. Finn folded his hands.

"Good day, sir. I want to see the selection of your finest cars, please."

Kyle did a thumbs-up.

"Alrighty, right this way please."

We followed him, just hoping to find a good car. There was going to be automatic cars, but some outlaws tried stealing the first ever-made automatic car and it blew up on them. So, we've stuck to traditional cars.

Finn almost squealed like a girl.

"Ooooh! I want that one!" He insisted.

We looked to see what he was pointing at and saw a black sedan. Oh Finn...

"Can we get it? Can we get it? Can we get it? *Pleeeeeeeeaaaasssssseee?*" Finn begged.

"Oh my God..." Sammy whispered, embarrassed by our brother's childish behavior.

I smiled at Kyle.

"How much for the sedan?"

Kyle beamed at our selection.

"Well, it's a mighty fine car, it would be around thirty Grand."

I raised my eyebrows and turned to my brother, who kept his smile. He looked like a toddler that had just laid eyes on a Christmas cookie.

"We'll take it," he said quickly.

"Finn!" I groaned.

"Alright. You can come sign a few papers up here, and you can pay cash. We don't take credit cards here."

Hallelujah! Welcome to 2222, folks! People didn't care if you just handed them ten Grand out of your pocket! If you had the money, it was usually fine... now, if it had been Doctor Kinderman from Black Gates...that was a whole other story. But Kyle seemed like a nice guy.

We approached the desk where he handed us a form. I signed my name

"Rosalina Ross."

Finn signed his name, "Ted Ross."

Sammy signed her name, "Selma Ross."

Kyle took our forms and grinned.

"Great! Now I will take the cash."

Finn handed him three wads of ten thousand dollars each. Kyle grinned wider, setting it in his cash box.

"Wonderful. Enjoy the sedan." He took out the keys from the drawer,

"Here you go."

"Thanks." I said, taking the keys, but Finn snatched them from my hand.

"Thank you." He said and hurried to the sedan,

"Yes! You're my baby! Yes!"

—

We got some groceries and faked our same names. Things were finally looking up now that we had disguises. But there was one thing that stood out to me.

Hanging on a telephone pole was a wanted sign for me.

Patient 606- Wanted Dead or Alive- prize is 20k.

That was me, I suppose. Patient 606. My Black Gates number. Finn patted my shoulder.

"Don't worry, sis. I saw three of them back there for me.".

After that, it was mostly just driving around.

We pulled up by a gas station and stopped to revive our car. Sammy went out to load the car with gas. I sat in the passenger seat while Finn sat at the wheel.

"My baby's gonna get full of oil."

He so far talks to our sedan like it's his child. He's not crazy. He's Finn. Finn tapped his finger on the wheel.

"Victoria...what do you say we get a house? For all of us?"

I looked at him, wide eyed.

"Are you crazy?"

"Yes," Finn answered,

"But I feel like this is our chance. I just robbed a bank and we have more money that we know what to do with... we have our fake names and disguises..."

I couldn't believe what he was saying. He continued talking,

"Victoria...we could be with the rich! We could go with the rich people and never have to worry about gov's ever again!"

I faced him now, I am pretty sure he was going money crazy.

"Finn, we just saw several wanted signs. Some were for the Black Gates massacre...I saw one for robbing Trotter's place, and *you* are also wanted for robbing the Waterville Bank! That old guy must have finally figured out who you were. Just because we have disguises and fake names does not mean we will be able to keep them forever!"

Finn was confused,

"What are you saying?"

"I'm saying that even though we are disguised, we will end up committing crimes again...it's what we do. Surely you of all of us, would know that." I pointed out.

Finn averted his eyes to his feet.

"Yeah, I know."

It was then that Sammy banged on the window with her fists.

"Finn! Let me in!" She screamed.

He hurriedly unlocked the door as I spun around in my seat.

"Sammy! What's wrong?!" I demanded.

Sammy sputtered the words out.

"H-H-H-Howlers! In the gas station! They're eating one of the employees! That alpha Howler with the half face is with them!"

Finn immediately turned the key to our sedan and sped away. Just as he did, several Howlers ran out of the gas station. They barked, growled, and howled. Just like wolves.

Finn was going fifty miles an hour. I was getting pissed.

"Finn, go faster, they are right on our heels!" I yelled.

The car screeched to sixty-five miles. Howlers could run very fast. It's how the government designed them. I saw the alpha in the mirror.

His face terrified me. I honestly was not sure if it was a boy or a girl, but I would just call it a "He" for now.

The alpha leapt for our moving car and hopped right on top of it. Its claws went right through the roof! Sammy screamed and tried to find a gun in our trunk.

"Hang on!" Finn shouted, going eighty miles now.

The alpha did not fall off. Another Howler leapt at our car and ended up launching right through the glass of our trunk. Sammy screamed again, this time even louder because she was reaching in the trunk for a gun.

The Howler had only half of its body reaching inside the vehicle because the glass of our trunk held it in place.

The alpha was trying to rip the top of the car off with his enormous claws. I was trying to find something to throw at the Howler launched in our trunk window. I looked up and screamed when I saw a Howler on Finn's side trying to get in.

"Finn, look out!" I screeched.

Finn saw the face of the Howler trying to get through to his side and he screamed, too. He quickly jerked the car and it wheeled all the way around, knocking the Howler away from him. We saw in the mirror that the alpha had fallen off too.

One Howler was still lodged in our back window.

"I think it's dead!" Sammy called from the back.

We drove as quick as we could. Finn suddenly hit the brakes to see us becoming surrounded. A couple Howlers must have jumped over our moving car to stop us.

The alpha stood right in front of our car. He ran his claws against the road, and I could have sworn I saw sparks fly out from the metal of his claws. I could tell it was pissed, just by looking at one half of his face. The other half was just a skull.

I could hear it growling from inside the car, which was totally torn up.

"We're surrounded..." Finn whispered.

I had locked eyes with the alpha. It was almost like facing a bully. You had to look them in the eye to confront them. Well, in this case, it wouldn't be a confrontation.

"Run it over," I ordered.

Finn looked at me like I had spiders crawling out of my nose.

"Are you out of your mind?!" He exclaimed.

"I said run it over, Finn!" I wasn't messing around.

Finn hit the pedal and the car zoomed forward, instead of hitting the alpha and a couple of his pack mates, they all jumped over the car. Finn kept driving forward. I looked at the endless land of country and road ahead. No other cars, just us and the Howlers. They were not going to win.

They all chased us, trying to bite our tires and leaping onto the car again. Finn drove so fast, the Howlers started to slow down.

I didn't even know where we were anymore.

"We gotta lose them!" Finn hollered over the noise from the car.

I tried hard to think of something. That's when Sammy rolled down one of the windows and fired a gun. Finn turned back but at the same time tried to keep a steady hand on the wheel. I was blown away.

"Sammy, where did you get that?!" I pressed her.

"In the trunk," She answered, firing again.

A Howler fell to the ground, rolling away from our sedan. The others kept chasing us.
Finn tried to watch the sides of the car to make sure one wouldn't run beside it again.

"They can't keep chasing us...we're gonna eventually run out of gas again." I said.

"Yeah I know." Finn replied.

He suddenly looked like he had an idea. I saw him looking at a bridge that was up ahead.

"Finn..." I spoke uncertainly.

"Alright, I need everybody to hold on!" Finn ordered.

"Finn, seriously!" I snapped.

I knew what he was thinking, this was not smart at all. Finn's side smile returned.

"Bite me, government."

We saw the bridge had a chain across it, meaning it was off limits. There was a sign that said:

WARNING! DO NOT CROSS! BRIDGE WILL COLLAPSE!

"Finn don't!" I screamed.

Sammy just held onto everything she could, eyes wider than pizzas. Finn sped up so fast that he broke the chain. Immediately, when our car began going over the bridge, we could feel it breaking from underneath.

"Oh my God!" I shrieked, followed by cursing at the same volume.

I saw the pavement crumbling beneath us. It was unreal to watch. Finn was going ninety-five miles now. The Howlers were falling behind.

So was the bridge. The whole thing was collapsing from behind our car. It split as though it were an earthquake. Finn glared at the remainder of the bridge that we had to go.

"Come on!" He groaned.

"Look!" Sammy gasped.

We looked back and saw the Howlers falling with the bridge crumbling behind us. Finn stopped the car and we looked back.

There were no Howlers. None. They were all gone.

We slowly grinned at each other.

"I can't believe it..." Finn sighed, astounded.

"We lost 'em." I echoed.

Sammy was still wide-eyed and attempted to gather herself together.

"I need to get some air..."

She opened the car door and stood outside. Finn and I joined her, taking in the air.

"I can't believe I'm saying this..." I spoke up,

"Finn, you are a genius."

Finn side smiled with pride.

"Why thank you."

The three of us then heard gunfire and we all jumped out of our skin. Finn uttered unnecessary curses. We saw someone approach us. He had a gun. I checked to see if Sammy had hers, but she must have left it in the car. I observed the man that came up to us.

A couple others followed him. They were all armed.

"Alright, put your hands in the air!" The man in the lead ordered us.

We all did as we were told for once. I tried making a mental image of this man in my head.

He was Asian, his skin was sallow, and his hair was short and black. He wore a white coat with a black undershirt and black pants. His men all wore black and had masks on.

"I am Shang Han, son of Zhu Lee. You all are gonna have to come with me." He said in a controlling way.

His men all approached us, grabbing our arms and attempting to bring us to a black vehicle.

"Let us go!" I hollered.

Finn was trying to fight back. I had to use all the skill I could possibly possess. I used my knee to jab one of them in the gut and then I twisted the other man's arm. Finn did the same thing and Sammy head butted one of them. Shang Han fired his gun in the air and our brief acts of self-defense halted.

He was a terrifying man.

"There will be no need for violence."

His tone was scary and light.

The remainder of the unharmed men roughly grabbed us and I saw one man club Sammy in the back of the head, knocking her out. Before I could yell, I was clubbed, too.

———

My head pounded in pain.

Shang Han looked at us in his rearview mirror of his black car. His guards or soldiers- whatever they were- sat with us.

Me and my sibling's hands were now cuffed and ached like you wouldn't believe. My head thumped with pain while I leaned against the window.

Seeing it gave me an idea. I glanced at my brother and sister, and then back at the door of the moving vehicle. I couldn't say anything to them because there were guards sitting in between each of us. I knew what this car was; a limo.

I wanted to go out like a hero, so I decided to say one thing.

"Finn, Sammy." I whispered.

They looked at me, along with the guards. I gave a small nod.

"I'll come back for you, I promise."

Their eyes widened.

"Wait- "

Before I could hear their exclaiming, I opened the car door and went flying out. I heard shouting in the distance, but everything went black after that.

—

Finn and Sammy sat in the car.

"*Victoria*!!!" Finn hollered.

One of the guards held his mouth shut. Sammy tried to move forward and go out the door as well, but Shang Han already spun the car around, the vehicle screeching. Everybody held on as he chased after Victoria.

—

I unconsciously opened my eyes a touch to hear the loud scream of something.

I saw Shang Han's car coming right towards me. I stood up, weaponless and too weak to run. This is what defeat felt like. Not being able to escape. I shouldn't even be so down about it. I've lived in facilities for over half my life.

It halted, and Shang Han got out of the car almost as fast as it stopped.

"Get in the car!" He told me, pointing a handgun at me.

I raised an eyebrow.

"No." I replied.

Shang Han scoffed, nodding to his guards who came out with my brother and sister, guns pressed to their heads.

"Let me repeat that again..." Shang Han said lightly,

"Get in the car, or it will be just you for the ride."

"Just get in the car, Victoria!" Finn half yelled at me.

"You, shut up!" The guard told him fiercely.

I rolled my eyes. I lost.

"Fine." I said bitterly, walking forward.

Just when I did, I saw Shang Han lower his gun.

It was then that I realized he was not an outlaw. If he was, he wouldn't lower his gun when I chose to come with him. This dude was either from the poor class, or he was a rich dude.

He could be for the government, but he didn't seem like he was. When he lowered his handgun and held it in his right hand, I grabbed it and twisted his arm.

"Ah!" He groaned.

I raised his arm up behind his back and that's when the real action happened. I opened the cartridge and loaded it quicker than lightning and I fired. I shot all eight of his guards before they could even fire at me. *Boom, boom, boom.* They all fell. My siblings looked like they could bow down and worship me like a Goddess.

Shang Han looked like he wanted to break me in half.

"Those were highly trained professionals!"

He also appeared astounded,

"How did you-?"

I smiled.

"I'm Victoria Hartley. You seemed to know that, why don't you figure out how I did it?" I suggested.

I now pointed it at him.

"I want you to tell me what you want with us, who you work with and-"

"And where you got that awesome car!" Finn interrupted me.

Shang Han kept his hands in the air.

"Please, I am a runaway, a rich guy! I was kicked out- disowned by my parents. That was two years ago, I was only eighteen. I had no money- I heard later that you three were wanted for twenty grand each..."

"It's different now." Finn side smiled,

"I'm wanted for thirty grand, Victoria is wanted for twenty-five, and Sammy is still wanted for twenty."

Shang Han closed his eyes, exasperated by our brother. Who wasn't, honestly?

"So, I needed some money...the limo was originally mine...a gift from my parents years ago...I hired some poor people to put together some costumes and bear weapons and be like my bodyguards. We all traveled together to find you, and I told them they could have some of the money." Shang Han continued.

"That's messed up." I grumbled.

"Yeah I know." Shang Han sighed,

"I'll do anything...just please don't kill me."

I stared at him, keeping the gun aimed at his forehead. This man was twenty now, disowned by his own family. I groaned quietly.

"Alright." I agreed,

"I won't kill you. But you will work for us now, got that?" I asked him.

Shang Han nodded quickly.

"Yes, Yes! Of course."

"And we want your car." Finn added.

"Howler's tore ours to shreds, basically."

Shang Han sighed.

"Okay."

I slowly lowered the handgun and stuffed it in my bra.

"Get in the car." I demanded.

Shang Han rushed into the back of the car and sat down. I now faced my brother and sister. Sammy's eyes were full of tears and she walked up to me. Immediately, she slapped me across the face. Sparks flew, and I gasped. Finn was a little shocked but crossed his arms. Sammy pointed a finger at my chest.

"You were gonna leave us, Victoria."

"Yeah, I know." I admitted,

"I promised I would come back...I was going to rescue you all when I could get backup."

"That's the dumbest excuse anyone could ever give." Sammy spat,

"May God almighty forgive you! Because I know I never will!"

I was shocked to hear her say the things she just said.

"Sammy..." I whispered.

Sammy's lips quivered, and she cried.

"We promised each other we would never abandon one another, whatsoever! It's always been us, all the time! That's how it's gonna be all our lives! Or at least, it was how it was supposed to be..."

Finn nodded.

"Yeah that was a low move, Victoria." He told me.

"Look, guys, I'm sorry, alright?!" I waved my hands in the air.

Sammy shook her head.

"You better be, Victoria Hartley. Never do it again!" She ordered.

I walked up to my sister, consoling her.

"I'm sorry..." I whispered.

Sammy trembled.

"I'm sorry I hit you." She apologized,

"I get scared when we separate...I don't want to lose you like when we lost mother and dad."

"Okay..." I said in her shoulder as we hugged.

Finn patted his pockets.

"Can we go in that awesome car now?" He asked us.

Sammy and I smiled and nodded.

"Yeah, let's go." I agreed.

We walked to the car, and at that time, everything seemed perfectly fine.

We drove for the rest of the day and night, once morning dawned on us, we found ourselves in need of some food. I drove through the woodlands, on a path. The trees were blessed with green leaves springing from their spindly branches and the air was calm and inviting.

"I'm starving!" Finn paced agitatedly.

"We finished the last of the groceries," Shang Han grumbled as did his stomach.

I kept my eyes on the path ahead.

"It's okay, guys. We will get food," I promised.

"That's what you said yesterday," Finn retorted.

I was becoming agitated.

"Well, what do you want me to do about it?" I raised my voice.

"This is a forest..." Shang Han observed.

Finn rolled his eyes,

"And?"

"That means there could be berries or nuts around here." Shang Han added.

I closed my eyes, groaning quietly. Why didn't we think of that? When you get hungrier, do you also get stupider? I stopped the limo and we all got out. Sammy seemed to be watching for berry bushes.

"I wonder if there could be any around," I murmured.

"If there were, they would be deeper in the woods." Shang Han pointed out.

That meant we would have to leave our limo. Leaving your vehicle could be around the dumbest thing you could possibly do nowadays.

My stomach urged me enough to agree.

"Fine," I said,

"Let's go."

Finn patted the limo goodbye.

"We'll be back soon," he promised it.

We walked off the trail and into the woods.

It took about an hour, but we eventually found raspberry bushes at long last,

"Thank God!" Finn groaned, immediately grabbing berries and stuffing his face.

Juice ran down his chin.

We followed suit. I sighed with relief now that I got my food, as soon as I felt content, we heard a low growl. We all exchanged glances.

"What was that?" Shang Han whispered.

His question was answered almost right away. At that moment, dozens of Howlers emerged from the bushes.

Including the alpha.

"How are they still alive?" Finn whispered, pissed off.

The alpha began to snarl. I saw from where the Howlers were standing, we only had three different directions we could go. South, East, and West.

"Okay..." I began,

"Shang Han and I will run West, Sammy will run East, and Finn will run South."

"Victoria, no!" Sammy whispered sharply.

"Yes!" I hissed, not in the mood for arguing.

Two Howlers howled loudly, and I shouted,

"*Go!*"

We ran in the directions I told them to go.

The Howlers all separated, a couple on each of us. The alpha and two other Howlers chased Shang Han and me. We had to leap over logs, swing off fallen branches, and hurry up hills to escape them.

"You have a gun, Victoria!" Shang Han hollered while we ran,

"The handgun you took from me! Shoot the Howlers!"

"I can't!" I hollered back,

"I gave it to Sammy yesterday! I had to go to the bathroom, so she held onto it! I never asked for it back!"

Shang Han looked like he wanted to punch me in the face, but we were running so he couldn't.

As we ran, we heard the loud roar of something up ahead.

"Is that what I think it is?" I yelled.

Shang Han grinned while we ran.

"It's a river!" he exclaimed.

While we ran forward, we saw the river. The only problem was, we'd have to jump off a cliff to land in it.

"We have to jump!" I told Shang Han.

The Howlers continued trying to bite us while we ran and dodged their quick nips.

"I know..." he replied.

I was glad he didn't argue with me. That was a first.

Shang Han and I raced forward and plunged off the cliff. Our bodies hit the cold water sooner than we thought.

Part Four

Sammy walked alone through a field. She had been on the run for days, nights...it felt like a week. She tried and tried to find her brother and sister, but she could not find them.

After the Howlers attacked, Sammy had climbed up a tree and shot them with the gun Victoria left her with. She only had one bullet left.

She felt hopeless, lost, scared, and starving; not to mention having no idea where to go and dared not ask for help. She had looked in the woods for her siblings for too long, that was until she made her way out into a field.

The sun burned her skin. It must be either spring or summer.

Sammy had not encountered any Howlers since she was with her siblings and Shang Han, the new man Victoria took in.

Her hands shook with hunger and fear as she made her way through the tall yellow grass. Her clothes were becoming worn out and her hair had not been brushed for a while.

There was nothing but sky.

All of that changed when she felt a prick of something, like lightning. Was she just now struck? Did thunder hit her, and lightning strike her skin? No.

She looked down to see an electric chain wrapped around her like a rope. It stunned her, and she fell into the grass, shaking and jerking one way and then the other. As everything became black, she thought she saw two people stand over her.

—

Her eyes blinked open to a dim room. Was she on a bed? She hadn't felt something so soft in ages. She glanced to her side and saw a small table with a modern-looking light sitting atop it. She tapped on the button and it turned on to a nice orange light. She sat up in bed, her skin stinging with scratches.

"Must be from the chain..." she told herself, touching a couple splinters in her arms and must have been on her sides, because they stung, too.

Her head hurt as well, probably from hitting it too hard on the ground. She looked around the room. It was a small room with rush floors, a bed that she lay in with a blue blanket and white sheets, a nice window, and a dresser by her nightstand and lamp.

What was she doing here?

Sammy turned her body and attempted to get out of bed, shuffling over to the window to see that it was barred. Outside was nothing but field, until she looked down from her window.

There was a huge fence that seemed to be surrounding the entire house she was in. At least, she thought this was a house. The two immature, pale, boys that had shocked her unconscious were down below.

One of them had the chain that must have shocked her.

She was trapped.

The door opened, and Sammy spun around. A girl stood with a tray of tea and crackers.

"You're awake!" The girl exclaimed.

Her voice was high, and she looked like a china doll. Her black hair and porcelain skin were complemented by bright red lips and blue eyes. She wore a sweater and jeans of the same colors.

"Mother insisted I bring you some tea. She did not approve of the boys using the shock chain to bring you here." She set down the tray.

Sammy sat back down on the bed, taking the crackers and eating them slowly.

"Who are you?" She asked.

The girl smiled,

"I'm Jane."

Sammy quietly nodded.

"I'm Sammy Hartley." She said.

Jane's eyes widened.

"*The* Sammy Hartley? My, I wouldn't go telling people your real name if I were you."

"I honestly don't care if people know my real name or not," Sammy replied, eating another cracker,

"I do not like to lie."

Jane chuckled.

"Then I suppose you picked the wrong occupation as an outlaw, since you don't like lying."

"It wasn't my choice," Sammy sighed.

"What do you mean?" Jane shook her head with a patient smile,

"We all know what you and your siblings have done. The whole country has! For heaven's sake, we even know what happened with you trying to kill Joseph Stonewall!"

"Heh, everybody knows that," Sammy scoffed,

"And believe it or not, I tried killing Joseph Stonewall because he killed our father years ago."

Jane clicked her tongue,

"I guess it did not work out then. Since you ended up shooting some other guy instead."

"What do you want?" Sammy did not really like this Jane person.

Jane shrugged defensively.

"I just wanted to bring you tea. Mother told me to."

Sammy's eyebrows furrowed.

"Can I speak with your mother?"

"She's not just *my* mother," Jane huffed,

"She's everyone's mother."

Sammy felt confused. Everyone's mother?

"What do you mean?"

Jane closed her eyes,

"You'll understand at supper. Get on some proper clothes. There are a pair in the dresser. Mother wants you to look your best."

Who was Mother? This whole thing was weird.

"Okay," was all Sammy could say.

Jane gave a small smile and left, closing the door. Sammy stood up and abandoned her tea and crackers, going to the dresser and opening it to find a robin's-egg blue shirt and brown shorts.

She took off her clothes, which were pretty much rags by now, and changed into the fresh pair. They smelled like the laundry her mother used to do for them..

Once Sammy was ready, she even saw a small hairbrush on the dresser top. She eagerly ran the soft bristles through her blonde hair, which was now growing. Finally, Sammy straightened her glasses, smiling.

She knew she had to get out of here to find her brother and sister, but for now she would go down to dinner and meet this 'Mother' Jane had told her about.

Turns out this place was a house. It was more like an enormous mansion. All the halls contained portraits of a woman. She was young and beautiful with fair skin and rosy cheeks. Her curly locks of hair were the color of gold and her smile was gorgeous. She posed with three children in almost all her pictures. Two boys and a girl.

They all looked so happy. But when Sammy finally went down the stairs after going down at least three hallways, she entered the dining room when seeing it on her way down the stairs. She could not believe what she saw.

At a long, dark, oak table were at least thirty kids and even adults. They were all sitting with a plate and silverware before them. Sammy's heart nearly skipped a beat. There were many people of different ages. The oldest person of the group must have been thirty.

At the end of the table there sat a woman. She looked middle-aged. And to Sammy's horror, it was the beautiful woman from the pictures hanging in all the halls. Except now, she looked terrifying.

Her golden locks were now almost completely gray and gone from her head.

Her face was one of the crinkliest faces Sammy had ever seen. She wore makeup, but looked terrible with it, and an old white sweater and jeans. A strand of pearls adorned her neckline. She offered a dull smile,

"Ah, the new child is here." She announced Sammy.

Sammy nervously entered the dining room, which was an open space. All the people at the table looked up at her. She gave a tiny nod and smile.

"You must be- "

"Don't act like you don't know me, dear!" The woman chuckled,

"I'm the Mother! And these are all my children, including you! Welcome to our home..."

Sammy didn't know whether to run or to just go with it.

"Nice to meet you, I'm- "

"Sammy Hartley." Mother nodded,

"Jane notified me."

Great. Sammy was now annoyed by Jane, more than what she had already been anyway. Some people whispered amongst themselves and others just stared. Mother pardoned them.

"I apologize for the children's excitement. You're the first outlaw child we've had here."

When she saw Sammy's nervous look, she chuckled again.

"No worries, darling. We won't turn you in. Family doesn't simply turn one another in for a reward."

This woman had to be mental, but Sammy was glad that she wasn't being turned in. Mother waved her hand.

"Please, have a seat. Dinner is about to begin."

Sammy walked over to one of the empty chairs and sat next to two people at the end. One a boy and one a girl. The boy was African American. He had a kind face, but the hard look he had in his eye contradicted it.

The girl had tan skin and sandy blonde hair and bright green eyes. Sammy gave them a smile and the girl smiled back, but not the boy.

"So, you're an outlaw, huh?" The boy asked gruffly, running his large hand through his thick, black hair.

He seemed tough, you could mistake him for an outlaw.

"Yeah," Sammy answered,

"So, are all of you poor people? Or..."

"Some of us," the boy responded,

"Some are even rich people that loitered outside their neighborhoods. Must have been curious of the outside world, I guess."

"Maybe..." Sammy muttered.

The girl leaned forward, wanting in on the conversation.

"I think it's cool that we have an outlaw here!" She whispered excitedly,

"I'm Rachel."

Sammy shrugged.

"You already know my name." Turning to the boy, she asked,

"And you are-?"

"Charlie," the boy grumbled.

The food arrived. Two teenagers brought it in. Sammy came to realize that it was the two guards she saw out the window.

"Ah, children!" Mother grinned,

"We waited for you! What kept you?"

Both boys respectfully folded their hands and looked to the ground.

"We apologize, Mother. The cornbread was almost burnt, and we needed to go to the shed and get more milk for the fridge."

Mother said nothing but waved her hand to two empty chairs and the two boys loaded the table with the trays of food and then sat down. Mother chuckled nervously. Man, this woman loved to chuckle, Sammy thought.

"Sammy, I'm afraid these two children were the ones that used the shock chain on you... I personally do not approve of it, and my sons will apologize to you for the inconvenience."

Both boys looked Sammy in the eye.

"We apologize for the inconvenience." They said at the same time.

Sammy touched the stinging cuts on her skin.

"It's alright."

When she turned her gaze to the food, her mouth watered.

Ham, cornbread, mashed potatoes, rolls, broccoli and cheese, and applesauce.

Sammy reached across the table and took the salt and pepper as the mashed potatoes were passed to her. Rachel smiled and giggled at the portion size Sammy took.

"Lordy, you take enough to feed a herd of elephants!"

"Shut your trap!" Charlie snapped.

Sammy didn't care what Rachel said. She and Jane both got on her nerves now. Charlie was okay. Sammy took a glance at all the people around the table.

"Don't worry, it's exactly what it looks like." Charlie said.

"Like what?" Sammy asked.

With a slight eye roll, Charlie answered;

"That woman, or "Mother" took all of us captive. Those boys over there took you in because that's what they do."

Sammy twiddled her thumbs, she always did that whenever she was nervous.

"Why would she do something like that?"

Charlie took a bite of ham.

"You obviously saw all the pictures on the walls...the pictures of the beautiful woman with the three children?"

"Those were her children, weren't they?"

"Yep." Charlie said under his breath,

"Nobody truly knows what happened, but everyone assumes they're dead. I mean, they're not around here, right?"

Sammy took a bite of mashed potatoes. They oozed with butter.

"Is there anyone who does know what happened to Mother's real kids?"

Charlie contemplated that question a few moments.

"Ask Jane," he answered.

"She's been here the longest. She might know something. We've all tried to get it out of her, but she's not intimidated by us...maybe since you're an outlaw, she'll be intimidated by you."

Sammy let out a long breath.

"Okay...I'll try to get something out of her."

Charlie nodded,

"I believe her room is next to yours. Your room was the last one available...at least, I think. Not sure though. Mother will capture more people anyway."

—

Jane sat before her mirror and brushed her hair gently. When she looked up, she saw Sammy leaning in the doorway.

"Sammy, hi!" She exclaimed.

Sammy did not respond, but only approached her slowly.

"Jane, I have a question."

Jane tried to play as coy as she could.

"About...?"

"About Mother," Sammy responded quickly.

Jane stood up.

"What do you want to know about Mother?"

Sammy closed the door and smiled.

"What happened to Mother's real kids, and why is she taking random people and pretending they're her children?"

Jane looked down and Sammy became annoyed.

"You know, don't you?"

Jane nodded.

"Yes, I do."

"Tell me." Sammy insisted.

"No."

Sammy came closer.

"You better tell me..." she threatened.

Jane scoffed, but nervously,

"Or what?"

"I'm an outlaw, I could do anything. Trust me." Sammy answered.

Jane's lips curled.

"If you want to know...you will find everything you need in Mother's basement."

Sammy felt chills go up her spine.

"The basement?" She questioned.

When Jane dipped her head, acknowledging it was in the basement, Sammy closed her eyes briefly and sighed.

"Is it bad?" Sammy asked.

"What do you mean?" Jane questioned her.

"Is the way her children died bad?"

Jane struggled to find her words for an answer;

"Let's just say every death of a person is bad...but this was just awful."

Jane brushed her pants with her hands.

"That's all I'm gonna say, you can please leave now."

Sammy turned to take her leave and closed the door quietly behind her.

"Sammy!"

Sammy nearly jumped out of her skin when she saw Mother coming toward her down the hall.

"Why aren't you in bed, child?"

Sammy shrugged, putting on a fake smile.

"I'm sorry, Mother, I was just making my way there. I had to say goodnight to Jane first."

Mother smiled back, opening her arms.

"Well...give your mother a hug, then!"

Sammy was so creeped out by this lady already, how long had she even been here? A few hours at the most? Although, that shock chain knocked the daylights out of her.

"Mother, how long have I been here?" She asked.

Mother tapped her chin.

"Oh, let me think...two weeks, I should say..."

Sammy wanted to drop to the floor. Two weeks?! She had been out for two weeks?!

"Oh..." was all she could say.

Mother smiled and held out her arms once more.

"Now," She said,

"Come give your mother a hug."

Sammy knew she had to play it calm. She slowly walked towards Mother and they embraced one another. Sammy wanted this to be over. It may have been a few hours that she was awake, but she had to get out.

But how?

The whole house was surrounded by an electric fence.

She had to find a way out. Surely, there was some way she could get out. She remembered those two boys that took her captive said something about a shed. Maybe there was a switch in there that she could shut off the electricity in the fence.

But first, she wanted to find out what happened to Mother's real children. It was obvious they died, but how? What made this woman so evil?

When Mother finally let go, Sammy gave her a curt nod before hurrying off to her room to go to sleep.

—

The next morning, Sammy sat in the kitchen chopping carrots and onions. Charlie was feeding the fire. Rachel and Jane were there, too.

Sammy had asked Charlie about the switch to turn off the electric fence.

"You're right, it's in the shed." Charlie answered,

"But the shed is guarded day and night by those two boys. And..." Charlie struggled to finish his sentence.

Sammy stopped chopping the vegetables.

"And what?"

Rachel finished the sentence for him.

"Well, someone tried to go in there to flip the switch...Mother found out, and the girl was brutally murdered."

Jane kept her eyes on the bread she was making,

"Mother tied her to the fence while it wasn't turned on...but then she turned it on to 2,000 volts."

Charlie threw the last log into the fire.

"I wasn't there at the time...but everyone had to watch."

"Meaning I saw it." Jane cut in,

"Since I was the first one here."

Sammy felt a little bad for Jane. No one should have to watch someone die by being electrocuted, let alone go through it.

"Now Mother has those two boys guard the shed." Rachel added.

Sammy set all the chopped carrots in a bowl.

"How long have you been here, Jane?"

Jane bit her lip.

"Five years." She answered quietly.

Sammy stopped again.

"Did you say five years?" She asked, bewildered.

Jane slowly nodded.

"I've basically gotten used to it."

Sammy shook her head.

"Well you shouldn't."
"Oh, what are you gonna do?" Charlie challenged her.

Sammy tapped her fingers on the table.

"I'm not only gonna get myself out, but now I'm gonna get all of you out."

She threw the chopped onions in with the carrots.

"But first, I want to find out what happened to Mother's real children."

"Why does that matter?" Jane asked.

Sammy smiled meekly.

"I have lost someone I loved very much, too. Maybe you all have as well. This woman has. But if I can find out what happened to make Mother so horrible, maybe I can find a way to help her."

"You're quite nice for an outlaw," Rachel commented.

Sammy batted her long eyelashes.

"Believe it or not...I was not always an outlaw."

That was all she said.

———

Nighttime struck the fields and Mother's house quickly. Sammy was forced to kiss that old hag goodnight and pretend to go up to bed. But now she knew that she had to find out the truth.

She crept down the hall, praying that the floor would not creak. Charlie, Jane, and Rachel all knew what she would do tonight. But no one else.

Sammy wasn't sure if she trusted her new friends, but they were all she had.

Sammy had never really had a best friend, or a friend at all. Only her brother and sister. She told herself that they would be all she ever needed. They were enough for her. But Sammy had always wanted to know what it would be like to have a friend.

People nowadays did not make a lot of friends. They were too busy trying to survive.

Sammy finally found the stairway to go to the main floor. She snuck down the stairs and stayed alert for the sound of other footsteps or any sign that someone may be near.

She saw dozens and dozens of pictures with Mother alongside her three children.

All were of them smiling, laughing, hugging, and in action; like running together or playing.

Seeing those pictures caused Sammy to think of her parents. Like usual, whenever she thought of her parents, she thought of their deaths. She would find the man that killed her father. That Joseph Stonewall guy.

Maybe her siblings were on their way to finding him.

"No!" She whispered to herself.

They would be trying to find her. But she would forgive them if they tried to find Joseph Stonewall instead. He was more important than her. He needed to be found and killed by one of them. Then their father would be avenged.

Sammy kept searching for some door that may lead to the basement. She saw the dining room, so she knew she was near the entry of the house.

There was a door right next to the entry on the east side of the room. Sammy hurried over to it and opened it. Just a closet.

She groaned quietly. This house was huge, would she ever find it?

She saw another door on the west side of the room. It had been just storage.

After walking down towards the kitchen, she wanted to double check and make sure the other door in that room wasn't the basement.

It wasn't. Just a pantry.

She thought deeply, exiting the kitchen.

Just when she walked out, there was a door right across from her. She approached it, slowly turning the knob.

Locked.

This had to be it. This had to be the basement. But she needed a key. She froze. She wondered if her new friends already knew that she was supposed to have a key.

She angrily hurried back to her room and did her best not to slam the door.

—

Sammy did not talk to Charlie, Jane, or Rachel at breakfast, nor lunch. But when dinner finally arrived, Charlie set his glass of water down.

"What's going on with you, Sammy?"

Sammy huffed,

"I looked for the door to the basement...I'm sure I found it...but I need a key."

She gave her friends a dark look.

"Did you guys know that I needed a key and didn't tell me?"

Charlie, Jane, and Rachel looked down. Sammy rolled her eyes.

"I'll take that as a yes." She sighed,

"Why didn't you all tell me?"

Charlie exhaled slowly,

"It's because the location of the key is somewhere you would not want to go to."

Sammy twiddled her thumbs.

"Where is it?" She asked, annoyed.

Jane jerked her head towards Mother, who sipped her cup of tea.

"It's in Mother's room." She answered.

Sammy let out a long sigh. She had to get that key. She wanted to know the truth about this woman and why she did all these things to these people; taking them, pretending they were her children, so many horrible things that would make up a sick woman.

Sammy wiped her mouth and folded her hands.

"Well I gotta get that key, then..." she whispered.

Charlie raised his eyebrows.

"Seriously?"

Sammy was becoming fed up with everything. She wanted out.

"Look, you can question me, hide things from me, and lie...but I am doing this, and I am getting out...with or without you."

Jane set down her fork.

"I thought we could come with you," she protested.

"You can. But I won't have people slowing me down. Once I set you all free, I need to go. Do you understand?" Sammy asked quietly.

Mother could not hear their conversation.
At least she got the location of the basement door right. But now she had to get the key.

After everyone went to bed, Sammy snuck down the hall for the second night in a row. She could pretty much remember where the kitchen was in the house by now. Sammy hurried down the stairs and made her way to the kitchen. Mother's room was down the hall from the basement door. She got that information from Jane, luckily.

When Sammy finally found Mother's room- she knew because there was a door that had the word MOTHER carved into it. It terrified her, but she didn't want to focus on carvings. She needed the key to the basement.

"Please don't be locked..." she whispered to herself.

She carefully turned the knob and the door silently opened. Thank the lord. Sammy entered the room to reveal a king-sized bed with a black canopy covering it. She saw Mother through the lacy canopy draped over her enormous bed. She was sound asleep.

Sammy saw a dark oak dresser and decided to look there first. She carefully opened drawer after drawer. She only found clothes as a result. Except the bottom drawer contained something she had not intended to find.

Letters. Unopened, returned letters.

Sammy took the envelopes, letting her eyes adjust to the darkness. She blinked over and over until she could see what it said:

To Joseph Stonewall.

Sammy nearly dropped the envelopes on the floor but kept her grasp. Why was Mother writing letters to Joseph Stonewall? She tried to read the date of when these were returned:

2211

That was eleven years ago. Sammy needed to take these and read them. She normally hated prying, but these were addressed to the man that killed her dad.

Sammy quietly closed the drawer. She had not actually seen an envelope in years. Sammy checked to see if Mother had woken up.

From the canopy, it looked like she was still asleep. Sammy walked over to Mother's nightstand and opened the single drawer. Her heart skipped a beat. To her great relief, there was a chain of keys. The basement key had to be one of them.

Just when Sammy closed the drawer, she turned and stopped.

Mother.

She was laying there, her cold eyes fixated like lasers.

"What are you doing, Sammy?" She asked.

Sammy didn't know whether to run, knock her out, or do both.

"I..." She struggled to find words.

Mother jumped to her feet, grabbing her shoulders.

"How could you do this?" She shouted,

"Pry into my own personal affairs, this is none of your business! How could you do this to your own mother?"

Sammy felt a blackness of hatred sweep over her like a threatening wind.

"You are not my mother!" Sammy snapped.

"I am so!" Mother was furious.

She stared at the floor and began pacing like a mad woman. What was wrong with her?!

"That man..." she growled.

"That man will go to the devil for what he has done! Joseph Stonewall... may he rot in his grave, if God hasn't put him there already!"

Sammy wanted to run, but she watched Mother's eyes blacken and her frail body shake.

"He did this!" She cried in horror,

"My poor babies!"

"So, he killed them?" Sammy asked, wanting answers.

Mother's face became grave and angrier than Sammy had ever seen in a person.

"Give me my letters and keys now!" Mother leapt at Sammy, but Sammy dodged her.

Sammy ran like hell was chasing her. She heard Mother make a loud thump when she hit the floor. She also heard footsteps coming from upstairs and the voices of some of her "children." All Sammy knew was that those voices were not those belonging to her friends, so she kept running with her stolen items.

Sammy hurried into the kitchen and hid in the pantry. She peeked through the lock hole to watch. She heard the wailing cries of Mother and some people consoling her.

Until footsteps were heard again. They traveled all over. It was like thunder. Sammy shook in the closet, trying to see what was going on in the darkness. How many times has she hidden like this? Hundreds, probably. Sitting here made her think of when she hid many years ago...waiting for her dad to come out from the grocery store with some food that they had been aching for.

All she got instead were gunshots. Along with her dad's body being dragged out after by a few men. Sammy saw those two guard boys enter the kitchen with FlashPads. FlashPads were a modern flashlight invented in 2163.

Sammy had to find a better place to hide. She saw all the shelves and got an idea. The two guard boys entered the room and Sammy watched them from below. She was stretched across the ceiling between two shelves.

They shined the FlashPads around the small room, and to Sammy's dismay, they pointed them right at her on the ceiling.

"Hey-!" One of them yelled.

Sammy swung off one of the shelves and onto the floor. Stuff fell from the shelf as Sammy grabbed one of the boys and shoved him into the other one. They were back on their feet almost immediately before Sammy could throw something at them.

One of them tried to punch her and Sammy ducked, allowing the boy's fist to connect with the wall. He groaned and the other one threw Sammy down. Sammy kicked him in the gut from below. The boy grabbed her leg and dragged her out into the kitchen.

The other boy limply followed.

Sammy broke free by violently kicking her legs and jumping to her feet as one boy charged at her.

The two went clashing into one of the counters. She could hear rushing footsteps coming down the hall. Sammy locked her legs around the boy's neck as the other tried to pull her away from him.

Until it got even more intense.

Charlie, Jane, and Rachel came bolting in; as a Godsend. Charlie attacked the boy that tried pulling Sammy away from the other one. Rachel helped Sammy up and Jane punched the other boy in the face.

"Come on!" Rachel shouted, running with Sammy to the stairs.

They ran past some people, who whispered nervously. Rachel swung the door open to her own room.

"Hide in here!" She told Sammy.

Sammy ran into the room and hid in the closet.

"Thank you." She said to Rachel through the door.

"Yeah, don't mention it." Rachel replied hastily.

Once Sammy was the only one in the room, she took silent breaths.

She knew she was not alone.

The door slowly creaked open and she heard slow footsteps come in. There was slight whispering, but Sammy could not hear what was being said. All she heard was a shaky voice.

"Sammy..." the voice cooed.

Sammy held her breath. Mother.

"Sammy Hartley..."

Sammy peeked through the lock hole of the closet and her eyes widened. Mother held a gun in her hand. She wouldn't shoot her...would she?

"Sammy, my dear, I don't want to make this difficult." She warned.

How did she know that Sammy was hiding in here? She must have seen Rachel hide her. Mother cocked the gun.

"So, I'm gonna give you a deal... if you come out, I will let you go." She proposed.

Yeah. Heard that one before only a million times.

Mother turned to the closet, slowly smiling.

"Sammy..." she repeated,

"You know you can't escape me...I'm your mother..."

Her voice became dark and more disturbing than what it already was.

"You can't escape your mother."

Sammy squeezed the doorknob with her hand. This woman would never be her mother. Her real mother was a warrior Kinderman. She was braver than this old hag would ever be. Sammy saw a can of hairspray. It may not be much of a weapon, but her only other option would be clothes. Clothes weren't much of a weapon.

Sammy swung open the door and sprayed Mother right in the face.

Mother screeched and fell to the ground and Sammy walked up to her.

"*You- are- not- my- mother!*" She screamed and then dashed out of the room.

She had to get to the basement. Sammy held the envelopes and keys yet and searched and searched for the right key. There must have been forty-something keys. She tried each one frantically and got the door open by the tenth key.

The wood door creaked open and she shut it quickly. She couldn't lock it on the inside, so she just had to hurry. The basement had such steep stairs. Sammy clenched the railing with her items and stopped when she got to the bottom.

She pulled on the light to turn the dim bulb on.

Sammy took a long breath.

In the basement was a huge amount of water. It must have flooded a long time ago. Sammy took a step into the black water.

She wasn't sure if she should do this. But something stopped her hesitation when her eyes fell on the only thing that mattered. There was a switch on the other end of the basement.

A switch to turn off the electric fence. The one in the shed had been a fake! Mother must have known that one girl was going in there and made everyone believe their way out was through the shed. Those boys guarded the shed day and night for nothing. Mother killed that innocent girl years ago just to freak everyone out.

Sammy had just found the real way out. Unfortunately, she now had to trudge through this awful, murky black water. Sammy made her way through, trying to keep the envelopes from getting wet. The water went up to her waist and made splashes that she couldn't control. Until her foot hit something.

"What is that?" She exclaimed, trying to reach down and feel for what it was.

It did not feel right. Sammy held her breath and went under water. She could not see a thing, sadly. She felt around with her hands and she could feel something. She grabbed onto something hard and thin. Maybe it was a pole or something.

She ran her hand down it and stopped when she realized that it was an arm. Sammy came up screaming.

There's a body down there! Sammy dove back under and felt the ankles of another child right next to the other one. Oh my God.

Mother kept her children preserved down here.

This woman needed mental help. The only thing was, where's the third child? Mother had three children.

Sammy hurried for the switch and was just about to pull it when the door swung open. Mother stood there with her gun, furious and eyes bloodshot as she hobbled down the stairs, quicker than she looked.

Sammy had only a few moments to stare in terror until she heard thunder boom from in front of her. She could have sworn she saw fire. But when she looked down all the storm went on in her gut.

A rain of blood dripped down and into the murky water. Sammy didn't feel a thing right away. Her hand cranked the switch and the power of the electric fence was off.

"No!" Mother shouted.

People ran when they heard the gunshot to see what happened. Charlie led the way and saw the switch.

"Get her!" He hollered,

"Get her, and we're free!"

People yelled and tackled Mother down the stairs. Charlie, Jane, and Rachel hurried to Sammy, who leaned against the wall, holding her gut.

"Sammy! Come on, stay with us!" Jane urged her.

"I'm okay." Sammy gasped.

"Man, that looks bad." Charlie said.

Sammy jerked her head to the door and past the people that were attacking Mother.

"You gotta get me upstairs..." Sammy told her friends,

"You gotta get yourselves up there too. We are all free now. The electricity in the fence has been turned off. You all have nothing to be afraid of anymore."

Tears came to Jane's eyes and she embraced Sammy.

"Thank you." She whispered,

"For bringing us freedom."

Sammy smiled.

"Hey, it's what we all want, right?"

Charlie lead Sammy through the black waters and helped her limp up the stairs.

"We gotta get you help." He told her.

Sammy patted his shoulder weakly,

"Just go save yourselves."

"No. We need to get that bullet out!" Jane insisted.

Rachel nodded in agreement.

"Sammy, it has to come out."

Sammy could not protest. It would hurt terribly, she knew that.

She looked at the bloody hole in her body.

"Okay." She murmured.

Charlie patted her knee.

"It'll be okay. We ain't medical professionals, but we are older and know a thing or two about surviving. I've been shot and had to take out the bullet on my own."

That satisfied her enough. She didn't know that about Charlie. What a good friend.

"Okay." She repeated.

Charlie helped her sit against the wall of the hallway. Jane and Rachel both too each of Sammy's hands. Charlie walked over to the kitchen and came back with a bottle of alcohol and a knife.

"Okay, my friend." He said aloud,

"Hang in there."

Charlie then began the long, painful process of removing the bullet.

—

Charlie watched Sammy as she slept on the floor and examined the envelopes that she had with her. They were addressed to Joseph Stonewall. Mother had been disposed of and they found the bodies in the basement. The third body remained missing, so the others were still looking for it. Charlie counted the envelopes. There were three.

He hesitated on reading them but wanted to know what had been going on. He opened the first one. The handwriting was in cursive, and very bad. It had dried tear drops on the paper as he read to himself:

Dear Joseph,

I ask you plainly as to why you have done this. Why have you taken my two children?

Charlie's eyebrows furrowed. Didn't Mother have three children? What was the third body downstairs that they were still trying to find? He faced the letter again.

As your mother, I only pray you bring back your little brother and sister. They don't want any part of your government ways. This confuses me greatly. We have always been rich but lived as outcasts from the neighborhoods. I have always taught you that the government was not to be trusted. How could you do this?

I pray that you will come to your senses, Joseph.

Love, Mother.

Charlie anxiously opened the next one, breathing quicker.

Dear Joseph,

I know you left this family long ago. You were my oldest son. I have pictures of you and your siblings on the walls. I also have a picture of us all together on your thirteenth birthday...the year you left us.

You don't need to take your brother and sister, too. So, help me God, Joseph Stonewall, don't do something you'll regret.

Mother.

This was all too weird. Mother was Joseph Stonewall's mom? He had to tell Sammy once she woke. They just killed Joseph Stonewall's mother. He read the final note, chills creeping down his spine.

Dear Joseph,

The fact that you couldn't save your brother and sister haunts my mind. You sent the bodies back to me to have a funeral for them. You could not save them from your allies? This betrayal will not be forgotten by this family.

I will never forgive you.

Charlie set the notes down and took a long breath. He leaned over by Sammy and shook her awake by the shoulder. Sammy weakly opened her eyes.

"Hm?"

Charlie held up the notes.

"I got something big to show you."

Part Five

My eyes opened to the bright sunlight. Pine trees surrounded me, and I could still hear the roar of the river.

Did I wash up somewhere?

I turned my head and saw Shang Han lying there next to me.

Where were we?

I suddenly remembered: The Howlers. We hurled ourselves off a cliff and into a river, so I knew we must be far from them now. A huge wave of nausea washed over me when I sat up.

"Ugh, Shang Han, wake up!" I groaned.

Shang Han still lay there like a slug.

I tried to crawl to him but felt an incredible amount pain come over me instead.

"Oh, my God!" I screamed, looking at my legs.

One of them looked fine, but the other had a bloody bone sticking out of it. My mouth opened in a moan. I fell back and stared at the sky, tears running down my face.

"Shang Han!" I called desperately.

Shang Han did not budge. Was he dead? I hope so. He was a pain and we only just met. I stared at the clouds. Was I going to die? I needed to find my brother and sister. I should be getting up. My stupid leg would really hold me back.

It felt like icicles were piercing my skin and tearing it apart.

"Shang Han, wake up!" I yelled as loud as I could through my dry throat.

He did not even stir. I turned back to the sky and took deep breaths. I needed water and food, not to mention medical help for my leg. I inhaled and exhaled slowly. I coughed and turned on my side, throwing up sour liquid. My gut turned and ached.
I was miserable and in some of the worst physical pain I had ever experienced.

I turned back to the sky and saw that someone stood over me. I could not see the person's face because of the light on their body. It looked like a shadow. I could tell the person was a man by his muscular form.

"You alright?" He spoke up.

I thought this guy was an idiot. Did I look alright?

"No." I answered,

"But I know you."

The man laughed a little,

"Really? Who am I?"

I locked eyes with him.

"You're Joseph Stonewall."

The man smiled;

"So, you *do* know who I am. Is it a good thing or a bad thing?"

I scoffed, "let's just say you better be glad my leg is broken so I can't stick my foot up your ass."

"Wow." Joseph put his hands on his hips,

"You must *really* dislike me. Is there a reason?"

He was the reason for my dad's death. I clenched my fists.

"You- "

Before I could say anything, the wave of pain rushed back to my leg and I moaned loudly. Joseph looked down at my leg,

"I better help you out with that." He reached out to scoop me up.

"Don't come near me." I spat.

Joseph picked me up bridal style and began to walk away with me.

"Too late for that." He said.

We passed Shang Han.

"Wait," I said quietly,

"Shang Han...he's with me...we can't leave him."

"He's alright," Joseph told me,

"He's alive and we will get him. But he's not the one with a broken leg."

I sighed, squeezing my eyes shut from the torture my leg gave me.

"How are we gonna fix it?" I asked.

"We will go to headquarters." He answered.

I could not help but notice how strong he was, carrying me. I must be around 150 pounds. Joseph was very strong.

"Headquarters?" I questioned him.

Joseph nodded curtly,

"It's where I've been staying with a few others. They're rebels. I assume you won't tell anyone?"

"Yeah, whatever." I responded, really feeling the torment of wanting to find Finn and Sammy.

"How could you be so dumb as to tell me that you rebel against the government? What if *I* worked for the government?"

Joseph cocked an eyebrow.

"And am I supposed to believe that?"

I groaned a little in agony.

"Touché."

After a small silence, I spoke up again,

"I thought you were loyal to the government."
Joseph shook his head,

"Not anymore. They betrayed me badly." Was all he said.

My eyebrows furrowed. What happened? I remembered distinctly that he said he was loyal to the government the day he killed my dad. He specifically said, 'we don't want no outlaws around here!' Why was he helping me?

"You know I'm an outlaw, right?" I tried to sound intimidating. It clearly failed.

Joseph shook his head again,

"yeah and I know who you are. You're Victoria Hartley."

Now I was impressed.

"How do you know?" I challenged him.

I was disguised. How did he know who I was? Joseph shrugged.

"I've only been catching outlaws since I was thirteen. I can study a person on a wanted sign better than any gov around. I could tell by your facial features, the way your eyebrows curve." He smiled cleverly,

"Your eyes."

I was not satisfied, but I still talked to him anyway.

"So, you're not working for the government...and you still kill outlaws?"

Joseph kept his eyes ahead of him.

"Well, I basically am one now, so no. I've stolen from all kinds of places with this new group of mine."

Joseph held onto me tighter, so I wouldn't slip from his arms. I need to find Finn and Sammy. Dear God, let my leg heal quick.

"Don't worry...I'll come back for your friend."

"He's not my friend." I said back,

"He's just a pain I can't seem to get rid of."

Why would I worry about Shang Han? Was he my family? No. Was he my friend? No.

"You know, you remind me of myself." Joseph chuckled.

That made me angry.

"If I am like you, I would want you to kill me right now." I replied coldly.

Joseph remained very quiet and nothing else was said for a while. We must have walked for another ten minutes before I saw a shack in the distance. I almost wanted to laugh.

"That's your headquarters?"

"Yep," Joseph replied proudly,

"I've been hiding out here with a few other people for the past two months."

I studied the man carefully. He was not the Joseph Stonewall I imagined. He was much kinder. I still hated him for who he was, but he was very handsome, and I could not help but stare at him a little. He looked like a man around twenty-five. I was just estimating his number of years he's lived in this screwed up world. His face was chiseled and very nice to look at due to its charming features. His hair was black and naturally slicked up, looking like one of those stunning men they used to call models. His eyes reminded me of grass in the summer, they were so green and lush. He had some gristle around his face, but it only made him ten times more glorious.

"Why are you staring at me?" He asked curiously even though he wasn't even looking at me.

"I just really hope you'll be struck down dead if I close my eyes and open them again." I blinked several times.

Joseph chuckled.

"Yes, I understand quite well that I am not on your A list."

I nodded.

"Yeah and don't try to take advantage of me while I'm injured. I'm not telling you anything about me."

"What's to tell?" Joseph exclaimed,

"You poisoned everyone back at Black Gates Facility, stole from Pine Shawl Inn, your brother robbed a bank and you all faked your identity!"

My eyes widened.

"How does the government know we faked our identity?!"

Joseph snorted,

"They don't, but I do. Like I said, I can read outlaws in and out."

I growled at another prick of pain.

"I can do the same...for everyone except jackasses."

"I swear, you are quite feisty," Joseph observed as we entered the small room.

"Yeah well- "

I stopped talking when we entered the room. Four men sat at the table. All of them looked intimidating, but intelligent.

"Gentlemen," Joseph announced,

"we have a visitor. Treat her kindly and help her out; she fractured her leg."

"Yes, of course," one of the men replied quickly and hurried into a closet. They brought out a gurney.

I smiled nervously,

"I guess they are like doctors." I realized.

"We are experienced, madam." One man said,

"My brother and I at least. We have a camp a little further down."

I raised my eyebrows,

"Camp?"

"Yes, we have a camp too." Joseph told me,

"Sixty men are there...a couple of women and children too. All of us are against the government."

I shook my head, staring into his eyes.

"Not you." I said lightly.

He sighed.

"Come on, I told you I stopped when- "

He furrowed his eyebrows.

"You seem like you know so much about me..."

I smiled a little.

"I know everything about you, Joseph Stonewall."

"Yeah, that's right. But how?" Joseph asked me.

I swallowed hard,

"You've done so much." Was all I said.

That only confused him more.

"What-?"

"Alright, Miss, we need to operate on your leg. If you would lay down, we are going to put you out."

I laughed a little.

"How can I trust all of you?"

Joseph patted my shoulder. I wanted to slap him in the face for touching me.

"Nothing will happen to you. I promise." He reassured me.

I never trusted anyone. I had been stupid this whole journey. I couldn't disguise myself, fake my name, fight people to survive; no matter what, people would learn who I was.

I couldn't think of that now. All I could think of or pay attention to was the blackness that surrounded me.

Once I woke, I saw a bowl of tomato soup next to me. I saw my leg; bloody and elevated on two pillows. It was kept in a cast. Maybe I would be alright after all. Joseph walked in.

"I thought you might be hungry," he proposed.

I glanced at the bowl of soup. Smelling it made my nose tingle and my stomach rumble.

"How do I know you didn't poison it?" I interrogated him.

"Oh, so I'm *you* now?" Joseph replied smartly.

I hated him. He was a little piece of work and I hated him. He killed my dad, he insulted me, and I wanted nothing more than to take that bowl of hot soup and throw it at his face. I jerked my head towards the soup.

"Give it here." I instructed.

Joseph held up his pointer finger.

"Say please." He ordered.

"Heh. That's not happening. I don't say please." I said firmly.

"Then you don't get soup." Joseph said back.

I almost gave him the finger, but I was too weak. I locked eyes with him again. Joseph gave me a hard look.

"I suppose locking eyes is a habit of ours," he observed.

I kept my hard gaze on him as well.

"I guess." I replied coldly.

We stayed silent. I looked from him to the soup. I was starving. I needed food. I wanted food. I had to have food.

I sighed, rolling my eyes;

"Please," I said with clenched teeth.

Joseph smiled with a touch of satisfaction,

"Better."

He handed me the soup and fed it to me. The man that killed my father, feeding me soup.

I ate it as quick as I could. After eight bites, I weakly plopped my head back on the pillow.

"Leave me now." I whispered,

"Go tend to my friend Shang Han."

Joseph stood up.

"You got it."

"How is he, by the way?" I quickly asked.

Joseph smiled a little.

"He's fine. Just very weak. We have some women feeding him back at camp."

I looked at my leg

"How long must I stay in bed?"

Joseph sighed,

"A long time Victoria."

I closed my eyes in despair and Joseph left. I had to get to my siblings. But first things first:

I had to kill Joseph Stonewall.

—

I slept uncomfortably last night; my leg was drifting me in and out of sleep like a raft on an ocean of pain.

I did not know what day it had been or what time it was. It felt like twelve years. Joseph finally walked in with my breakfast.

"Hello there, sleeping beauty," He greeted me with a chortle.

I gave him the darkest glare I could conjure as he set the tray down. Toast with a small bowl of butter and a knife to spread it on. I stared at the knife. Joseph pulled up a stool and took the knife to spread on the butter for me. I could not take my eyes of the sharp tool.

"The women in the kitchen kicked me out...so I have to butter your toast here."

He gave me a wink.

"I better keep the knife away from you, outlaw." He joked.

He set the knife back on the tray and handed me the plate of toast. I tried not to gawk at the knife sitting on the tray. I weakly took the toast and bit into it.

"How long have I been here?" I asked.

Joseph wiped his hands on his pants and thought.

"Hmm...I think a week and a half now."

I swallowed my food before biting into it again. I was hungry.

"And what day is it?"

Joseph could answer that a little quicker:

"April 19, 2222."

I perked up,

"It's my birthday." I said quickly, not that I cared that he knew. I just thought out loud. I'm seventeen.

"Happy Birthday." Joseph cheerfully exclaimed.

Seeing him happy made me mad. I looked away, my head spinning from worry. What could have happened to my brother and sister? Did they die? I'd throw myself off a cliff if they died.

Joseph folded his hands, probably considering if he should leave. I kept glancing at the knife. I couldn't stop. I wanted this man dead. I wanted to avenge my dad. Joseph stared at me.

"Why do you hate me so much, Victoria?" He asked me again.

Hopefully if I told him, there would be no interruptions this time. I kept my eyes on my lap.

"Answer me something first before I tell you anything."

"Okay," Joseph said willingly.

I took a slow breath and asked him,

"Why did you have the bloodlust to kill so many people? I know you claim they were outlaws...but they were still people. They still had lives that you took."

Joseph looked down. It was quiet for a long time.

"You know, Victoria, I had a tough childhood. From the moment I was thirteen, my heart and mindset changed. I became hardhearted. I did this because the government manipulated me as a child."
I listened closely as he continued explaining himself:

"The men I talked to were kind of like cops without badges and they served the government. They..." he took a breath,

"Let's just say they got me to do bad things...and ended up leaving me to Howlers."

"What bad things did they get you to do?"

Joseph shook his head,

"I will not tell you that. Not now."

I locked eyes with him.

"What makes you think I'll be here long enough for you to tell me?" I questioned him.

Joseph shrugged, keeping his eyes on me. A smile played his lips.

"Not sure. But something tells me you'll be here awhile."

I furrowed my brow.

"Are you...flirting with me?"

Joseph shrugged again.

"Maybe...maybe not."

I laughed a little. Was this guy out of his mind?

"Well, you're very bad at it." I said frankly.

"I guess." Joseph chuckled.

He picked up the tray and set my plate on it.

"Get some rest," he told me.

I stared at him as he left, I tried to get one last glance at the knife.

—

I twitched in bed anxiously tonight.

'I wonder where dad is.' Finn said in a hushed voice.

It was then that we heard some gunshots in the store. It wasn't uncommon to hear those lately. We just waited for dad. I saw some people running away over the hills, but none of them were my father. We just stared at the back window that he had gone through.

No one came out.

We waited one minute.

No one came out.

Two minutes.

No one came out.

I opened my eyes a few moments. How many times have a dreamt this? Ten times? A hundred times? A thousand times?

A million times?

I drifted back to sleep:

I stood back, frozen with shock, anger, and sadness. Sammy climbed on Finn's knee and he picked her up to look.

'Daddy!' She cried, tapping on the window.

I ran over to them, grabbing them both by their arms and running with them to the front of the store. That's when we saw it.

Two men dragged our dad's body out onto the parking lot. I covered Sammy's mouth and held her tight, so she wouldn't scream and run to our dad. Finn clutched my arm and we sat huddled behind the wall.

This was not happening. I tried reaching for a glass of water to calm my nerves down; but my glass was empty. I limply closed my eyes again.

I could hear the men conversing with one another.

'You really got em didn't ye Joseph?' One man with a Scottish accent said.

My heart burned with hatred as I stared at this "Joseph" man that killed my dad.

Joseph grinned.

'Yeah I did! We don't want no outlaws around here!'

My eyes burned with tears. The Scottish man patted Joseph on the back.

"Ye did really good, lad."

Joseph waved his hand to beckon people over. People that were apparently loyal to the government. And Joseph was one of them.

I was beginning to sweat. I thought of Joseph. He was so wonderful, and I refused to see it. How could a man so wonderful be so evil? How? My mind wandered. He was so sweet. He was so gentle now. Did he have a twin? A whole other side of him?

Did I like him?

God, I couldn't like him, I hated him! It was out of the question. Could a girl like the man that killed her father? It wasn't logical.

"Come on, Victoria, you hate the man." I whispered to myself.

No, you don't! My mind screamed.

I sat up, ignoring the ache of my leg. I had to stop. I couldn't like him no matter what. I had to hate him even more. That was what I would do.

—

It had been a week and I was colder than ever towards Joseph. He visited me less because of my hateful attitude. I was glad for that on the outside, but deep down, I was hurting and only feeling worse.

I had kept track of the days now. Ever since Joseph told me what day it was.

When I got better, Shang Han and I would get out of here. I couldn't stop dreaming about what happened. It was almost like the closer I got to Joseph, the more vivid the dreams got. So, I tried to hate him even more. I knew he was confused and didn't understand. I wanted to tell him, but I felt like he wouldn't even care if I did.

He had killed so many people. Why would my father be any different? I suppose he looked like an outlaw for stealing food...but he was just getting rations to feed his family.

The door opened, and someone entered. I prayed it was Joseph, but to my surprise, it was Shang Han.

"Hey!" I exclaimed.

"Hello, Victoria." Shang Han replied.

He looked much healthier and happier.

"How's your leg?" He asked.

"How'd you-?"

"A lot of people know about you in the camp. Joseph talks about you a lot."

I blushed a little. *Stop that!* I wanted to order myself.

"He does?" I tried not to smile.

Shang Han nodded.

"Yeah, he thinks you are fun to spend time with and that you're an outlaw legend."

I scoffed then,

"That's not Joseph."

Shang Han sat down.

"He told me you were acting very bitter towards him."

I glanced at him.

"Don't worry about it. Where is he now?"

Shang Han thought a second:

"He's getting your lunch. He will be here- "

Joseph walked in. He saw Shang Han. Joseph meekly smiled.

"Oh. Hello. Um...Could you-?"

"Yeah." Shang Han understood as he got to his feet and turned to me,

"I'll see you later, Victoria."

"Yeah, bye." I said quietly.

Once Shang Han was gone, I didn't even look at Joseph. He set my tray of food down and faced me.

"Why are you acting this way, Victoria?" He asked me almost sadly,

"I know you kind of disliked me before...but now you completely hate me...did I do something wrong?"

I must have given him a dark look. I could feel my heart burning like fire and my eyes swell with tears.

"Wrong?" I could barely whisper,

"You have done so much...so, so much wrong, Joseph."

"Like what?" He asked me in an exasperated tone.

I sniffed, a couple tears falling from my eyes.

"You killed my dad..." I whispered in despair,

"He was a good man...he only wanted to get food for his starving children. And you killed him. You shot him down like he was nothing! He-only-wanted-to-feed-his-children!" I choked.

Joseph was horrified.

"I..." He murmured.

I wouldn't let him say anything, I only ranted more and sobbed harder.

"I saw the whole thing...you dragged his body out and shouted that you were loyal to the government! I was only nine years old! My brother was seven and my sister was four!"

I had to gasp a few breaths as Joseph tried to reach out to me, but I pulled away.

"Don't touch me! Never touch me! You're nothing but a killer. A *murderer*! Do you know what it was like to have to bury your father at nine years old? Or to hear your four-year-old sister ask, 'what is daddy doing in the ground?' *Do you*?!"

Joseph let out a shaky breath, eyes watering. I didn't care; I only felt angrier with every word I shot out at him.

"Victoria, please," he whispered.

I leaned forward and slapped him. It made a loud noise and he immediately touched his cheek in shock. After a gasp, he glared at me.

"Listen to me," He said firmly.

"No!" I screamed.

"Listen. To. Me." His voice was stone cold.

When I stared at him, he huffed,

"Look, I was a bad man back then. I did the most unforgivable things. They were terrible...I know that. And what I did to your father- "a tear rolled down his cheek,

"I'm so sorry."

I watched him as he scooted closer.

"I know I was bad then...I know I can change though. I've been a changed person the past seven months or so!"

"You are still bad." I spat, "And you are not sorry, and you are not a good person, and you can't change! You are what you are! A murderer!"

Joseph, as hurt as he was, scooted close as he could and touched my face.

"I know I was a monster." He whispered,

"I know I was bad in your eyes...I know I-"

I became lost in his eyes. He was becoming lost in mine, too. I held his hand to my cheek. He sniffed and so did I.

"But can such a bad person love you?" He asked me.

I leaned in and touched his cheek with his bristle against my soft skin. He leaned in, too. I wanted to fight it, oh god, how I wanted to fight it. Our lips pressed together, and my mind screamed. My hands caressed his jaw and his hands stroked my hair. I had passed the point of no return.

Never had I before felt passion for someone like this, though. I cared for this person. Was that wrong?

—

I woke up the next morning, rubbing my eyes. I turned next to me and saw Joseph was gone. My heart beat a little faster, but I tried not to worry. I basically accepted what happened: I loved that man now. He loved me...he told me.

As suspicious as I was of people, I believed him.

I turned on my other side and saw a note. It was addressed to me. I reached out from over the blanket and took the thin sheet of paper.

Opening it, I read:

Victoria,

I don't know how to begin this letter. I know you say you loved me, but I feel in my heart that you still hate me for what I've done.

I mean it, I've changed, really.

I admit, I have feelings for you. I have for a while. I know I've known you for about a month, but I feel that time does not matter. If you need me, I will be in camp. There are crutches by the bedside if you want to come find me.

Love, Joseph

I smiled a little and looked over at the end of the bed to see wooden crutches. I sat up willingly. I wanted to try using the crutches. It would be good for my leg, I think, anyway. I needed exercise. I grabbed my sweatshirt from Joseph and slid it on after I sat up and scooted down the bed slowly. It hurt my leg a little, and I clenched my teeth.

"Come on," I urged myself.

I reached out and grabbed my crutches, smiling widely.

"Yes!"

I looked at the dirt floor. I held the crutches tightly and stood up. Slowly, step by step, I began moving across the room.

Once I made it to the door, I swung it open and let the sunlight blind me. Clouds scattered across the blue sky and pine trees were divided among the land and the grass stood tall and thick.

I moved along the beaten trail. Soon enough, I saw many tents and campfires around in the wooded area. My ears perked up to the sound of music. Happy music well played. It sounded like a fiddle and a couple other instruments. It came from a larger tent, probably the largest in camp. There was even something I hadn't heard in a long time. Laughter. But not just laughter, happy laughter.

I walked inside and entered the room. People were dancing, laughing, conversing, eating, and children were playing. Children. I hadn't seen children in years. Some people looked up; their smiles did not leave their faces. I saw Joseph, he sat with a small girl on his knee.

"Victoria!" He exclaimed.

He set the child down and walked swiftly to me. He kissed me and smiled at everyone.

"This is Victoria, guys." He introduced me.

People waved and said hi. It had been ages since I'd encountered such a friendly group of people. Maybe a person every now and then, but not people. I waved a little, and Joseph kissed my head.

"Well, come on! We are throwing a celebration. Someone had located where some fellow government-supporters are, and we are gonna wipe them out. We hadn't found any gov's for two months. This is a great thing!" Joseph told me excitedly.

I faked a smile, but deep down I wanted to talk to him alone about everything that happened last night. He brought me to a table filled with food. There must have been dozens of things there to eat. I chose a couple rolls and a turkey leg. Joseph took a bite of an apple with a smile.

"You look beautiful," he said to me.

I took a breath.

"I need to talk to you."

His smile faded,

"Is everything okay?"

I took his arm,

"Come on."

We stepped outside the tent and once I leaned on my crutches, I faced him. He stuck his hands in his pockets.

"What do you want to talk about?"

I sighed,

"Look, about last night…"

Joseph closed his eyes and looked down.

"Ah, Victoria..." He sighed,

"Let's just forget the matter."

I blinked several times.

"Okay, well, you know we cannot be together, right?"

Joseph looked like he knew I was going to say that but acted sad anyway.

"Why not?"

I shook my head.

"You know why." I said,

"You killed my dad; how could we be together?"

Joseph stayed quiet awhile and did not look at me.

"I know...but..." he locked eyes with mine,

"I think I actually love you, Victoria."

Deep down, I loved him too, but I decided to replace my gentle behavior with anger, as usual.

"We have only known each other for a month!" I told him, even though it didn't really matter,

"And it feels like-!" I calmed down a moment, closing my eyes and taking a breath,

"And it feels like I've known you for years."

Joseph smiled a little.

"You basically did." He came closer,

"Like I said in my note, if you read it, I feel in my heart you still resent me for what I did to your father...and I will always regret all the terrible things I did. But I feel a special guilt for the pain I caused you and your family."

I crossed my arms.

"You mean to say- what was left of my family?"

"Yes!" Joseph exclaimed,

"I could cry a river, apologize a million times, punch my fist through a thousand walls, roar like a lion until I could scare away every man and woman and child around me out of shame for what I've done- and if you want me to do ANY of those things, tell me now!"

I was about to cry,

"Wow...cheesy." I chuckled, followed by a few tears.

I touched his face and stroked his dark hair.

"I feel like this would be more meaningful in time if we hadn't known each other only a month in person...but I know that you do mean it, right?"

Joseph nodded and hugged me with a kiss on the head.

"I love you, Victoria." He said.

We kissed passionately and locked eyes when we broke apart after a few moments.

"Want to go to the party now?" He asked me.

I smirked,

"I guess, and with this whole ambushing on the gov's thing...I want in." I insisted.

Joseph kissed me again and grinned,

"I couldn't find a better partner."

I looked into his eyes for a long time. And remembered him saying something about the government betraying him and he did something awful.

"Please tell me what happened." I suddenly begged him.

"What do you mean?" Joseph glanced side to side.

"You mentioned you did something horrible with that group of outlaws-what happened? You said you left home at an early age, too." I reminded him.

Joseph closed his eyes.

"Fine." He decided to tell me,

"I left with the corrupted government when I was thirteen. My mother searched for me, soon giving up. Our group became starving when the rightful government came after us, for we had been manipulators, and for that we had to be put to death. We hid away in the wilderness- penniless, as a matter of fact. So, one man had an idea that I..." He stopped to take a shaky breath.

"I could sell my younger brother and sister to the rich people as servants and make some money... instead things turned for the worst. When my men and I came to the tall electric fences of the neighborhood, their guardsmen started shooting at us in alarm. I threw my brother and sister in the way and fled to save my own life. Some of my men were killed as well. I finally retrieved their bodies and ordered a couple of my men to bring them to my mother, so she could bury them. Deep down, I never forgave myself. It had been a desperate time. I still don't forgive myself." He finished his story with tears running down his cheeks like spreading wildfire.

I was shaking to the bone. How awful. Joseph reached out to take both my hands.

"Oh, my love... if you no longer want to be with me, I understand. Frankly, I wouldn't blame you."

I held up my hand to pause him from speaking,

"I just need time to think about it." I told him.

Joseph held his tongue and gave me a nod. He kissed my head and took my hand.

"Let's go inside."

With that, we entered the room once again, my mind spinning. How could I do what I have done with a man with a past such as that?

"I challenge Joseph Stonewall to a fight!" A man called.

Joseph stood up, removing his arm from around my shoulder.

"Oh please, Walker, you couldn't survive a race with a tortoise, and you want to challenge *me* to a fight?"

"You bet!" Walker called loudly,

"I wanna challenge you to a fight and win it, too!"

People whooped and began to gather in the center of the room to watch them fight. Joseph and Walker circled one another, eyeing each other darkly. Joseph's biceps shimmered in the glowing light of lanterns and outdoor campfire light gleaming through the slightly opened door.

By the look of his gray hair and beard, Walker seemed to be in his fifties and wore cheap biker clothes.

"I'm gonna rip out your heart and make you eat it!" Walker yelled.

I did not like this man.

"Oh, go eat your own words," Joseph retorted.

"Stop talking, start hitting!" One man yelled.

Joseph chuckled, and Walker sneered,

"You heard the man."

With that, Walker ran headfirst into Joseph. Like a bull.

They both clashed on the ground with a loud thud, both men groaning. Joseph grabbed Walker by the neck and rolled on top of him, punching him three times before Walker could throw him off. People had to back off, so they would not be in the way of the two men.

Joseph jumped to his feet and kept his fists at the level of his chest. Walker got up too and took a few breaths. He was already winded. I watched them both. I was still troubled over the whole thing with Joseph already. Now there was a possibility of him getting beaten up by a fat man who got winded one minute into a fight.

Walker waited for Joseph to make the first move. Joseph yelled and attempted to punch him in the face, but Walker grabbed him by his sides and threw him down. Joseph's head slammed against the dust.

He groaned and stood up. Walker was still laughing, thinking he had won. But Joseph proved him wrong. Walker was brutally punched in the face. So hard, in fact, that he fell right to the ground.

"Ah!" He yelled, clutching his nose,

"You broke my nose, you bloody- "

"Joseph won!" Someone yelled over Walker's cursing.

People cheered as I ran to Joseph. He was going to have a massive headache, if he didn't already. He planted a kiss on my head.

"I need a drink." He grumbled.

I grinned. A drink? I hadn't had one of those in ages! I followed him over to a bar stool on my crutches.

"Can I have one?" I asked hopefully.

Joseph tossed me a bottle of vodka.

"Normally I would say no, but I know you would take it anyway. So here."

I grinned and took the bottle.

"It's been a long time." I said, staring at the bottle of clear liquid,

"I got you back now, baby!"

I unscrewed the lid and began chugging it. But that was before I remembered how strong vodka was. I used to drink margaritas from the store. Vodka was not sweet at all, it tasted like rubbing alcohol. Joseph laughed when he saw my face scrunch up.

"Oh my God, that is strong!" I gasped.

He laughed and took the bottle to take a drink.

"Yeah. This is the good stuff. I got this from a man back in Zeeland, Michigan. This is pure gold."

I snatched the bottle and took a long drink.

"Well, God bless Michigan!" I announced.

"Amen!" Joseph echoed.

I watched him, and he looked into my eyes. So much had happened between us. So much. I knew if or when my siblings found out about Joseph— and I knew they would whether I told them or not— there would be hell to pay.

Part Six

Finn sped down the road, almost as fast as when the Howler's were chasing him and his siblings while they were in the car.

He had managed to get away by losing the Howlers—God only knows how—and circled around back to Shang Han's limo.

Finn was okay with Shang Han. He had a cool car. It must have cost a fortune. Then again, when did Finn *not* worry about money?

Money was always on his mind. It was a disease that could almost never be cured, but it could not kill him either. There was no antibiotic to get rid of it. It could only be self-motivation. Finn didn't have a lot of that. He just got his way or there would be vengeance.

The limo screeched against gravel, but Finn kept a steady hand on the wheel. There was nothing but open road ahead of him. He had to find his sisters. That was his top priority.

Until he heard a faint voice in the distance.

It sounded like a cry for help. Finn stopped the car and turned the key to stop the engine. He listened carefully.

"*Help!*" He heard a woman scream.

"Holy-"

Finn turned the key again and the engine roared loudly. He sped up, opening his window for some air in the heat of the day. He followed the sound of the cries. It grew louder the closer he got.

"*Help me, someone, please!*"

Finn saw a person silhouetted in the glare of the sun.
It was a woman...and she was pregnant. She saw Finn in the car and began waving frantically.

"*Hey!*" She called in a wail,

"Please help me, sir! Please!"

Finn stopped the car and jumped out as soon as it stopped.

"Ma'am!" He called, running over to her,

"Ma'am, what's wrong?"

The woman was gorgeous. Her white blonde hair hung wavy and shimmery in the sunlight. Her skin was fair, and her eyes were blue. Her face had tears cascading down it. She looked like her belly was about to pop.

"Sir, I need your help! My water broke...I need help delivering the baby."

Finn had no idea what to say. He couldn't just leave this woman standing here. He was no medical professional either, though. Finn let out a small breath.

"Okay."

He swung open the back door to the limo and waved his hand.

"Hop in."

The woman clutched her belly and scooted way back into the seat, laying down. Finn could still sit back there, so he did. He shut the door and left the windows open to let in air.

"What's your name?" Finn asked.

"Eleanor...Eleanor Rigby."

Finn cocked an eyebrow.

"Are you serious? Like the old Beatles song?"

Eleanor rolled her eyes.

"Yes! His last name is Rigby and he is a huge Beatles fan- so he named me Eleanor! Eleanor Rigby!"

Finn chuckled.

"People these days." He muttered.

Eleanor waved her hands in the air.

"Okay, okay, I've introduced myself! Who are you?"

Finn was not about to reveal his identity, so he took a breath,

"My name is- "

"Wait...are you Finn Hartley?!" Eleanor exclaimed, leaning forward to study him closer.

Finn touched his hair which would be growing back soon. How did she know? Maybe this plan of disguise was not as smart as he thought it would be.

"No..." Finn lied.
Eleanor was about to say something, but her mouth opened in a gawking moan.

"Is it coming?" Finn asked.

"No, it's a contraction," Eleanor answered in a huff.

"Oh, lord, soon the baby is gonna be crowning!"

Finn was confused again.

"Crowning? Is this a royal baby or something?"

"No!" Eleanor moaned.

Finn sucked in his cheeks,

"How come you ain't scared of me?"

"What are you talking about, Finn?" She groaned as she held her stomach tightly.

"My name ain't Finn." Finn said, exasperated.

"Yes, it is. I know your face from all those wanted posters hung up around here." Eleanor argued.

"Well whatever. How come you ain't scared of me?" Finn repeated his question.

Eleanor clenched her teeth; maybe one of those contract things were coming back.

"Well, you are being very kind by helping me. That proves you're not entirely a bad person," she answered,

"Oh my God! This is killing me!"

She reached out,

"Take my hand, Finn! Please!" She begged.

Finn awkwardly took her hand.

"You know..." Finn said,

"When I have some pain or stress going on, it helps to talk about it... that's what my dad used to tell my sisters and I anyway."

Eleanor took a breath, her face red and glowing from the pain she was in.

"I'm guessing you want to hear what class I'm from?"

"Yeah. I do." Finn admitted.

Eleanor sighed.

"Well I was with the rich folks. My daddy Franklin Rigby was the richest man in our neighborhood. He inherited all his money from his great grandfather. Any who, I was supposed to inherit his remaining money next since my older brothers are all douchebags. I am my daddy's youngest child. Now he's dying and-" Eleanor had to stop explaining her background to let out another gasp, "So I was next in line for his inheritance. Until things turned around and I had a relationship with one of his colleagues. Resulting in my preg-*ow*!" She screamed in the end,

"When my daddy found out, he disowned me, and now I'm out here all by myself..."

Finn was very interested in this story.

"Who was the man you had a relationship with?"

Eleanor huffed.

"Do you always ask such personal questions?"

"Yes." Finn answered plainly,

"Who is personal? Never met him."

Eleanor rolled her eyes as she moaned a little,

"His name was Joseph Stonewall."

Finn froze.

"Who?"

"Joseph Stonewall." Eleanor repeated,

"I didn't know it at the time, but he was loyal to the government and was just using my dad's money to buy food and supplies for outlaws."

Finn blankly nodded. He couldn't believe it. Eleanor and Joseph Stonewall were lovers. This baby was Joseph's? Eleanor gasped louder than she had before and grabbed the seatbelt and squeezed the daylights out of Finn's hand.

"How long ago was this?" Finn asked.

"A year ago." Eleanor answered.

"Oh God, I think it's coming!" She cried, then gave Finn a look that almost made Finn want to run,

"Look… could you go look down there to see if it is coming?"

Finn thought he didn't hear her right again.

"I'm sorry...you want me to go and check to see if the baby is-?" He didn't want to finish the sentence.

"Yes!" Eleanor answered loudly.

Finn did not want to do that. He slowly went over by her long white skirt she was wearing and lifted it up. He only peeked briefly and set it down again.

"It's all good." He said quickly.

"Finn! I need you to watch for the baby!" Eleanor yelled in agony and in annoyance.

"Look, Eleanor Rigby, I have done a lot of things in life- but one of the things I would rather not do...is watch a baby come out of your skirt!" Finn said defensively.

People say you never know what to expect in a day. Finn would let that quote go on his gravestone after this happened. Eleanor sighed desperately.

"Finn, please."

"I need your help...please."

Finn saw the desperation in her eyes. Normally, he hated begging. But this woman was in serious need of help. Not to mention she was beautiful. So, he sighed and watched for the baby.

"I'm going to wash my eyes out with soap and water after this..." Finn grumbled.

"Oh shut up, it ain't that bad." Eleanor snapped, until her face turned red and she screamed like one of those chicks in a sci-fi horror flick.

Finn's eyes bulged out of his head.

"Oh my God."

He wanted to faint. He tried looking away the whole time and let Eleanor squeeze his hand to death, but he had to watch the baby. Eleanor was puffing in and out for breath.

"I swear...Finn, don't make stupid decisions." She sighed, looking at her belly.

Finn sighed, "A little too late for that, honey. You saw all my wanted posters, right?"

"Yeah, and I saw your eyebrows...yikes." Eleanor cringed.

"Okay, okay, I'm not photogenic." Finn retorted.

Eleanor watched the roof of the car and looked more miserable than ever. Finn held her hand a little more gently. Eleanor closed her eyes tightly.

"How old are you, Eleanor Rigby?" Finn loved saying her last name because it was the name of a song by the oldest band in history.

"Seventeen." Eleanor answered in an exhausted sigh.

Finn moved a strand of hair from her face and she smiled at him. So beautiful... he thought to himself.

"Thanks." Eleanor said gratefully,

"For helping me."

Before Finn could reply, Eleanor screamed in pain. It burst out of her like a bomb.

Sweat formed on her face in big drops as if her head was a storm and sweat was a rain of agony.

"God, it's coming, Finn!" She huffed.

Finn was now more than determined to help her.

"Push it out, Eleanor!" Finn urged her.

Eleanor yelled, pushing with all her might. Finn waited, watching carefully. He could see the head and a ton of blood rush out from her. Eleanor's nails dug into Finn's hand. He did not complain because her pain was probably the worst pain she had ever been in before in her lifetime.

Eleanor remained silent for a few moments before sighing and a few tears streamed down her cheeks before screaming in complete discomfort to what was happening to her. Finn continued to dry her face from sweat and tears. Not to mention he would check for the baby.

Soon enough, a tiny body slid out into the world. At first no noise was made until after a couple seconds; then a loud cry filled the back of the limo. Finn smiled, amazed at what he witnessed.

It was witnessing the beginning of a person's life. This little baby could be an outlaw, a poor person, a rich person...the baby could even work for the government one day...

Finn held the baby in the air, who was bloody and slimy.

"Eleanor, meet your son." Finn announced, handing the baby to his smiling mother.

Eleanor weakly grinned.

"He is the most beautiful thing ever..." she whispered, almost to where Finn could not even hear her.

She sounded so weak...so frail...instead of being red in the face, she was ghost white. Finn looked at the skirt Eleanor had worn. It had gone from white to almost completely crimson. Crimson with her own blood. Finn slowly became horrified. Eleanor smiled weakly.

"Finn...we gotta call him Nehemiah. It's always been my favorite name."

Finn smiled, he wasn't sure if his eyes were watering or not.

"That's a good name."

Eleanor kissed her baby softly.

"Finn, I need you to take him...to my father...Frank Rigby. Go north... just keep going north..."

Finn didn't believe this. Frank Rigby, Eleanor's dad, was a rich man. He lived in one of those neighborhoods that was surrounded by electric fences. Plus, the man disowned her! Would he welcome this baby?

The baby began to cry again, and Finn realized Eleanor had died. She was alive one minute, dead the next. Finn slowly took the baby, trying hard not to cry. He stared at the child. It was the most beautiful baby Finn had ever seen: his small tuft of brown hair, his button nose, his small beady eyes. He was just gorgeous.

Finn's heart immediately softened.

He held the baby tightly.

"Nehemiah Rigby, I promise I will get you home."

—

Finn sped in the limo with the baby crying in his arms. It was almost impossible to drive with a baby. Eleanor's corpse remained in the backseat. He did not want to leave her out in the grass. She did not deserve that. She had to be buried.

He passed a couple of cars.

Go North.

He remembered Eleanor telling him to keep going North. Don't turn at any road. Keep going forward.

Nehemiah continued to cry. Finn could not keep calling him Nehemiah. That name was hard for him to pronounce. Whenever Finn tried too coo his name, he never pronounced it right.

"Calm down Ne-hi-mi-ae."

"It's okay Ne-hemi-ae."

"Don't cry Nae-em-iah."

How did you pronounce his name? He tried to think back to how Eleanor said it. He just could not remember it. Finn had an idea.

"I know...I'm gonna call you Nemo for now." He decided.

The baby didn't care. All he did was cry. Finn tried to watch his driving. He became experienced after stealing his first car at eleven years of age.

He still could not believe this was Joseph Stonewall's baby. Eleanor had a baby with that monster. Finn could still remember what Joseph looked like. He made a mental image of him in his mind the day Joseph killed their father.

Joseph Stonewall was very muscular, with dark hair and fair skin. Now that Finn thought about it, he realized baby Nemo looked just like Joseph.

Finn could not direct hate towards this child, though. It was not the baby's fault it looked like Finn's sworn enemy.

Before he could continue his thoughts of disbelief, he saw a neighborhood in the distance. Finn's entire body became speckled with goosebumps.

"Wow..." Finn whispered.

There must have been nine houses. All of them mansions. They formed kind of a cul-de-sac. The house in the center stood out the most to Finn. It was the largest, most beautiful house he had ever laid eyes on.

Finn stopped the car to stare at it. The other eight houses remained on the other side of the grandest house in even rows of four. He saw trees in the neighborhood, along with nicely cut grass and budding blossoms.
All this beauty remained behind an electric fence at least seventy feet high. He saw guard towers outside the neighborhood, too.

"Great." Finn grumbled.

He drove a lot slower now, and when he got close enough, he took a crowbar from the backseat and slid it in his belt for protection. He held baby Nemo securely and got out of the car. A couple seconds after he got out, he heard a voice:

"Stop right there!"

Finn froze and looked around immediately. Four guards rushed out at him with guns.
They were all pointed directly at his head.

Baby Nemo began to wail in Finn's coat that he had stolen a little while back.

"Calm down," He told the guards gently.

"Who are you?" One of them demanded.

Finn hoped and prayed they did not already know him like Eleanor did.

"My name is not important," Finn declared,
"his is."

Everyone turned their attention to the baby.

"Your baby?" One guard asked in an annoyed tone.

"Not my baby," Finn said with a hint of smugness,

"Eleanor's. Eleanor Rigby's baby."

The guards all lowered their guns grudgingly.

"Eleanor has been exiled."

Finn jerked his head toward the limo,

"Eleanor is dead. She died having the baby."

The men whispered quietly amongst themselves and two of them headed towards the vehicle.

"Dead." One guard announced after he had opened the door.

The lead guard, which is what Finn would call him, sighed.

"Come on." He huffed.

Finn smiled and followed the men up to the electric fence.

"Open the gate!" Lead guard called.

A gate?

There was a screech of iron and two large doors opened.

"Woah." Finn mouthed in disbelief.

He could hear the twitter of birds and the buzz of bees as he entered the luscious green landscapes of the rich people's world.

"You'll find Frank Rigby in there," the guard pointed to the grand house Finn had stared at.

Finn grinned again, patting the baby.

"Thanks."

He hurried over to the mansion door, running up the three cobblestone steps. He knocked on the hollow, dark wood. It only took a few moments before he and baby Nemo were answered by a tall bald man.

"Can I help you?" He bellowed.

Finn tried to sound as polite as he could:

"Hi. Are you Frank Rigby?"

"No. I'm his butler. Mr. Rigby is out of sorts now and is not taking any visitors."

He eyed Finn in a rude manner.

"Come back later."

Before he could close the door, Finn stopped it with his foot. Now the butler was really annoyed.

"Sir, I believe- "

"I have Frank's grandchild here," Finn interrupted.

The butler gawked at the two for what seemed to be hours on end. He finally snapped out of it and opened the door a bit wider.

"Come in."

Finn entered the house with baby Nemo, smiling. The inside was just as glorious as the outside.

"This house is really something else," Finn observed.

There were things Finn had only dreamed of seeing. Things that their father had told them about after he had met a rich man himself. Finn saw a tall metal clock that chimed four in the afternoon.

He saw an east room with a large table and twelve chairs on each side, plus one on each end. Paintings hung on all the walls; massive paintings that should have belonged to royalty.

The West room had two very fancy couches, a fireplace with a moose head mounted in the center above the roaring flames. There was also a TV. At least a seventy-inch. Finn marveled at the grand staircase before him.

"Right this way," the butler guided him up the steps.

Nemo began crying and Finn had to hush him quietly as he followed. The butler led him down an eastward hall. The end of the hallway revealed a massive door bigger than the other doors. The butler knocked quietly and was answered by a raspy voice.

The door opened, and Finn's eyes fell on a man that lay on a king-sized bed. He looked as though he were dying. Dark loops were formed under his eyes. His skin was pale...almost like Eleanor's when she died.

Other than that, the man had aged like fine wine. His face had a large, white mustache that matched his thin white hair. His lips were dry and cracked. He glared at Finn and the baby.

"What is this?" He demanded.

The butler stood next to Finn,

"This boy has something that you may be interested in seeing," he said, and left.

Finn was outraged.

"Wow, very specific!" He called after the butler.

Frank Rigby's glare darkened, and he folded his hands.

"Come here." He instructed.

Finn slowly approached the old man cautiously. Mr. Rigby squinted his eyes.

"You sure have a lighter voice for a grown man..." He commented,

"Now, why have you come here?"

Finn glanced down at baby Nemo and faced Mr. Rigby calmly.

"See this baby?" He asked.

Mr. Rigby blinked a few times.

"I'm not blind...so clearly I do."

Finn side smiled.

"This is your grandchild." He said.

The curious look dissolved on Mr. Rigby's face into anger.

"Get out of my house."

Finn did not budge.

"Look, sir. I know you disowned your daughter..."

"Heh. Yeah..." Mr. Rigby almost chuckled,

"Glad I did too. She really shamed me. She had been lovers with one of my comrades. Now...she had that abomination there." He gestured to baby Nemo.
Finn felt that it was not fair to judge the baby for his daughter's stupid decision.
"To think...I gave her everything. She got much better treatment than her

older brothers did. I granted her ten personal servants. She had a will of millions. She would one day inherit my entire estate...and she fooled me, boy. That's what she did." Mr. Rigby ranted.

Finn stared at Mr. Rigby, completely horrified. Mr. Rigby folded his hands.

"Now I lay here...dying. People say I'm sick, but that's all bull. I am a dying man. I have a sickness, that's for sure. I really do not have long...and I have not told any of my staff. I most likely have a month. And an open will to give someone."

"Yeah well, keep it. You disgust me." Finn scoffed.

"I beg your pardon?" Mr. Rigby demanded.

"You heard me!" Finn exclaimed,

"The way you treat your flesh and blood is terrible! This baby here is your grandson! His name is...Nehe- Nehe-mayo."

"Nehemiah...?" Mr. Rigby assumed.

Finn nodded.

"Right. Ne-heh-miah."

"She loved that name," Mr. Rigby grumbled,

"Another thing about my daughter Eleanor...she promised to wait to have children until after marriage. She promised! Well, that only proves what her promises are worth! She will burn for what she has done! Wherever could she be now?" He glared into Finn's soul,

"Did you-?!"

"No!" Finn answered straightaway,

"I was driving by in my limo and I saw her. She was crying for help and was gonna have her baby! I couldn't just leave her! Then she told me to bring baby Nemo to you!"

"Nemo?" Mr. Rigby questioned him.

Finn glanced at the baby who was now fast asleep.

"That's what I nicknamed him."

Mr. Rigby said nothing but began a long and terrible coughing fit. It almost scared Finn to watch. Mr. Rigby yelled something Finn did not understand, and the butler ran in with some tea. Mr. Rigby drank it quickly then fluttered his hand to tell the butler to leave. Once the butler was gone, Mr. Rigby wiped his mouth.

"She's here...isn't she?" He asked quietly,

"My daughter Eleanor is here?"

Finn's lips tightened,

"Your daughter is dead, sir."

Mr. Rigby made a face that let Finn know he had been stung greater than the betrayal he went through with his daughter.

"Dead?" He murmured.
He tossed his teacup aside and it landed on the floor, crashing into many pieces. Baby Nemo woke up and began bawling.

"Let me hold him," Mr. Rigby insisted.

Finn looked up in shock over the sounds of wailing. He was not sure if he could trust Mr. Rigby with the baby, but he was the baby's grandfather. Finn carefully handed the infant to the old man, who took him as if he were a robin's egg. The baby stopped crying almost immediately. Finn folded his hands nervously,

"I think I best be going, then."

"Oh, no. You must stay!" Mr. Rigby exclaimed.

Finn stopped before the doorway and took a few steady footsteps towards the bed.

"Sir...I have to find my two sisters. You see, we were separated."

Mr. Rigby grinned wryly.

"You're funny. Haven't I just told you how my family is with me? Your sisters probably found something else to do." He said.

"No, they wouldn't do that. We love each other. We've been together all our lives." Finn protested.

"So have me and my family." Mr. Rigby said back, patting the baby gently.

"I beg your pardon, sir, but I'm not you." Finn pointed out.
"Not yet." Mr. Rigby replied swiftly.

Finn stayed planted to the ground.

"I'm sorry?"

Mr. Rigby carefully handed the baby back to Finn, which confused him more. He couldn't hold the baby again, he had to leave.

"I said not yet." Mr. Rigby repeated,

"Boy, have you ever dreamed of being rich?"

Finn did not want to believe what he was asking. He could be asking if Finn would be his heir! That would be crazy! Insane! All Finn ever thought of was his sisters, money, and cars, in that order. .

"Sir, you just met me." Finn mumbled.

Mr. Rigby sighed desperately.

"I know that. I just met you, but you have impressed me greatly. You helped my daughter deliver this grandchild and you have brought him back to me. You barely know us. It proves you have a good heart...unlike my wicked children. You must help me, boy. Help me raise this baby to not be wicked like my daughter...please..."

"Sir, I have to find my sisters!" Finn insisted.

Mr. Rigby seemed to be thinking of anything to convince Finn to stay.

"I know I sound insane...what more to expect from a dying man? I'm begging you, boy."

Finn looked from the dying old man to the sweet baby that lay in his arms.

Mr. Rigby locked eyes with Finn.

"If you do...you can inherit everything." He whispered,

"My millions...my cars...my house...everything! Once I am dead, anyway."

Finn looked at this man as though he had lost his marbles. Which he had. Sure, this man was probably just desperate because he was dying and thought the worst of his own children, as unfair as that was. Finn was a total stranger to him. But all those millions...all those cars...this house...this house enchanted him the minute he saw it.

Where did he get all that stuff anyway? It's 2222!

Finn looked back to Mr. Rigby.

"You just met me!" Finn repeated in shock.

Mr. Rigby smiled a little.

Finn bit his lip and the longing look on his face gave Mr. Rigby an easy answer. Mr. Rigby chuckled a little.

"Many folks do...but they never can. Those electric fences that surround our neighborhoods keep everyone out! Nobody gets in here...except you, I suppose. I'm guessing my little grandson there got you in?"
Finn smiled a bit.

"Yeah." He answered,

"One of your guards let me in when I told him the baby was related to you. I'm sorry for the loss of your daughter...within the brief time I knew her, she seemed amazing."

"Heh. Right." Mr. Rigby scoffed,

"Amazingly idiotic."

Finn frowned. Eleanor Rigby was a wonderful young woman. She just made a mistake was all...she was blessed with a son. Mr. Rigby held out his weak and frail hand.

"The wealthy world awaits you..." he whispered,

"Join me."

Finn stared at the old man's hand.

And gently accepted it.

I will leave eventually, he promised himself. I will leave and go find my sisters. I just have to say I'll be here. After the old man dies, I'm out.

Finn released the handshake and held the baby tighter. Mr. Rigby gave Finn a curt nod.

"Now...what do they call you, boy?"

Finn slowly handed baby Nemo to his grandfather and said,

"You'd probably heard of me; Finn, Finn Hartley."

—

I tossed and turned that night.

Two men dragged our dad's body out onto the parking lot. I covered Sammy's mouth and held her tight, so she wouldn't scream and run to our dad. Finn clutched my arm and we sat huddled behind the wall.

I could hear the men conversing with one another.

Joseph grinned.

"Yeah I did! We don't want no outlaws around here!"

My eyes burned with tears. The Scottish man patted Joseph on the back.

"Ye did real good, lad."

"I am Joseph Stonewall and I am loyal to the government!"

I sat up in bed, gasping for breath. I glanced at Joseph, who lay next to me, fast asleep. That was the twentieth nightmare in a row. I had been with Joseph almost two months in his camp.

The fact that he killed my father lingered on my mind the whole time. I loved him. Though loving him was like eating a poison apple; it was tempting, but it would be the death of me...

What am I doing?

I was so sick of having these dreams. My mind always screamed at me to stop and leave him.

What was I doing here?

I needed to find Finn and Sammy. They were my siblings! I had known them all my life and they were probably looking for me, too. I sat up, limping over to a drawer where a few of my new outfits were and tried to find a bag.

I kept watching for Joseph as he stirred in his bed. I had to get Shang Han and then we would be out of here. I saw a small bag that would probably only fit a few things; so, I decided to take one outfit, a handgun, and some cash. Joseph had some that he probably had stolen after his days of being with the gov's ended.

With Joseph and I together, I knew everything there was to know about him. I knew where he kept everything, too. I took a pair of jeans and my favorite shirt.

I looked under the bed and saw a handgun laying there. I needed bullets along with it. Luckily, I knew just where to go.

I opened the drawer again and dug under all of Joseph's clothes. I found two packages of bullets. I decided to take one and fit it into my bag along with the outfit and the handgun. Last of all, I needed some cash. I walked over to the corner of the room and dragged a stool over to his wardrobe and climbed on top of it to peek.

On top of the wardrobe were some bills and coins. I smiled, taking it all and clenching it in my fist. I opened my hand and counted the money. Forty-six dollars and thirty-nine cents.

Once I had my belongings, I headed for the door, not looking back.

—

After I had woken up Shang Han, we left the camp before dawn. We stole a motorcycle parked by a pine tree that had the keys already in the keyhole left there by a dumb jack.

"It's really too bad we're leaving," Shang Han said disappointedly as I struggled to drive on the road.

I was not experienced with a motorcycle whatsoever. I only knew how to start one because my dad used to have one and he would sit me on his lap and let me "drive" it.

"Why?" I asked him.

"Because...I think it's kind of cruel what you're doing. Joseph loves you."

I rolled my eyes.

"He doesn't *really* love me."

When I said that, I was not only lying to Shang Han, I was lying to myself.

"I don't know..." Shang Han mumbled.

I ignored him and kept my concentration on my horrible driving.

We drove for hours. Until the motorcycle stopped all the sudden.

"Oh, come on!" I groaned.

"Looks like it's out of gas." Shang Han observed.

I closed my eyes.

"Shang Han...what's the date?"

Shang Han thought a minute,

"Not sure, why?"

I sighed, covering my eyes to hide my tears.

"Has it been one month or two months since I've been separated from my brother and sister?"

Shang Han sighed.

"I'm not even sure anymore."

I rubbed my sore eyes and sniffed.

"Shang Han, what am I doing?"

I took a shaky breath and paced back and forth.

"What am I doing? I had relations with the man that killed my father! Who does that? If my siblings find out, they will hate me forever. I should have stuck to looking for them. I'm sure they are out there, terrified! Terrified because their sister hasn't found them yet!"

I walked over to the lifeless motorcycle and sat down, crying. Shang Han was stunned.

"Are you on your period or something?" He mumbled.

I wiped my eyes, taking deep breaths.

"We have to keep looking for them, Shang Han. I don't know where we are, or what time of day it is, but we need to keep looking."

Shang Han walked over to me and laid a hand on my back.

"It's gonna be okay, Victoria. You are a strong woman. You can get through anything. You couldn't look for your brother and sister because your leg was broken. You also can't help that you love Joseph...no matter what, you can't change what he's done...and yeah, your siblings are gonna be very angry." Shang Han glanced downward,

---

Patient 606 161

"Who says you have to tell them?"

I scoffed,

"I was already planning on it."

Shang Han took my arm and stood me up.

"You ain't a bad person for loving someone." He pointed out.

"I don't love him." I whispered angrily.

"I hate him."

"Now, we both know that's not true." Shang Han said.

I remained quiet for some time. Until he touched my cheek briefly.

"You are strong, and beautiful, and-" he stopped himself mid-sentence,

"You can get through anything."

He walked over to my bag which had fallen. I stared at him a long time. Shang Han smiled and handed it to me.

"Let's go." He whispered.

I stared at him while I accepted the bag and following him.

—

We walked for the next two days. I was tired, thirsty, and hungry. I looked at Shang Han, who was exhausted too.

I kept thinking of Joseph no matter how hard I tried not to. I thought of the way he touched my shoulder, kissed me, held me...I just thought of him in general.

"Victoria..." Shang Han whispered, stopping me.

I rolled my eyes, snapping out of my daze.

"Yeah?"

"Look." Shang Han pointed to a figure in the distance.

I peered out through the harsh glare of the sun.

I could not believe what I saw.

"Oh my God..." I whispered,

"It's Sammy."

I came in close contact with my sister at long last. We faced each other in awe. As if we were from totally other planets. My sister was bloody and had dark circles ringing her eyes. A bandage was wrapped around her crop top. Was she shot? I wonder how she managed that...

We stared at each other, tears filling both our eyes. A smile came to her face and she hurried towards me. We embraced one another tighter than ever. I felt an immense wave of relief wash over me.

Part Seven

(Three Years Later)

IT IS 2225. THE WORLD HAS PLUMMETED FURTHER AS EACH YEAR PASSED.

VICTORIA AND SAMMY HAVE BEEN ON THE ROAD LOOKING FOR FINN, WHO IS NOWHERE TO BE FOUND. SHANG HAN STILL STAYS WITH THEIR GROUP.

VICTORIA HAS NOT TOLD SAMMY ABOUT HER LOVE FOR THE MAN THAT KILLED THEIR FATHER BUT WORRIES THAT HE WILL FIND THEM, AND HER SISTER WILL FIND OUT.

AFTER FRANKLIN RIGBY PASSED AWAY, FINN INHERITED EVERYTHING AND CONTINUES TO RAISE BABY NEMO RIGBY, WHO IS NOW THREE YEARS OLD AND IS FIFTEEN YEARS AWAY FROM INHERITING HALF OF FINN'S ESTATE. FINN HAS BEGUN HIS OWN EMPIRE AND EXPANDED THE RICH NEIGHBORHOOD, HAVING EVERY SINGLE WEALTHY MAN, WOMAN, AND CHILD FROM THE ENTIRE UNITED STATES MOVE TO HIS NEIGHBORHOOD, WHICH IS NOW A NEIGHBORHOOD OF 667 HOUSES.

THE GOVERNMENT HAS BUILT 110 MORE FACILITIES AND THE UNARRESTED OUTLAW COUNT IS LESS THAN 5,000.

THE POOR HAVE ALL LIVED THE SAME HARD LIFE, TRYING TO SURVIVE NOW THAT THERE ARE FEWER STORES AND PLACES TO GO. THE GOVERNMENT HAS BEEN TOO FOCUSED ON CATCHING OUTLAWS TO DO ANYTHING ABOUT THE GROWING NUMBER OF LOWER-CLASS PEOPLE.

MAY 2225 GO PLACIDLY.

The sun glared at my skin, reddening and burning it. My outfit did not help; everything I wore was black, which looked good with my auburn-dyed hair.

Sammy, now fourteen, matured very nicely and was ten times more beautiful than I. She still wore the same thickly-framed glasses and now had long, curly blonde hair.

Shang Han looked almost the same except he had a goatee.

"We need a car," he groaned,

"I can't believe our other one got stolen. This is driving me crazy!"

"How many wanted signs do you think we passed for stealing that car?" Sammy asked out loud.

"Like, sixty." I answered straightaway,

We kept walking through the grassland as the sun beat down viciously on our bodies.

—

Nighttime always came as a blessing. I loved to watch the moon and the stars. Not to mention, the air was much crisper.

The only thing was, whenever I marveled at the stars, I thought of Joseph. I would think of our nights of watching the stars, as corny as that sounded. I laid on the ground, trying to find sleep. Shang Han snored loudly, and Sammy sat up.

"Victoria...why won't you tell me what happened in the time we were separated?" She sighed,

"It's been three years. I know you said you and Shang Han went through something terrible, but you two can tell me. I'm sure it's not that bad. Like I've said multiple times, I ended up meeting Joseph Stonewall's mother! Need I remind you; *Joseph Stonewall* is the man that killed our father. So basically, I met the murderer's mother!"

I agitatedly sat up.

"Sammy, you ask me to tell you what happened for the past three years almost every other week! For the thousandth time, I'm at the end of my wits, and I cannot tell you what happened! I'm sorry, but Shang Han won't, either!"

Sammy sighed, laying back down.

"It's not fair." She mumbled,

"I told you everything that happened to me and all you have the guts to tell me is that you went through something terrible but won't even go into detail!"

I rolled my eyes.

"Yeah well, life isn't fair so get over it, will you?"

Sammy let out a long sigh before rolling over and going to sleep. I stared at the stars. Sleep evaded me.

—

I saw myself standing in a mirror. I faced myself, wide eyed. A person approached from behind me. It was Joseph.

"Victoria..." Joseph whispered.

"Joseph?" I whispered back.

His hand touched my shoulder gently, stroking my hair and moving behind my shoulder.

"Why did you leave me?" Joseph spoke quietly in my ear.

I shook a little.

"I had to leave you...you killed my father; I can't be with the man that killed my father." I replied.

He turned my cheek to face him, pressing his lips to mine. I responded by kissing him back. Once we broke apart, he smiled a little.

"Come back to me, baby." He whispered to me.

I shook my head,

"I can't...",

"I'm so sorry, but I can't."

Joseph reached out and took my face in his hands.

"I love you." He said,

"I'm gonna find you."

"No!" I whispered sharply.

My eyes watered, and I faced him with determination.

"Find someone else. Find someone who will love you. It can't be me."

I caressed his jaw.

"It can't be me." I repeated.

Joseph kissed me passionately until I was out of breath.

"It can't be me." I said again.

"I will find you." Joseph promised,

"I'm coming."

I sat up in a deep gasp.

The sun peeked out from just below the pine trees in the distance. The sky still had stars, but they were quickly fading.

"Shang Han! Sammy!" I whispered sharply,

"Wake up!"

My sister's eyes snapped open, along with Shang Han's. Sammy seemed angry that I woke her up.

"Victoria, what-?"

"We need to leave." I ordered,

"We need to leave now!"

"Why?" Shang Han rubbed his eyes.

I shook my head,

"I can't explain! We just need to go!"

When Sammy and Shang Han stared at me, I became angry,

"Let's go now!"

With a small groan, everyone got up.

—

Even after a few days, the heat of summer was so unforgiving on us. My sunburn was ten times worse and I simply wanted nighttime to come so the darkness and crisp air could cool my skin.

"It's so hot." Shang Han groaned loudly.

"Oh, hang in there." I snapped.

Sammy sweat through her clothes as she tried to fan herself with her wet shirt.

We kept walking. A large group of ducks flew across the sky.

"Looking at those ducks remind me of home..." Shang Han commented calmly.

"Ducks remind you of home?" Sammy questioned.

"Back when I was rich, my family had a small pond outside of their house. It was so beautiful... ducks would nest there and swim in the water. I used to feed them. They were so peaceful."

I smiled at Shang Han who returned the smile back to me.

We turned back to the ducks. A shot echoed through the morning peace. One of the graceful ducks fell to the earth below without a sound.

I stood there with the others, horrified. Who would be so horrible as to shoot an innocent creature like that? My answer was revealed. Through the bright sunlight, we saw him.

We saw Finn.

Finn had a rifle clenched in his hand and a look of pure shock on his face. A couple other men came up from behind him with hunting rifles, too.

We all stood there, absolutely dumbfounded.

"Victoria?" Finn spoke quietly.

He walked over to us and touched my face with a grin and tears coming to his eyes. He walked up to Sammy.

"Sammy?"

Finn had changed. Like all of us. He was seventeen now. He seemed way older. He must have been six-foot-something now, due to his appearance. His smile remained handsome and his eyes were still chocolate brown. His hair had grown and stood up, probably because of fancy gel.

My God.

My brother looked like some rich man!

"Finn, where have you been all this time?" I demanded.

I was in no mood for sappy stuff. I wanted answers. Finn tightened his lips.

"I have been running the Rigby estate, along with building my empire. But right now, I am duck hunting."

I was not sure whether to interrogate him more, or to just slap him across the face. My throat swelled along with my anger.

"Finn *Hartley, we have been looking for you for three years, and you've been building some damned empire*?!" I yelled.

"How have you not been arrested by the government yet?" Sammy asked, not believing any of this.

Finn clapped his hands once.

"The reason why you or the government could not find us was because our huge empire is hidden. You see, I have all the rich people from the United States of America living in my neighborhood. I have an empire of six-hundred-and-sixty-seven houses!"

I scoffed, scanning my brother with my eyes from head to toe.

"So, money really is more important than family," I observed.

"Victoria, you know that is not true!" Finn exclaimed,

"I tried to find you; I really did!"

"Seems like you would have had enough guards to help look for us," Shang Han sneered.

Finn turned to Shang Han as if he didn't notice him before.

"Hello, Shang Han." Finn greeted him with a touch of boredom in his voice.

Shang Han faked a bow,

"Well, hello, your majesty."

Sammy snorted, but I held my glare. Finn faced me now.

"Victoria...Sammy...Shang Han...come to my home. Come to the Rigby estate. I'll explain it all there."

"What is the Rigby estate?" Shang Han rolled his eyes,

"Who are the Rigby's?"

Finn raised his hand.

"Like I said, I'll explain there."

—

We walked about twenty minutes before we came to a forest. Finn smiled widely.

"There used to be no trees around here," he began,

"We have them all grown in. Another way to hide our empire."

"Quit saying empire like you're the emperor of China," I snapped.

"I will call it whatever I want." Finn replied calmly.

"I thought rich neighborhoods have electric fences. I don't see anything..." Sammy said.

Finn smiled at her and we came to some sort of tunnel.

"Right this way," he guided us.

The men that had followed Finn while he was hunting shot us dirty looks. They clearly thought we didn't deserve all the attention Finn was giving us. We walked through the tunnel with nothing but curiosity. I was still pissed at Finn, as was Shang Han, but Sammy seemed enchanted by this empire Finn spoke of.

The tunnel was a short walk before we made it to paradise. A surreal, magical paradise. All of it remained behind a screen, which must be the electric fence, that stood at least sixty feet high.

"That fence is seventy feet high!" Finn vocalized my thoughts.

He put his hands on his hips, the rifle strapped around his shoulder, and looked up.

"Alfonso! Open the gates! I'm back with my family!"

Alfonso gave us a smile and pressed a button that made a loud beeping noise before the fence opened to us. I stared at the beauty and wealth that casted a spell on me. Mansions as tall as sycamores stood proudly in line next to each other. The grass and trees grew green and luscious within the area. We stepped onto the cobblestone path. People walked around and conversed with one another as if life was peaches and cream. Which, around here, it must be all the time.

"Here, we are all people with millions or billions of dollars and live in harmony," Finn said proudly.

"Where do you get all the food and supplies to run your neighborhood?" Shang Han asked.

"We pay people from overseas to ship the supplies. Places like Europe, China, and South America for the fruit, anyways. They need the money to manufacture goods. It's really quite complicated to explain," Finn answered.

"Well, what about the money?" I asked loudly,

"I'm quite interested to know where all this money came from to build this...empire?"

Finn smiled at me. It was the same side smile he always had when he was being clever.

"All I can say is how I received the money I got."

"Do explain." I commanded him lightly.

Finn waved his hand to a house that must have been the biggest I had ever seen in my entire life. My mouth gaped as Finn hurried up the short steps to the front door.

"Here's my little cabin in the woods." He bragged.

The men that were duck hunting with Finn had gone back to their own homes, so it was only me, Sammy, and Shang Han left to see Finn's beast-of-a-house.

Once we entered, I feasted my eyes on the luxurious home. I could see many hallways and rooms in the distance but the thing my eyes first fell on was a massive chandelier hanging from the ceiling, almost like the ones in churches.

"This is insane." Sammy murmured.

"This is bigger than my old house, that's for sure." Shang Han added.

Finn turned around and straightened the collar of his fancy blue shirt.

"Why yes, I suppose this is the grandest house in all of the United States. Perhaps the entire world."

I didn't like this new, evolved Finn Hartley. He never sounded greedier. His weak spot for money had ruined his heart and torn it to shreds. Before I could say anything, I heard the pitter-patter of feet coming from upstairs. To my surprise, a small boy came trotting down the steps and held onto the railing. A huge smile pulled up the corners of his lips.

"Daddy!" The child exclaimed.

I looked behind me to see if there was some man that was the little boy's dad, but to my even greater surprise, the little boy ran into Finn's outstretched arms.

"Nemo! Come to daddy!" He replied, kissing the boy's cheek.
My mouth dropped open. Sammy's wide blue eyes expanded. Shang Han only laughed a little.

"Finn Hartley..." I whispered,

"What in God's name did you do?"

"It was bound to happen..." Shang Han mumbled.

Sammy nudged Shang Han aside and stepped forward.

"Finn, who is that?!"

Finn picked up the small child who tried to hide his face in Finn's shirt.

"This is my son Nehemiah. I call him Nemo because his name is too hard for me to say ninety percent of the time."

Nemo waved shyly before kicking his legs to be set down. Finn laughed.

"Demanding, like me."

The maids that had apparently followed the child downstairs chuckled with Finn. I balled my hands into fists.

"Who is the mother of this child? I want to meet her right now!" I ordered.

Finn held up his hand again.

"She passed away a few years ago. Actually, while she was delivering Nemo." He explained.

I did not know how to react, so I simply folded my hands and took a breath.

"Well I am sorry, but Finn, how could you be so idiotic as to have a baby at your age?"

Finn chuckled.

"This child isn't really mine," He explained,

"I adopted him after his mother died. I found her on the side of the road when I was looking for you and Sammy. She was in labor."

I closed my eyes.

"So, you returned the baby to his family, why didn't you come back and keep looking for us?!"

"Because the grandfather of the baby, Frank Rigby, told me if I stayed with him and his grandson...I could inherit everything!" Finn answered.

Sammy looked so hurt and it broke my heart to see her reaction. I was just as hurt as she was. Shang Han was annoyed.

"So, it's exactly what I thought..." I mumbled,

"You gave up on us, so you could have enough money to satisfy God almighty himself!"

Finn pinched the bridge of his nose.

"I know it sounds so wrong...but I was doing it for my son!"

"He is not your son!" I snapped.

That ticked Finn off.

"Listen here, Nemo is my son!"

He turned to the child who was standing there with his thumb in his mouth and a confused look on his face. Finn crouched down to Nemo's level.

"Why don't you go play with your toys upstairs?" He suggested in a friendly tone.

He gave Nemo's personal maids a nod and they took him upstairs to play. I crossed my arms bitterly to face my brother. His jaw was tight, and he pointed a finger at me.

"Don't you ever speak that way to me in front of my son." He told me with clenched teeth,

"He is only a child!"

I waved my hands in the air.

"What about the government?!" I exclaimed,

"What about running away? We don't want to be captured and thrown into another facility, do we?! Black Gates was our final straw, Finn! If we get caught, we will be put to death!"

Finn smiled at me.

"Oh, Victoria." He said,

"I've taken care of that...I am no longer wanted by the government because Frank Rigby paid for everything that I had stolen before he died. He is friends with people that work for the government and promised them that I would do no more wrong. But if I ever leave my empire, then they will be notified, and I could be wanted by the government again."

I was so disgusted with him that I could hardly speak.

"So, you allowed them to track you?" I whispered shakily.

Finn opened his mouth to reveal a blue tooth. A tracker.

"They put me to sleep and put it in...and I agreed to do this: To stay in this neighborhood. Then I would not be wanted by the government and I could live my life without running."

I was so angry I could feel my blood boiling under my flesh. I slapped Finn across the face. Sammy gasped, and Shang Han grinned. Finn touched his reddened cheek in shock.

"How dare-?"

"You are the most selfish, conniving person I have ever met!" I screamed.

I took a small and unsteady breath before I continued my rant;

"How could you do this? We have spent years and years looking for you! Now you sit high and mighty with the rest of the fools of this place. All your rich people are oblivious to what goes on in the outside world. There are hardly any outlaws left and here you sit, drinking your wine and raising a child that is not yours. By God, the hate I have for you is more than all the millions you have inherited! You say you have "freed" yourself but haven't even attempted to look for Sammy or me! What is wrong with you?!"

Finn listened to me and maintained a calm look, but I knew him better than that. He was hurt by my words. I knew he was. Finn came to me and Sammy and held out his hands for us to take them. I stared at his palm. He was still my brother. I still loved him, somehow, despite his arrogance.

Sammy and I took his hands. Finn smiled a bit.

"Come stay with me for a while. Forever if you must. I will see what I can do about letting you go..."

I shook my head.

"We will not stay forever, Finn. I am sorry, but I will not allow the government to track me and I do not want to feel trapped here. Like you said, if we permanently left this place...the government would want us again and if they found us...we would be put to death."

"Just like before...when we were always on the run." Finn nodded.

"Why were you out duck hunting, then?" Shang Han challenged him.

Finn grinned.

"Why do you think I had those men hunting with me?"

I dropped my arms in annoyance. The men Finn had hunted with were really guards to make sure Finn was not escaping. Finn was truly trapped in his own empire. It was confusing and wrong.

"Finn...we can get you out of here." I whispered,

"We can all run together...we can do something about your blue tracker tooth... just come with us." I pleaded.

Finn shook his head.

"I'm sorry, Victoria...but I ain't gonna try. It's way too risky."

He faked a smile at us.

"Come stay for a little while. It will be worth it...we can, I dunno, catch up?"

I closed my eyes, taking a breath.

"Show us to our rooms." I sighed.

Finn grinned and waved his hand to lead us up the stairs. Sammy kept a meek smile; Shang Han was just annoyed that I allowed us to stay.

—

Dinner was amazing. We sat in Finn's grand dining room and drank expensive red wine.

I'd never had wine (let alone expensive wine). Sammy held her wine glass eagerly while she gulped the liquid down. Waiters came out with our first course: chicken salad and crackers.

Shang Han stared at all the silverware placed before him. He chose his salad fork and ate quietly.

"You know, Finn, my family did not have this much silverware," he pointed out.

Finn blinked multiple times and set his wine glass down.

"Were you even rich, Shang Han?"

"Be nice." I murmured to Finn,

"He's helped us through a lot."

"I feel like he scorns me for everything I do." Finn muttered back.

I did not respond and ate my salad quietly. Nemo played with his salad.

"Dad, I don't want this. I want something gooder."

"Then don't eat it." Finn replied.

Nemo held up his bowl of salad and a servant took it away. It's funny how an adult would answer to a three-year-old. I watched, trying to keep control over myself and the secret I had kept from everybody. Only this secret was something Shang Han didn't even know.

"Victoria..." Shang Han murmured,

"Are you alright?"

I snapped out of it and Finn looked at me curiously. Sammy rolled her eyes.

"When we were all separated, Victoria claims that she and Shang Han had gone through something terrible. After three years...they told me nothing."

Finn finished the last of his salad and smiled.

"I'm sure you could tell your ol' brother, couldn't you?" He asked me.

I shook my head.

"No... I'm sorry...I don't like to talk about it."

Servants came over and took the salad away and gave us corn chowder.

"Why not?" Finn asked me.

All I could think of was my Joseph.

Not mine anymore...

"I just can't." I said as I ate a spoonful of my corn chowder.

"Daddy, I want to go play." Nemo broke the thick silence.

"No. The main course hasn't arrived yet. And I'm sure you want dessert." Finn replied.

Nemo pouted while he tapped his fork against his bowl.

"This isn't the main course?" Sammy asked as she gestured to her chowder.

"Oh, no," Finn laughed,

"We still have a way to go."

I played with my food quietly. Joseph haunted my mind.

I'm coming...

"It can't be me." I said aloud.

Everyone looked up.

"What?" Finn wanted me to repeat myself.

I looked at all of them with my eyes watering. You know that feeling where you want to cry, but you can't because you're in front of a group of people which makes it ten times harder to hold it in? I felt that way now. I stood up from the table and hurried away from the dining room.

Tears escaped my eyes as I sat on the balcony stairs.

I missed him. As wrong as it was to love him because of what he did, I missed him. I love him. Part of me worried that he was not even trying to find me. Maybe he moved on to someone else.

"Victoria?"

I looked up to see Finn standing there. He came and sat next to me as I sniffled and sobbed some more. Finn pulled a handkerchief from his pocket, handing it to me. Since when did Finn start carrying handkerchiefs?

"What's wrong?" He asked me quietly.

I remember back when we kept transferring to different facilities...I would tell Finn everything because Sammy was too little to understand. I could not tell him about Joseph. Because he was the man that killed our dad. Finn would never forgive me.

"Well..." I mumbled, wiping a tear from my cheek,

"While we were all separated, Shang Han and I went to a camp because I had broken my leg. We needed help."

I shook my head.

"Someone helped us, I should say. He was so kind...so special... I really loved him, Finn."

Finn's eyes grew wide and his lips parted.

"Who?" He asked me in shock,

"Who was it?"

My face reddened, and I bawled.

"I need to go lay down..." I whispered.

Finn reached out to stand me up.

"Come finish your dinner first." He insisted.

I hurriedly wiped my eyes and followed him to the dining room.

—

After the rest of the meal, which was medium rare steak, carrots, and fried apples, and a dessert of peach cobbler, I hurried up the stairs and into bed. Finn had told me which room to go to and I was more than ready to go to sleep.

Once my head hit the soft pillow, I bawled like a baby. Until I fell asleep.

I love you, Victoria.

I couldn't find a better woman even if I tried.

I'm coming...

—

I sat up in a cold sweat, gasping as my door opened.

The person that entered my room was none other than Finn himself, with a tray.

"Good morning." He greeted me cheerily,

"Or should I say afternoon? You slept the day away, Victoria!"

He set my tray of food on my lap. Eggs, bacon, and toast. I wasn't even hungry. I studied my brother curiously.

"What's gotten you all cheery?"

Finn offered a nervous smile.

"I wanted to wait to tell you...but oh, what the heck!"

He sat on my bed next to me and patted my hands.

"I realized last night that all you wanted was someone to love...someone to love you...and I understand that! So, I had some people get together and post flyers all over the area! I couldn't go, of course, but my guards did it for me!"

My eyes slowly widened,

"What are you saying, Finn...?"

"I'm saying I am going to be holding a contest...here, in the manor! A contest for your hand in marriage!"

I wanted to throw my tray of food at his smug little face.

"Are you out of your damn mind?!" I exclaimed.

Finn tried to calm me down.

"Now, Victoria, you are twenty years old! You need a suitor!"

I spent my seventeenth birthday with Joseph in his camp three years ago. Finn continued talking,

"I sent people on motorbikes and they are going to go all over and post flyers. Those who are interested will come here and anyone suspicious will be shot by my guards!"

"Finn, you have come up with pathetic plans in the past...but this is the frosting on the cupcake!" I yelled.

I wanted to be with Joseph.

"I know, it's crazy, but we will have guards making sure no one bad comes in. It will be a piece of cake!" Finn reassured me.

I still wanted Joseph.

"Victoria, I'm trying to help you! I have many fine men here who are already interested in doing these tasks!"

My eyebrows furrowed.

"What tasks?"

"It's more of a competition, really. Men from all over will be selected to compete for your hand."

"Selected? I thought they could just come!" I said.

"No, no. They will come, and my guards and I will hold conferences with each man that comes to the gates of my empire... the top three men with the most worth will compete for your hand in marriage."

I was getting a headache.

"How long will it take for you to select three men?" I asked.

Finn thought a minute,

"Probably a week or two. It takes time for men to travel of course, but my men will take them over most likely by bus after the flyers have been recognized. Don't worry, I'll figure something out."

I rolled my eyes.

"I'm sure you will." I said back.

Finn kissed my cheek.

"I'll see you later. Enjoy your food." He told me.

With that, he left.

Let's just say I had a good, long cry.

Part Eight

After being in Finn's home for another two and a half weeks, I thought more and more about Joseph. It killed me that I could tell no one about him only because I was afraid of being hated.

I would spend my days playing with Nemo and his toys. I never owned such nice toys like he had.

Finn burst through the door to his son's room.

"Marvelous news, Victoria!" He shouted.

I was so stunned by his outburst that I could hardly respond.

"W-W-What?" I stammered.

Finn waved three slips of paper in the air.

"The three suitors have been selected!" He announced.

I wanted to tell Finn that I wanted no part of this. I had tried a million times. He just would not listen.

"When do they start competing for me?" I mumbled.

"In two days," Finn said excitedly, "They are coming tonight. You will get to meet the three of them! I am positively sure that they will blow you away."

"Heh. I'm sure." I responded sarcastically, handing Nemo one of his toy trucks.

Nemo made loud crashing noises with his cars over me and Finn's conversation.

Finn had a sly smile.

"I'm sure there is one you may favor over them all..." he hinted.

I had no idea what that meant. I wished it was Joseph. But it wasn't. Therefore, I did not care.

"See you at dinner." I bid him.

That was his cue for him to leave me alone. Finn clapped his hands once.

"Right, then, see you at dinner."

Once he was gone, I turned to little Nemo, who kept playing.

"Your daddy can be ridiculous sometimes. You know that?" I asked him.

"I know." Nemo replied,

"He's funny, though."

"Yeah, he sure is." I agreed with him,

"You're three years old, right?"

"Yep." Nemo replied, bumping his toy car into my knee,

"I wanna show you my toy tiger now," he insisted, taking my hand and leading me up the stairs.

I followed Nemo to see his toy tiger.

—

I dressed myself in a nice, short, and white dress with white high heels. It was the outfit Finn wanted me to wear. Since it was pretty, I agreed.

I tied my hair into a braid, studying myself in the mirror.

What was I doing?

Why was I agreeing to this?

Well, no time to pout about it now. Because now would be the time I would meet the three men that may or may not end up marrying me. I made my way down the stairs and finally found my way to the dining room. This was such a huge house.

Finn sat at the end of the long table and raised a glass of red wine when he saw me walk in.

"You look amazing, Victoria."

A servant rushed forward to pull back a chair for me.

"Have a seat. The suitors will be here shortly."

Once I sat down, Sammy came in. She wore a nice blue dress and blue heels. Her diamond earrings were amazing.

"Sammy, you look wonderful!" Finn complimented her.

She thanked him shyly and sat down. I smiled at her.

"You look good, girl." I said nicely.

After looking around curiously, I asked,

"Where's Shang Han?"

Before Sammy could answer, Finn interrupted her.

"He's getting ready," he told me quickly.

I faced my sister, wondering something else.

"Do you know who the suitors are?" I asked her.

Sammy glanced downward nervously.

"I know one of them..." she murmured.

"Sammy, hush!" Finn whispered harshly but kept his smile,

"We don't want to drop any hints!"

"You did, a while back." I said to him.

Before Finn could reply, there was a knock at the door. It was opened by a servant.

"The suitors are here, sir." She told Finn.

Finn looked like he could squeal like a silly schoolgirl.

"Yes! Let them in, Gertrude!" He told his servant anxiously.

Finn got out of his seat when the door opened. Finn waved his hand at the first suitor.

"Introducing...Mr. Adam Harp. He's one of the wealthiest men in my empire."

Adam Harp stepped in the room. How could I describe Adam Harp?

He was tall, very tall. He must have been six-foot-two, at least, and wore very fancy clothes. His black shirt was slightly unbuttoned and revealed some dark chest hair. It matched his curly black hair. His skin was more on the tan side and he gave a dashing smile,

"Hello there, Miss." He greeted me in a low voice.

He was like that Filipino dream everyone had.

"Hello." I replied politely.

Adam Harp seemed like a man that got a lot of respect. I could not avoid his muscular arms...they reminded me of Joseph's. He still wasn't Joseph, and that was a big minus on his part. Finn smiled broadly.

"Mr. Harp is a man with a bank account almost as large as his heart. He plays the guitar and is quite the ladies' man. He claims he is ready to settle down and marry you. Not to mention, go through the tasks I've been planning. He is an honorable man."

Mr. Harp gave me another charming smile.

"You can take a seat, Mr. Harp." Finn said as he pulled back a chair across from me.

Mr. Harp winked at me and sat down. I tapped my fingers against the table nervously.

Finn gave me a witty smile. "This is the one I've been waiting to show you," he said excitedly.

Finally. I wanted to know who this anonymous man was. Finn told him to come forward and I stopped.

My eyes slowly widened.

"No..." I whispered,

"It can't be."

There before me...stood none other than Shang Han.

"Shang Han?" I whispered in disbelief.

Before Finn could say anything, Shang Han stopped him.

"Victoria...I'm going to be totally honest with you...for the past three years I've been with you and your sister...I felt things...I felt things for you, Victoria. I have cared for you and I am willing to compete for your affections." He told me.

I could not believe this. I was angry, shocked, and flattered all at the same time. Finn didn't care, he was so happy and excited to reveal that sick and twisted surprise.

"Well, I guess he summed it up." Finn said aloud.

I turned to Sammy angrily.

"You knew about this?!" I exclaimed.

Sammy waved her hands in despair.

"I'm sorry." Was all she said.

I shook my head at her and faced Shang Han.

"It is true...we have been together for three years. As friends...but Shang Han, you know the person I love! You know him! Why on earth would you still compete for my love anyway?"

Shang Han folded his arms.

"I personally did not think you two belonged together." He said honestly.

I was hurt by that. He saw me with Joseph!

"I see." I murmured.

Finn decided to change the subject.

"Well, we got one more suitor yet! Shang Han, you can take a seat next to Mr. Harp."

Shang Han sat down in a chair next to Mr. Harp, who glared at him. I could not look at Shang Han. Finn clapped his hands once to allow the last suitor to come in.

Another tall man entered. His clean, shaven face and darker hair belonged to someone I thought I recognized, but this man's appearance was slightly different. Joseph had a weak beard, basically just bristle. This man did not. But his face was still so familiar it looked like it could be him. The man wore a thick blue shirt and looked, well, very weak to be honest.

Finn smiled.

"This is Joey Stone." He began.

My eyes widened as I sat there with my fork. Shang Han looked the same way I did. Joey Stone- Joseph Stonewall.

It was him.

It was the man that I had run away from for three years. Joey gave me a warm smile.

"You must be Victoria," he said in a scratchy voice.

My eyes filled with tears.

"Hello." I could hardly speak.

Finn patted "Joey's" shoulder.

"This fine man worked with the medical field in helping injured outlaws. I personally found that touching. So that brought up his chances of him coming here tonight." He explained.

I wanted to laugh at my brother for falling for that. Joseph was one of the best liars that I knew. Finn continued speaking,

"Joey has always been fond of hard work. As any man should be. He gave a marvelous interview with my guards and me. So therefore, I chose him."

Finn drew back a third chair for "Joey" to sit at. He sat down and did not take his eyes off me. I have met my three suitors; Mr. Harp, Shang Han, and Joseph Stonewall or "Joey Stone."

Before any more thoughts could cross my mind, the food arrived.

—

Once the suitors, Finn, the servants, and Sammy were all tucked away for the night, I remained at the table, ready to sob hard. I felt betrayed, curious, and scared.

I felt betrayed because Shang Han was competing to be my husband, curious because I was almost certain that Joey Stone was really Joseph Stonewall and was scared because if he really was Joseph Stonewall, I was in deep trouble.

The fireplace by the dining room table roared loudly. My tears and endless weeping were making me sleepy. My eyes slowly closed. Until the door opened. My head raised immediately. There stood Joey Stone. He smiled at me.

"Ms. Victoria." He smiled gently,

"Why have you not gone to bed?"

I wiped my eyes.

"You can cut it out now, Joseph Stonewall. I know it's you."

I waited for the man to reveal himself, but he only looked confused.

"Joseph? Joseph Stonewall? I could never be that monster."

My eyebrows furrowed.

"So... you're not him?"

Joey smiled and pulled back a chair to sit across from me.

"I used to be..." He whispered.

I knew it. It was him. I reached out to touch his face.

"Joseph?" I whispered shakily.

Joey sighed.

"I used to be that man...until the person I loved left me...with some of my possessions...but mostly my heart."

I laughed a little, now holding his face with both my hands from across the table.

"You could be so cheesy, Joseph." I said.

He smiled at me again.

"Is it really you, Victoria?" He whispered; eyes filled with tears.

"Yes." I answered,

"Yes, it's me."

"God, why did you leave me?" He asked me.

I hurried to his side of the table and threw my arms around him.

"I'm sorry." I cried,

"I'm sorry! I thought I couldn't be with you because of what you did to my father long ago, but I realize that I love you too, and I want to be with you!"

Joseph held me.

"I looked for you for years! I never stopped looking!"

"I'm sorry I kept running." I answered in despair and shame.

"It's okay. I got you now." Joseph cooed.

"I can't believe Shang Han is trying to compete for my hand in marriage." I exhaled.

Joseph chuckled,

"Or that rich dude. He's a real dream come true, huh?"

I laughed.

"Yeah, I guess. You plan on beating them, right?" I assumed.

"You bet." Joseph replied,

"I'm going to beat those cowards and marry you, Victoria. I promise."

I brought my lips to his and he hugged me gently.

The next morning, I was woken up by one of Finn's servants.

"Miss Victoria? You are wanted in Finn's office." She said.

Finn had an office?

"Take me there," I ordered her,

"I have no idea where it is."

"Get dressed and follow me." The servant replied.

Once I was done dressing in my walk-in closet, I followed her down the stairs and through several halls. The servant knocked on a grand door. Finn replied in a muffled voice, and the servant opened the door to Finn.

Finn sat at his desk and was accompanied by Mr. Harp, Shang Han, Sammy, and Joseph AKA Joey.

"What is this?" I asked.

Finn nodded to the servant who left us alone and closed the door behind her.

"Victoria...there has been a major accusation: Sammy claims she saw you and Joey kiss and talk to each other last night...she also claims that Joey here is really Joseph Stonewall." Finn explained.

"It's not an accusation! It's a fact!" Sammy exclaimed,

"Our sister and Joseph Stonewall were kissing last night!"

Finn kept his eyes on me.

"Is that true?" He asked me.

Sweat began to take over my palms.

I have never felt angrier at Sammy. Shang Han stared at me with wide eyes. Mr. Harp just hoped this all was a big misunderstanding. Joseph gave me a small nod. I looked into my brother's eyes.

"Yes." I finally said.

"That was what you and Shang Han have been keeping from me for the past three years..." Sammy whispered.

"You were in love with the man that killed our father?!" Finn shouted.

A huge silence came over the room. Finn closed his eyes.

"Shang Han, Mr. Harp, leave us." He demanded.

Both Shang Han and Mr. Harp protested angrily, but Finn slammed his fist on the desk.

"*Leave now or both of you will be disqualified*!" He yelled.

Mr. Harp and Shang Han left then, but bitterly. Now it just was me, Finn, Sammy, and Joseph in the room. Joseph stood up.

"Guys, look, I helped your sister when she broke her leg and…"

"*Shut up!*" Finn hollered,
"You have no right to speak here!"

Sammy crossed her arms and faced me angrily.

"Victoria, we have spent years and years wanting revenge against this man! How could you love him?!" She cried.

When Joseph and I stayed quiet, Finn cocked an eyebrow.

"What do you have to say for yourself?" he questioned.

I helplessly waved my hands in the air. "I'm sorry." I sniffled.

"Being sorry will never make up for the horrible things he has done!" Sammy snapped,

"Hey, Joseph, did you know I met your mother? She's dead now!"

Joseph was shocked and hurt by the way my sister broke the news to him.

"My mother?" He whispered.

"Yeah!" Sammy shouted,

"You've been gone from her for decades! God only wonders if you'd even care! You would rather work for the government than be with your own mother! How heartless are you?"

Before Joseph could say anything, Finn took on a sly smile. He opened his office door and called for one of his servants. Soon enough, one of his servants came into the office with baby Nemo.

"See this child, Joseph?" Finn asked him.

"Yeah. Your point being...?" Joseph did not understand.

Finn turned to me with Nemo in his arms.

"Victoria...this is Joseph's son." Finn said aloud.

I thought I did not hear him right.

"What?" I whispered.

Finn looked at Joseph, who looked as surprised as I did.

"This is Joseph's child. Nehemiah Rigby." Finn repeated.

I looked at Joseph.

"Is that true?"

Joseph was astounded.

"Victoria...I swear to you...I had no idea that child existed until now."

Joseph stood up slowly.

"You said his last name was Rigby...so Eleanor had this baby?" He asked Finn.

Finn was disgusted that he was even speaking to his mortal enemy.

"Yes." He answered.

I felt so angry and betrayed. My heart ached to know why Joseph had a baby with someone other than me. I honestly should not even be surprised. Should I? He did not even know my secret. Joseph smiled at Nemo, who looked very confused.

"I have a son?" He smiled a little and reached out to touch the boy's face.

Finn backed away and set Nemo down.

"*Never touch him!*" He snapped,

"*Never set eyes on him! Never speak to him so help you God!!*"

When baby Nemo started to whimper, Finn picked him up again and hollered for the servant to come back. Once she did, Nemo was given to her.

"Bring him up to his room." He told her.

Once Nemo and the servant left the room, Joseph hit the desk with his fist.

"That is my child, Finn! Now that I am here, I want him back! What happened to Eleanor?"

Finn approached Joseph slowly. Sammy and I watched with wide eyes. The only difference was that mine were battling tears.

"She's dead, Joseph. She died giving birth to YOUR baby! You weren't even around, and I'm betting you don't even feel one bit sorry!"

"I am!" Joseph protested,

"But that little boy is my son and I want him, too! I want your sister *and* I want my son!"

Finn folded his hands.

"Well, you can't have him. Not anymore. He is rightfully mine. Frank Rigby, Eleanor's father, had Nemo go into my custody before he died."

"What is wrong with you?! That's my son and I have every right to have him back!" Joseph shouted.

"You have no rights here," Finn scoffed.

"You are sick and twisted! Just like Frank Rigby!" Joseph spat.

"And you're a snake to love my sister, despite what you did! Plus, got a wonderful woman like Eleanor pregnant!" Finn shot back.

"I took advantage of no one! I assure you! And I love your sister with all my heart, and I want to compete for her hand in marriage!" Joseph yelled.

"Not only did you kill our beloved father...you have been the demon that has haunted me and my sisters' minds for years! Sammy was arrested and brought to a facility for accidentally shooting a man when she wanted revenge against you! You are the evilest thing besides the devil himself! May God forgive you and Victoria for cooking up such a sinister romance!"

"*Enough!*" I screamed.

Everyone immediately looked at me. I balled my hands into fists and stood up. I looked from Sammy, to Finn, and to Joseph.

"I am finished with all of you! Sammy and Finn, I know loving him seems twisted to you, but I am in love with this man whether you two like it or not! You do not have to like him, but you must treat him like a human being! He has told me millions of times how sorry he is for all the terrible things he has done! But it was all in the past...and I realize that life is not all about getting revenge or hating someone for the rest of their lives...because if you do that...then you die unhappy and ten times worse than any enemy you have ever been against!" I spun around to Joseph,

"And *you* are one of the biggest liars I have ever met, Joseph Stonewall! I question the fact that you love me for many reasons now! The first one being that child! Which now I know what would have happened if *my* baby was born!"

Everyone held their gaze on me for the longest time. Joseph turned white.

"What?" his voice did not sound like his own,

"You slept with him?"

I turned to my brother and sister, "During the years Sammy and I were separated from you, Finn, I had a miscarriage."

Finn's rage was indescribable. Sammy stared at the ground with a look of despair. Joseph shook in horror.

"How could you not tell Shang Han or I?!" Sammy finally screamed at me,

"Victoria, I could have helped you! That's what sisters do! How could you keep that from us?!"

I did not answer, I only kept my gaze on Finn. Not even the man I loved. Just my brother.

Joseph kept shaking his head and I sat down.

"Victoria..." he tried to talk to me.

I held up a hand to silence him and continued to face my brother.

"I am the one being competed for; therefore, I should get a say on how the results of the competition will work!" I insisted.

"The only result is that you will marry the champion of the competition!" Finn told me sharply, struggling to even look at me.

"No." I shook my head,

"Here are my terms: if Joseph wins, then he will marry me *and* get to have Nemo! If he loses, *you* get to keep Nemo and do whatever you like to Joseph...and I will marry either Mr. Harp or Shang Han- whichever one of them wins."

Joseph looked at me as though I had lost my mind. Finn seemed as though he wanted to argue, but only smiled a little; which surprised me. Sammy stayed silent. Finn leaned forward.

"Well, then...that seems agreeable. Joseph, if you win, and that is a *big if*, you can marry my sister...and have Nemo."

Finn wouldn't forfeit that easily...he had to be plotting something.

"And... if you lose..." Finn gave a wicked smile,

"I get to keep Nemo...and you can never see Victoria again."

Of course, he would say that! I should have figured that. Joseph kept his eyes on me.

"Okay." Was all he said.

Finn pointed to the door.

"Out! Everyone!"

I walked out the door and Joseph tried to touch my shoulder, but I jerked away and kept walking.

Today was the day of the competition. I spoke to no one ever since Finn had called me down to his office. Sammy never looked at me, Finn never looked at me...but I didn't care. Because no matter how much the world despised me, I was glad everyone knew about me and Joseph. Everyone in Finn's empire was gathered in his grand ballroom for the great tournament. Finn's ballroom was enormous and could fit thousands of people. There was a great space left at the front of the ballroom where the competition would take place.

I was placed in a seat towards the front next to my brother and sister. My suitors all came out and faced us.

Mr. Harp, Shang Han, and Joseph.

Finn stood up and smiled.

"Welcome all! We now begin the trials for my sister's hand in marriage. I am not big on speeches, so let us begin!"
Wow.

Finn gave a twisted smile.

"The first task will be strength. My sister needs a strong man. So, I brought in some potato sacks that will be filled with bricks. You must climb up this ladder." Finn pointed to a very tall ladder.

"You will carry a sack of bricks while climbing up the wooden ladder...all the way to the top. If you do, you must climb back down and grab another sack of bricks. The first man who can carry three potato sacks up the ladder AND climb back down will win the first task." Finn said.

"How many tasks are there?" Shang Han asked.

"Three." Finn replied, "And you would either win all three, or two out of the three. If there is a tie, then there will be one more task...and you better hope no one gets a tie."

"That ladder looks very high," Mr. Harp observed,

"What if we fall?"

"Well the result could involve a broken back, neck, limb...maybe all three." Finn answered.

Is he crazy?! These men could die! Finn looked at Joseph. Both Shang Han and Mr. Harp asked questions; I suppose Finn figured Joseph would ask a question too.

"Do you have anything to ask as well, Joseph?" Finn asked with a fake smile.

"No." Joseph replied calmly.

Finn back up and glanced at the potato sacks. I watched him anxiously. He clapped his hands.

"Let the first trial begin!"

Everyone cheered as Shang Han went first. The ladder had two sides so Finn told Joseph to go too.

Once Joseph grabbed a sack of bricks, he began climbing on the other side. It looked like it strained their muscles very hard. Shang Han was ahead of Joseph.

"You will never get to marry her!" Shang Han shouted.

Instead of replying, Joseph kept his eyes for the top of the ladder.

"Let's just let the tournament do the talking, huh?" He said.

Shang Han, out of anger, used his foot to stomp on Joseph's hand from across the ladder. I gasped and stood up.

"That's not fair!" I screamed,

"He can't harm anyone in the first trial!"

"My sister is right, Shang Han." Finn called from below the ladder.

"Do not harm any other contestant!"

Shang Han made it to the top of the ladder along with Joseph. Both men made their way down to grab another bag. Shang Han brought two sacks of bricks and set them on his shoulders, trying to balance them as he climbed up the ladder again. Joseph did the same thing and the two both climbed at the same rate. Mr. Harp was just ready for it to be his turn.

Once the two of them made it up a second time, they slowly climbed down. Both were sweating and grunting for air. They seemed to be thinking about how they were going to carry the third sack of bricks. Shang Han looked at my brother.

"This is impossible!" He protested.

Finn smiled.

"It really isn't Shang Han. I had men test this trial already to make sure it was."

Joseph did not complain, He only adjusted the two sacks that already weighed his shoulders, and then grab the third one with one of his hands. With that, he began to climb the ladder. Shang Han rolled his eyes and copied Joseph. Once the two began climbing, I prayed that Joseph would make it.

Sammy kept glancing at me and rolling her eyes out of anger. I honestly wanted to get this stupid competition over with, so I could leave this place. I saw baby Nemo among the crowd; he was held by one of Finn's servants.

I tried to remember when Finn and Sammy and I were back at Black Gates, the place we escaped from.

I wondered if Howlers were near...If they lingered out in the wilderness and waited for one of us to come out of Finn's empire surrounded by electric fence.

The thought gave me shivers. So many Howlers escaped from Black Gates just like my siblings and I did. Now look at us; three complete idiots.

There was suddenly a cry of pain and I saw Shang Han had fallen from the ladder. He was not very high up, but he landed on one of the sacks of bricks. I stood up as Joseph began to climb down with his three sacks. Joseph won against Shang Han for the first trial.

Some men hurried over to Shang Han who stood up and clutched his shoulder.

"I'm fine!" He insisted.

He angrily pointed at Joseph.

"I will beat you in the next trial." He promised him.

He took a seat in the front of the crowd. Finn turned to Mr. Harp.

"Mr. Harp, you are the final contestant for the first trial. Joseph made it through, if you can beat him, there will be a tie. If you do not, Joseph wins the first trial."

Mr. Harp brushed his fancy pants with his hands.

"This will be easy, I assure you."

I rolled my eyes and Finn gestured to the ladder.

"Go ahead then."

Mr. Harp rushed for the sacks of bricks that lay in a pile and took one. Once he started climbing up the ladder, he began to sing.

"Hello, hello, hello, how low..."

"Shut your trap!" Someone in the crowd hollered, followed by a roar of laughter from many others.

Mr. Harp turned to them briefly and then sung even louder.

"With the lights out, it's less dangerous. Here we are now, entertain us."

Finn flinched at the sound of Mr. Harp's terrible singing.

My eyes grew wide. My God, he was already making it back down and going to grab the second sack. He did what my other two suitors did: he set both sacks on his shoulders and made his way up again. His singing sounded worse from the pain he must have been in.

"I feel stupid and contagious. Here we are now, entertain us."

"Seriously, man! Quit your singing or we'll all go deaf!" Someone else shouted.

People laughed again and now Mr. Harp shouted his singing.

"Hello, hello, hello, how low... hello, hello, hello, how low!"

Before he could finish his song, he made it to the top and somehow one of the steps to the ladder broke and he fell.

This time, he was very high up compared to how high up Shang Han was. There was a loud boom when he hit the floor, and a scream. Now everyone stood up. I covered my mouth and when men rushed over to him, one of them soon shouted,

"He's out cold!"

"Take him upstairs and get the doctor!" Finn yelled.

After Mr. Harp was hurriedly taken away, a huge silence filled the large room. Finn broke it with a nervous laugh.

"The second trial will be postponed until tomorrow morning at 10."

No one argued or protested. No one even cared to ask if Mr. Harp was still in. They whispered to one another as they departed from Finn's house. Shang Han stalked off and I was in no mood to speak to Joseph.

"Victoria." He tried to talk to me, but I hurried away.

—

Mr. Harp's back had broken, and he had a concussion. He would no longer be able to compete for my hand in marriage.

Now it was only Shang Han and Joseph Stonewall. I laid awake all-night last night. I did not eat my dinner, for I was too anxious to eat. My stomach hurt, and I was in a bad mood. My brother still did not want to talk to me, nor did my sister.

It had infuriated all of them to know I could have had a baby, and it would have been Joseph's. I did not blame them, either. I kept wondering what the second trial would be. Finn mentioned if they tied there would be a fourth trial and that they would not want it to happen. It concerned me even more that if Joseph won, I would marry him, which would be wonderful, but he would also get custody of baby Nemo. I could not imagine being a mother. Even though I could have been one to my own child.

I had no experience whatsoever. Plus, that child was born by Joseph's previous lover, which bothered me a lot. Nemo was a very sweet little boy, though. I could never hate him. Nor could I hate Joseph.

How could Finn allow the government to track him? He trusted that Frank Rigby dude to 'set him free' and now he was basically being stalked!

If anything happened to this empire or if he left it, Finn would be screwed.

Once morning arrived, I ate breakfast. I dressed myself up in a purple dress with black leggings and black heels for today. Ten o'clock arrived sooner than I thought. Everyone was gathered again, Shang Han and Joseph stood at the front of the ballroom. Finn was even more peppy than before.

"I am mostly excited for this part of the tournament because we will be doing a hobby that I have always enjoyed for the past few years of living here."

He held up a bow.

"Archery!" He announced happily.

Everyone cheered, and I relaxed a little bit. Finn paced around.

"This trial represents skill. The two suitors will receive three arrows and their own individual target. Whichever man can hit the target three times in the center or can get closest to it will win!" He explained.

"That sounds easy," Shang Han scoffed.

Finn chuckled.

"Let the second trial begin!"

Two targets were rolled into the room. One faced each man. Both Shang Han and Joseph were given a bow and precisely three arrows.

Shang Han loaded his first arrow and drew back his arm. When he released it, it hit the center of the target.

He grinned as the crowd cheered him on. Joseph loaded his first arrow, kept his eyes on the center, and shot for the middle, but missed. It hit very close, though.

Shang Han scoffed again and loaded his second arrow. He squinted hard and shot it, hitting a bullseye a second time, right next to his first arrow. Joseph drew back his arm with his second arrow and shot a bullseye as well.

I wanted to stand up and cheer for him, but I had to stay calm.

I was very shaky. Shang Han was succeeding with this trial. Shang Han also seemed to be squinting a lot. He suddenly had to stop a moment and clutch his shoulder. I remembered, he hurt his shoulder falling off the ladder the day before. This archery challenge must have been troubling him greatly.

"You okay?" Joseph asked.

"I'm fine." Shang Han snapped back.

I frowned a little. Shang Han had become so bitter over this trial. Just because of his feelings for me. I felt very responsible for this. But he knew I had feelings for Joseph. Shang Han drew his arrow back and released it. He hit the bullseye a third time.

Everyone screamed with triumph, clapping and cheering excitedly. Shang Han raised his bow in the air and cheered with him, giving Joseph a boastful smile. Joseph loaded his third arrow and aimed for the target. He had gotten one bullseye and missed the other time. Once he shot his third arrow, I cringed. It did not even hit the target at all.

Finn seemed very happy with the results of the second trial.

"Very good!" He congratulated Shang Han,

"I am very excited to say Shang Han won the second trial! The third trial will carry on this afternoon to determine the winner for my sister's hand in marriage! Now we will go to the grand dining room to have lunch! Everyone can go down the east hallway and take a seat!"

Grand dining room? What else did Finn have in his house? A bowling alley?

I stood up and Joseph tried to walk with me, but Finn pushed him out of the way and wrapped his arm around me.

"Hey sis." He greeted me.

I huffed,

"I figured you were still mad at me." I said.

He sighed,

"Let's just say I'm working on it. But suitors must keep hands off until the trials are over. I can tell that will be a huge issue for you and Joseph."

Angry at my brother's rude comment, I walked faster until I made it into the grand dining room with the others. The food was not too fancy, chicken sandwiches and tomato soup with peaches. I was able to eat some of my food while Sammy sat across from me. She sighed.

"Look, I know I have not been speaking to you lately, but I need to warn you about something..." Sammy whispered meekly.

I leaned forward when she did.

"Okay, what?" I asked quietly.

"I would be careful of Finn...I feel like he's planning something." She said.

"How do you know?" I demanded.

Sammy glanced at Finn down the table.

"Last night I heard him talking to some of the guards...if Joseph wins the competition...he will do something..."

I became worried,

"What will he do?" I asked nervously.

Sammy bit her lip.

"He's gonna kill Joseph if he wins."

I felt chills run up and down my spine. I wanted to kill my stupid brother. I know I told him he may do what he like, but I would never let Finn kill the man I would always have a place in my heart for.

This was so unfair.

Sammy now turned back to her food and I totally lost my appetite. I had to tell Joseph, but how? This was the final trial. My stomach churned, and I took a breath. I could not do anything because just then, Finn stood up.

"Now let us all return to the ballroom for the third and final trial!" He announced.

Everyone excitedly hurried for the ballroom. It took twenty minutes before I could get to my seat again. Shang Han and Joseph made their way to the front of the ballroom. Finn gave his "son" Nemo a kiss on the head before making his way to the front of the ballroom too.

Finn grinned at everyone.

"And now, ladies and gentlemen, we watch the third trial."

This was so wrong. I had to say something. Finn gave a grin.

"The third trial...is a trial of loyalty and trueness. I will ask you a few questions...and you two will give a proper answer. I happen to be an honest man and I will choose the answers I like the most."

He glanced at both.

"I will be honest despite any prejudices I may have."

"Drop dead." I uttered.

"First question: Say the government came for Victoria...and they were about to take her away... what would you do?" Finn asked.

Shang Han answered first,

"I'd shoot every one of them. No gov would be left standing." He guaranteed him.

Finn side smiled.

"Okay then..."

He now turned to Joseph.

"What about you, Joseph? I'm sure you'd say the same thing."

How could any of these rich people react to knowing that Joseph Stonewall was in the same room as them? They barely knew anything that went on outside their neighborhoods, that's why. Joseph smiled a bit.

"No." He answered,

"I would tell the gov's to take me. They could find me of some use. That's what I would do. I would save Victoria and have them take me."

Finn clenched his teeth a bit and glanced down. I was glad Joseph gave such a good answer.

"Moving on." Finn changed the subject,

"If I asked you what you both had to offer for my sister, what would the two of you say?"

Shang Han thought a moment, as did Joseph. Shang Han smiled,

"I would offer the entire world for her...a fine house, a good family, nice car, etcetera."

Joseph crossed his arms.

"I offer her myself. My love, my protection, my everything."

Finn rolled his eyes a little.

"Final question!" He said a little too loudly,

"Would you both be patient with my sister and honor and respect her?"

"Yes." Shang Han answered right away.

"Yes." Joseph also said.

My heart pounded against my chest and I wanted to yell what Finn was planning to do. Finn smiled broadly.

"Well with the results of these questions, I am more than pleased with the answers! Ladies and gentlemen, we have a tie!"

People all gasped, and both Shang Han and Joseph looked at each other with wide eyes. Joseph won a trial, and Shang Han won a trial, then they tied. Oh no...

Finn gave them both an intimidating look.

"The fourth trial will begin tomorrow morning. No audience is allowed except for Victoria and Sammy, my two sisters."

The audience angrily protested because they wanted to see the fourth trial. I had to speak up. I was not going to let Finn do anything to Joseph. I rose from my seat and yelled at the top of my lungs,

"Finn is planning to kill Joseph!"

Part Nine

Gasps filled the room. Finn's eyes were the size of meatballs.

"Victoria...I planned no such thing."

"That's what Sammy told me." I argued.

Finn glared at Sammy, who took a fearful breath.

"Sammy, why would you tell Victoria that?"

"Because I heard you!" She answered.

Finn closed his eyes.

"Sammy..." he sighed,

"I have no idea what you are talking about."

"Don't lie, Finn!" Sammy yelled,

"I have kept quiet about this whole thing for the entire time! No one asked me how I felt about this! I have dedicated my life to killing the man that killed our father, and now I must drop it because he is my sister's first love now! It's disgusting! I am ashamed of you, Finn, for even letting him continue with these trials! I know you two are feuding over Nemo and who gets custody of him, but God! That little boy is Joseph's actual child!" Sammy hollered.

"The man didn't even know he existed until a little while ago!" Finn yelled in disagreement.

"That's not my fault!" Joseph butted in,

"He is still my son and I will fight until the end of this damned battle to get your sister and him!"

I huffed.

"Finn, just tell the truth! Sammy said she heard you plotting something! What was it?"

Finn released a breath.

"I was planning to have someone take Nemo and hide him somewhere. I said if Joseph wins and tries to find him...they should kill him if he gets close to finding my son..."

I was aghast at what my brother just said.

"Finn how could you-?"

"But he's my son!" Joseph nearly shouted,

"He is not yours!"

"I am more of a father to that little boy than you ever were!" Finn exclaimed.

Joseph crossed his arms.

"I think we should have the fourth trial here and now."

Shang Han gave a curt nod.

"I agree."

Finn stared at them both for a few moments before sighing in anger.

"Fine."

He faced everyone,

"You all must leave. The results of the trial will be announced tonight."

The audience quietly left.

My heart pounded against my chest and I took short, quivery breaths.

Once the audience left, Finn turned to my two suitors.

"The final trial will be a test of championship. You two will fight one another to the death." He said blankly.

"What?" I murmured as Joseph and Shang Han glanced at one another.

I looked at the two competitors in shock.

"You two will go through with this?"

Shang Han sighed.

"If it means beating this jerk and getting to marry you, then yes." He told me.

"I couldn't have said it better myself." Joseph chimed in.

I glared at Finn.

"Why would you let them do this?" I almost shouted.

Finn did not respond, only waved his hand to one of the guards.

"Bring the swords."

Swords? Was this a medieval battle?

I sat next to Sammy who held out her hand. I took it and squeezed it tightly. I was terrified, and I wasn't even the one fighting. I felt like this was all some horrible nightmare, ever since I arrived at Finn's house. This must all be a bad dream.

Shang Han and Joseph were both given short, dagger-like swords.

I squeezed Sammy's hand tighter. Finn stood back and nodded.

"You two can begin."

Joseph and Shang Han circled one another. I didn't want to watch.

"It'll be okay," Sammy whispered.

Shang Han yelled and charged at Joseph, who blocked him with his blade. Steel clashed with loud bangs. It startled me with every blow dealt. Both men yelled and grunted, each wanting to beat the other.

As I watched them fight, I tried to picture a life with both of them.

If I married Shang Han, I would be forever sad that he defeated Joseph, who was the man I truly loved.

Shang Han was really a good man. This whole competition turned him into a terrible person. I could maybe find that good person again. We would probably live a well-to-do life if Shang Han could get his parents back. Or if Finn would let us live in his empire. Unlike my brother, I was not into riches and money. I liked the feeling of being on the run. That was something I learned after being at Finn's for a little while.

Running was the thing I did best. Running away from my problems and troubles. I was fast. I wondered where those Howlers were right now. They were probably all over the U.S.

Joseph slammed the blade of his sword into Shang Han's as they fought roughly.

My hand shook in my sister's.

I now pictured a life with Joseph. If he won, he would get custody of his son, if Finn didn't have anything to do with it. I'd be a stepmother, but I vowed to myself here and now that I would care for little Nemo. We would live in a small place, almost like the metal trailer I grew up in. We would raise a family and I could be a mom to my own children. I would want my brother and sister to be a part of my life, too. If Joseph won this ridiculous trial, hopefully they would accept it.

Shang Han edged his blade near Joseph's neck but was blocked by Joseph's. Joseph kicked him in the knee and Shang Han fell to the ground with a startled cry. Joseph lifted the tip of his blade to Shang Han's forehead.

I leaned forward in terror.

"Surrender, Shang Han." Joseph said.

Shang Han gave Joseph the deadliest look a man could give before throwing down his sword.

"Alright…" He spat,

"I *surrender*."

Joseph backed away, so Shang Han could stand up. Finn watched the whole scene in awe. Shang Han's face contorted into rage as he leapt in the air and kicked Joseph in the stomach. Joseph made a noise and dropped his sword. Shang Han caught it and thrust the blade deep into Joseph's shoulder.

"*No!*" I screeched.

Joseph sank to the ground like a rag doll. I fixed my eyes on Shang Han's blade that dripped with sticky blood. In my soul, I conjured a rage that filled my being with fire and hatred. Shang Han spun towards Finn in triumph.

"You see?" he barked,

"I won! Now your sister will be my-"

My blade ran through his heart. A gurgling noise escaped Shang Han's mouth as he flopped to the ground, his hands flying towards the slit that been engraved into his chest. Blood oozed from his parted lips as he fell into cold death.

No sounds came from my actions. Only silence. I looked at no one, except the blade I used to stab Shang Han.

"Victoria!" Joseph gasped in pain.

I snapped out of it and ran to my Joseph. He kissed me lightly and tried to speak, but Finn shouted over him.

"How could you do something so wicked?!" Finn screamed,

"You cheated! You phony! You cheated, she cheated!"

Joseph still consoled me and kissed me once more.

I turned to my brother.

"Finn, it's over. I demand that Nemo be given to his real father and I will marry Joseph."

Finn stared at me for a long time.

"Victoria..." He whispered,

"That is unfair. That is not how this trial works! Joseph would have to defeat Shang Han himself!"

I walked over to Finn and grabbed his collar.

"You will return Nemo to Joseph. And I will marry him." I repeated with clenched teeth.

Finn's eyes watered.

"How could you do this to me?"

I shook my head.

"You did this to yourself, Finn. None of this is our fault."

Finn had tears running down his cheeks. Joseph stood up with a sad look on his face.

"Finn." He said meekly.

Finn gave Joseph a look of hatred.

"Don't talk to me." He snapped.

Joseph had bloodshot eyes.

"Keep my son," he could barely get the words out from the pain in his shoulder.

I hurried back to Joseph and held him because I knew he was in agony.

Finn blinked multiple times with shock.

"W-What?" He whispered.

Joseph grunted as he began to cry.

"Keep my boy. He seems well with you."

He wrapped his good arm around me.

"From what I learned about this competition... I want Victoria. Finn, I do want to be able to get to know my son because he is really mine. But he knows you like you're his father...I don't want to take him away from you."

Finn smiled a little.

"Really?"

Joseph nodded.

"Yes, really."

I kissed Joseph's cheek.

"Are you sure?" I asked him.

Joseph looked at me and tried to force a smile.

"Yes."

Finn sobbed and hugged Joseph tightly.

"Thank you," he whispered,

"Thank you so much."

Joseph clenched his teeth.

"Of course."

Sammy walked to the front of the ballroom.

"Joseph Stonewall," she said loudly,

"I had promised myself one day I was gonna kill you. I had laid awake at night, and I ain't lying, I would have wonderful dreams about shooting you in the face or stabbing you in the heart like you did to me when you killed my daddy years ago!"

As I watched my sister get closer, I could see she was crying.

"And now..." she whimpered,

"Now you will marry my sister...because you claim you love her...and you are letting my brother keep Nemo...and I guess it proves you are not the worst person in the world like I thought you were."

I smiled a little and Sammy walked over to Joseph and me.

"Victoria, I'm sorry for getting so angry at you..." she cried,

"You deserve to be happy and we stood in your way...please forgive me."

I began to cry too as I embraced my sister. She looked at us both.

"May I be your maid of honor, sis?" She asked me.

I touched my sister's soft cheek. Her wide, blue eyes glowed.

"I would want nothing more." I replied happily.

Finn crossed his arms and walked over to me too.

"Victoria, I know I'm not dad...but can I walk you down the aisle?"

I didn't think I could be any happier than what I was right now.

"Yes." I said quickly.

I smiled at Joseph, who grinned. We kissed a quick and sweet kiss before I said to my brother,

"We need a doctor. Joseph needs his shoulder patched up."

Finn hurried for the door to get someone. I turned to Sammy,

"Where is baby Nemo?"

"With some of the servants, playing." Sammy answered.

"Make sure to have Finn tell him that everything's okay." I said.

I turned to Joseph and smiled a bit.

"Joseph and I have a wedding to plan."

—

Shang Han's body was buried by some of the guards. His gravestone was marked,

Rest in Peace, Shang Han Zhu. Born August 1, 2198. Died September 2, 2225.

I had to admit, I cried when I visited his grave. He'd been an old friend and would always be remembered. Finn was more than happy that he was able to keep Nemo. I was mostly excited to be married to Joseph.

Finn made sure the wedding would be spectacular. Everyone in his empire would be there and the wedding would be outside the house.

My dress was insanely fancy. The train must have been as long as a limo and was lacy like the dresses you would see on the angel statues at a chapel. It matched the sleeves, which were also long and lacy. Of course, the dress was white. Like snow.

The wedding would be in two days, the date being September 5, 2225.

Finn had all his servants cooking up a storm, along with making sure the house was spic and span. I had been spending every moment I could with Joseph. We had so much to discuss. Finn was allowing us to live in his home temporarily, but Joseph and I agreed that we would not live in Finn's empire.

Sammy wanted to come with us too, and of course we would let her. Finn did not want us to go, but we promised that we'd visit every now and then.

This all felt like a fairytale.

There was a small knock at the door, and I looked up from the book I was reading. Yeah, I was reading. Don't judge me! Nemo walked in the room.

"Hi, auntie Victoria..." he greeted me in a small voice.

I smiled.

"Hey, Nemo."

Nemo was holding his stuffed tiger.

"Do you like my tiger?" He asked me.

"Oh, yes, he's a strong-looking tiger." I replied, patting the stuffed animal on the head.

Nemo lifted his arms and I sat him on the bed next to me.

"Whatcha doing?" I asked him.

Nemo shrugged.

"There's some loud talking downstairs...my daddy Finn is down there, and he is yelling at some people."

I became a little worried.

"About what, do you know?"

Nemo nodded,

"They wanna kill Uncle Joseph."

I became horrified, but I tried to stay calm in front of the small child.

"Okay, Nemo, stay here." I told him as I stood up and ran for the door.

Sure enough, when I came downstairs, I heard shouting.

I saw three men stand in the main entry of Finn's house. Finn stood on the balcony staircase with his arms crossed.

"You three are ridiculous, why are you coming to me with this nonsense now?" He asked.

"Because we thought that horrible man would die in the competition for your sister's hand in marriage!" One of the men yelled.

"What is going on?" I asked them.

Finn turned to me and rolled his eyes.

"These three jackasses here are all upset that you are marrying the "infamous" Joseph Stonewall." He explained.

"It's a marriage that is an abomination to everyone!" Another man said aloud.

I sucked my cheeks in and slowly came down the stairs.

"If you three have a problem with my marriage, then you can leave and not come to my wedding." I said plainly.

All three men laughed.

"I don't care about your stupid wedding!" One of them said,

"In fact, I think this whole empire business is a fool's game!"

"Why do you think that all of the sudden? Everyone seemed to be on board with it." Finn asked, curious.

"Ever since you wanted to play this whole thing like a medieval kingdom!" Another one said angrily,

"Frank Rigby, the previous owner of this mansion, knew what he was doing! You are an ignorant seventeen-year-old who knows nothing! You sit around all high and mighty on your throne like you're the king of the world!"

Finn's lips tightened in anger,

"Well if you don't like it, you three will be banished. Guards!"

The guards all came over and Finn pointed to the three men.

"Throw these men outside the fence!"

The three men were seized by the guards and marched outside of the house.

"We're coming for you!" One yelled,

"There won't be any precious little wedding, sweetheart!"

Chills ran up my spine.

Finn straightened the collar of his fancy clothes.

"Don't listen to them, Victoria." He told me.

I gave a curt nod and stared at the door.

"Every time someone tells me not to listen, something bad happens. I'm going to tell Joseph."

"No!" Finn stopped me by grabbing my arm,

"We don't want a spectacle made from your fiancé! Just go back to doing what you were doing!"

I watched as Finn went up the stairs and out of sight.

I ran outside the house.

—

I knocked on one of the guard towers and a guard answered:

"Can I help you?" He bellowed.

I took a breath,

"I need to look at the outside world."
The guard sighed.

"You need to have Finn's permission to do this." He told me.

I glared at the guard.

"I'm his sister. I insist." I hissed.

The guard sighed and stepped aside so I could climb the ladder. Once I made it to the top of the guard tower, I peered out from the top of the electric fence. All I could see was the wilderness I came into with Shang Han and Sammy before we met up with Finn again.

This time it was different.

This time I saw something far out in the distance. A that gave me tense shivers. I saw the way the object moved and prowled...I knew what it was...

A lone Howler.

Of course, it was not alone. There had to be a pack close by.

I looked to my right to see more beautiful wilderness, but there was one problem.

Another Howler stood there too.

I rushed to look to my left. A third howler stood there. If there were Howlers near the front and the sides of Finn's Empire, that meant there had to be more guarding the back too.

We were surrounded.

We had to be. The Howlers probably tracked Sammy and I down. They could not get in these walls, but that made me think of what those men said.

'We're coming for you! There won't be any precious little wedding, sweetheart!'

The fear that lingered in my soul doubled. I hurried back down the ladder and told the guard to get my brother.

Once Finn and Joseph, along with Sammy, all ran to me, I told them to come with me to the guard tower. We all climbed up one by one until we all saw what was there.

"Howlers..." Finn whispered.

"Why are they here?" Sammy asked in a terrified voice.

"They are most likely here because of you and me, Sammy." I responded,

"They finally tracked us down."

"We were always running from them. For the past three years..." Sammy whispered.

"I know." I answered,

"But we are safe inside these walls."

"Hopefully." Joseph sighed.

——

Even though my siblings and Joseph and I were all nervous about the Howlers, the wedding continued.

And today was my wedding day.

Sammy helped me get into my dress as I looked at myself in the mirror. My auburn hair was tied in a beautiful bun, decorated by little white flowers to match my dress. I wore mascara with a little black eyeshadow and light pink lip-gloss just to touch myself up a bit.

I turned to my sister and hugged her tightly.

"You are too beautiful, Victoria." She said to me.

"Thank you, Sammy." I whispered.

Sammy was wearing a short blue dress with white heels and her blonde hair stayed long and curly. She straightened her glasses and patted my shoulder gently.

"I need to go out now. Finn will be here shortly." She told me.

"Okay." I responded.

She was right, too. Finn arrived two minutes after Sammy left. Boy did Finn look nice. He was a real looker in his white tux and dashing smile.

"You look amazing." He complimented me.

I chuckled.

"Good to see you áre wearing a suit." I observed.

Finn glanced down and waved his hand.

"Oh, this old thing!" He exclaimed,

"I don't look near as glamorous as you do."

I smiled tenderly at him and brushed his shoulder.

"Since when did you become so grown-up?" I asked him.

Finn beamed,

"I was gonna say the same thing to you, sis."

He held out his arm.

"Ready?"

I nervously took it and laughed a little.

"Yes."

We both walked down the hall and down the stairs to the open doors. A path of white rose petals guided us to the end of the walkway where Joseph stood with the minister. Enough people were gathered to fill the entire yard. We walked through the path as the sound of an accordion played.

Joseph smiled as he brushed his white tux with his palms. He stared at me with a small smile. I squeezed my brother's arm tighter.

When we made it at the end of the isle, Finn kissed my hand and left me to face the man I would be married to in moments.

"Today!" The minister began in an uplifting voice,

"We are gathered here to unite this man and this woman as one."

I gazed into Joseph's eyes. I loved everything about him. I loved how his eyes sparkled when he laughed. I loved how he held me close to him whenever I was scared or felt lonely. He always made me feel better when trouble awaited me.

The minister smiled at us both while he spoke his small speech. The entire time he delivered his message, I pictured the life I would have with Joseph.

I was so glad at how everything turned out in the end. I was here with him, all these people, my family. Joseph was now part of my family.

We loved each other dearly, and I knew that. The minister turned to Finn,

"I need the rings now, Mr. Finn Hartley."

I almost forgot about the rings! I wondered what my ring would look like. I was about to turn to the someone who had the rings, but instead we all stopped when we heard a whoop and a yell.

I averted my gaze to see one of the three men that were at Finn's house a few days ago. He was yelling loudly from outside the electric fence that he had been banished at. Finn was furious that the wedding was interrupted.

"What is the meaning of this?" He demanded with a raised voice.

The man laughed like a maniac.

"Hey, little pretties!" He called,

"Told ya I was coming!"

Joseph and I both looked at each other and then back at the man outside the fence. The man laughed a little again.

"The Howlers got my other two buddies! But I hid from 'em! Y'all are surrounded, my friends!"

I closed my eyes as everyone began to panic and whisper to one another in fear. We did not even tell the other civilians of Finn's empire about the time we saw the Howlers. The man laughed.

"Finn Hartley, your little game is all over now! I paid one of your rebellious guards two million dollars to cut the power on your precious electric fences! I'm sure you've never paid him that much in his entire life!"

Finn gasped.

"You cut the power on the fences!" He yelled at the guard that betrayed us all when the man pointed at him.

The guard only shrugged weakly and the man kept laughing.

"And now..." he took out a machete from his weapon belt and grinned madly,

"Now we will let the Howlers feast!"

"No, don't!" Finn roared, along with many others.

It was too late.

The man sliced his machete through the fence, which tore a huge hole.

He raised his arms in the air.

"Let the fall of Finn Hartley's Empire begin!"

Just as he finished his declaration, a Howler leapt at him and devoured him. The man did not even have time to cry out. At that moment, many Howlers dashed into the empire through the hole in the fence.

I screamed and picked up the skirt of my wedding dress to run. Joseph ran with me and we hurried into Finn's house. Finn and Sammy followed us with Nemo, who was crying.

Once we were in Finn's house, we barricaded the doors shut with two chairs that were in the corner of the entryway.

"Oh, my God." I cried,

"We're gonna die!"

"Hey!" Joseph took my face into his hands,

"Listen to me! We are not gonna die, do you hear me? We will survive, you know why? Because we are together. We thrive on life; we thrive on everything we can. Don't lose heart to fear now, Victoria, Come on!"

I took his hand and we all ran into Finn's dining room. All I could hear was screaming and the barking from Howlers outside. I was trying to rip the train of my dress off. Finn reached for a butter knife on the table and helped me. Once the train of my dress was pretty much chopped off, I huddled against Joseph.

Finn huffed.

"Sorry your wedding is ruined, guys." He said to us as he held Nemo in his arms.

"Hey, don't worry about it." Joseph responded.

All the sudden, Sammy screamed when a Howler broke right through one of the windows of the dining room. We could not believe who it was, either.

The alpha.

That terrifying beast with only half of a face. The other half was just a skull. I remembered him from a couple different occasions. He growled lowly and approached us; one paw after the other.

"Is it that same freaking alpha from three years ago?!" Finn exclaimed.

"Yep." I replied quickly.

The alpha began barking and charged for us.

"*Run!*" Sammy screamed and we all scurried out of the dining room.

Because of how fast the alpha had ran, he swerved right into the wall and was delayed chasing us.

"Go for the living room, I have swords in there above the fireplace!" Finn ordered as we hurried away from the alpha.

Nemo cried loudly in fear and Finn ripped one of the swords off the mantle. He pointed it at the alpha, and he stopped and growled at the sight of the blade pointed at him. We all stood behind Finn. Joseph reached up and took the other sword that had lain over the other above the mantel.

I glanced at the fire, which was still lit a little, and then I glanced at my brother and Joseph who were defending us with the two swords. The alpha Howler tried to swipe his claws at the sword and Joseph bravely swiped the blade at the alpha's foot.

That only pissed the alpha off. He barked and snarled at us.

I saw three fire pokers and had an idea. I took two of them and reached out to take one of the burning logs. With all my might, I thrusted the log at the alpha and it hit him square in the snout.

He howled loudly and we all opened one of the doors to run down a hallway I had never seen. Joseph shut the door quickly as the Howler continued to howl and whimper.

"Follow me, I know this hallway!" Finn insisted as he clutched a sobbing Nemo in his arms.

Finn turned on one of the lights, so we could see where we were going. Soon, we were far down the hall and we hid against the wall. Finn gasped quietly, like he thought of something.

"I have an idea! I know there is a room around here that opens to the backyard. We can sneak around front and take one of my cars." He told us.

"Do you even have a key?" I asked him.

He smiled and took a few car keys from his pants pockets.

"I always hold the keys to my babies in my pocket."

I shrugged.

"Sounds like you." I said quietly.

We fell dead silent when we heard footsteps. Nemo whimpered, and Finn covered his mouth. I peeked around the corner to see the alpha sniffing for our scent on the ground. Finn jerked his head quietly and we all tiptoed down the hall. Joseph still held his sword and my hand as we hurried as quietly as we could.

That did not last long because we heard the alpha growl from behind us. He faced us with a terrifying look. His skull nearly glowed in the dark. Joseph had held Finn's sword as well and he pointed both blades at the ferocious beast.

"Run." He told us,

"Run now, and I'll catch up."

"Joseph, no!" I whispered in a terrified voice.

Before anything else could be said, the alpha leapt for Joseph and he yelled,

"*Run!*"

Finn grabbed my arm and we all ran for one of the doors. Finn swung it open and we stumbled into the bright daylight. He made sure we were all there. Me, Sammy, Finn, and Nemo were all present. Just not my Joseph.

"I need to go back there!" I cried.

Sammy grabbed me tightly.

"He said he would come out and he will!" She reassured me,

"But right now, we gotta find Finn's car and get the hell out of here!"

When we ran to the front yard, Finn stared at his empire in despair.

People had lit torches out of rakes or garden tools wrapped in cloth and oil. They used the torches to ward off the Howlers. Some of it failed because houses were on fire now and people were killed and dropped their torches.

Screams and sounds of items breaking filled the air. Howlers barked and snarled, munching on the bones of the deceased.

Finn sighed,

"A whole empire...gone..." He murmured.

I laid a hand on his shoulder.

"I'm sorry, Finn." I whispered.

Finn tried to fight back tears while we all ran to find one of Finn's cars. Three had been destroyed, but two were still there.

"We're taking the red van." Finn told us,

"The truck won't fit all of us."

He was sad to see his fancy cars in ruin.

"Sorry, babies." He said to them.

I opened the car door to let Sammy and Nemo in first, then I got in. Finn turned the key and we began to drive.

"What about Joseph?" I asked concernedly.

We then heard yelling and saw Joseph run out of the house. The alpha was not behind him, and I mustered up some hope.

Joseph leapt into the passenger seat and gasped for breath. Finn began to drive forward.

"What happened?" I asked him.

Joseph took my hand from behind him and answered,

"I sliced the alpha's back leg and it stopped chasing me. My shoulder is much worse."

I closed my eyes.

"You were healing fine after we gave you stitches..." I said.

"Victoria it's only been a few days since that happened." Sammy pointed out.

"Yeah, I guess." I replied.

Finn kept his eyes ahead as we busted through the hole in the fence. Finn sped the car up after that. No Howlers followed us. They were too busy destroying my brother's empire. Finn's expression was so broken. Like he had lost everything he'd ever known.

Nemo's head popped up and he tapped on Finn's shoulder.

"Daddy?"

"Yeah, Nemo?" Finn replied dully.

Nemo reached into his pocket.

"I never got to do my special part..."

Joseph and I glanced at each other.

"What special part, baby?" I asked Nemo.

Nemo responded,

"Daddy was making me bring you and Uncle Joseph the rings."

He pulled two gold rings from his pocket. I gasped, and Joseph grinned. Both rings did not look the same even though they were both gold. One ring was broad and three tiny circular diamonds were engraved into it. The other ring had a single diamond in the center and sparkled in the sunlight.

Sammy smiled excitedly.

"You guys! We can still have the wedding! We have the rings!"

"That's ridiculous, we need a minister." Finn said in a depressed voice.

"No, no, stop the car!" Joseph insisted.

Finn pulled over and we all got out.

"Everyone gather around!" Joseph ordered.

Everyone surrounded Joseph.

"Nemo, may I have the rings?" He asked him nicely.

Nemo handed Joseph the two rings and Joseph took both of my hands. We locked eyes exactly like we used to back at his camp. His suit was tarnished and his hair askew, but his eyes still sparkled like they always did. My bun looked atrocious, my dress was torn and itched my skin from the sweat coating my body from running.

This was my wedding day.

Joseph took the small ring with the single diamond in the center and smiled at me.

"When I place this ring on your finger, I will now and forever call you my wife."

I smiled with tears cascading down my cheeks and I took the broad gold ring with the three tiny diamonds in the center and spoke shakily,

"When I place this ring on your finger, I will now and forever call you my husband."

Sammy cheered and raised her arms in the air.

"You may kiss the bride!" She squealed.

Joseph bent down and kissed me passionately.

Finn smiled at us and Nemo cheered with Sammy. I'm pretty sure the sun shined even brighter that day...

Part Ten

It had been about 3 months since me and Joseph had gotten married. The date was December 7, 2225. How do I know this? Finn's fancy little vehicle has the date on the touch screen. Of course, the vehicle is a van, which, according to Finn, is not a fancy car.

"Remember when some bozos came up with the idea of automatic cars?" Sammy snorted.

"They weren't bozos, they were idiots." Finn replied lowly.

Finn was still depressed about being betrayed in his empire. He constantly wondered what would happen to the rich people. He also felt hurt that there were people in his empire that despised him and would do what they had done.

My brother felt like a failure to let his empire fall to shreds.

"Aunt Victoria, when can we stop? I'm sick of riding in the car." Nemo complained,

"I want my toy tiger and my bear and all my other toys."

"Honey, your toys is back at the house which is burning to bits." I told Nemo.

That only made Finn more upset.

"I'm such a failure!" He cried.

"Oh, here we go again." Sammy groaned.

"You're not a failure...you just screwed up." Joseph tried to make Finn feel better.

Finn scoffed,

"Yeah...and because of me the entire rich population is vanquished."

He wailed even though he wasn't actually crying,

"I'm a real hero!"

"Yes, you are!" Sammy said positively.

Finn hit the pedal faster and sped the car up.

"Can you turn the heat up? It's freezing!" I exclaimed.

"It's winter, of course it's freezing." Finn retorted,

"I gotta get gas. Maybe we can find some kind of abandoned gas station or something."

"How did we fuel our cars again?" Sammy asked me,

"You, me, and Shang Han walked most of the three years we've been separated from Finn."

"We had cars every so often." I said,

"We would just unload if it ran out of gas."

"Back when the three of us were together," Finn spoke,

"Remember we would cover our faces and drive through a gas station the government worked at? I almost got caught that one time but got away with being some young adult named Ted Rosencrans."

"Oh yeah!" I chuckled,

"Finn you would not believe how many cars me, Sammy, and Shang Han stole!"

"How many?" Finn asked.

"Too many." Sammy replied.

Joseph was doing a craft in the back. Nemo moaned.

"I want my toy tiger." He sighed.

Joseph handed him a piece of his leather jacket that he had stolen off the road. I smiled. He had tied the leather with a string to make a weird doll.

"Here, this should do it for now." He said.

Nemo studied the "toy" for a second.

"It's not my tiger...but I like it."

Joseph laughed a bit.

"If I was mistaken, I'd say he acts a lot like you, Finn." Joseph chuckled.

Finn smiled briefly before concentrating on the road again,

"I gotta get gas." He mumbled.

While Finn tried to look for any sign of a gas station, Nemo looked at Joseph.

"I gotta ask you something." He said to Joseph.

Joseph folded his hands,

"What's up, Nemo?"

Nemo tried to give a serious face, but he was so cute, he was failing.

"Are you my real daddy?" Nemo asked quietly.

The smile left Joseph's face, along with mine. Finn stared at him in his rear-view mirror.

Joseph released a breath.

"Nehemiah Rigby...I was once your father, yes... but Finn has been more of a father to you than I had ever been. The only thing I had done for you was bring you into this messed-up world and make you a doll. Finn has done so much more. I want you to understand that."

"I do. I love my other daddy." Nemo reassured us,

"But what about my mommy? I never knew her. Did you have me, Uncle Joseph?"

I chuckled and so did Joseph. Finn did a bit, too. Sammy rubbed Nemo's small back.

"No, you had a mommy." She said.

I waited for Joseph or Finn to say something.

We all knew that this had to be said. Nemo would ask about his mother. We just did not think it would be now.

"Your mother died when she had you..." Joseph said bluntly.

"Joseph!" Finn exclaimed,

"He's three!"

Joseph closed his eyes,

"Right...sorry...your mother...she um... went some place for a little while."

Nemo smiled.

"When will she be back?"

Joseph glanced nervously at me.

"Um...let's just say you two will see each other again someday."

Nothing else was said for a while before Finn grinned and pointed at something in the distance.

"Person!" He said excitedly.

We all tried to see through the falling snow out the window.

"Looks like an elder." Finn observed.

Sure enough, it was. An old man as a matter of fact. The man had tan, wrinkly skin and wore a red coat and blue jeans that were dirty and matted. His silver goatee matched his long, silver hair. Finn slowly stopped the car and rolled down the window a touch.

"Want a ride?"

The elder grunted with a small nod and got in the car. Sammy, and Nemo and I all scooted over.

The aged man smelled of smoke and pine. Finn began to drive again, and Joseph turned to the stranger in our car.

"Where are you heading?"

"North." The man answered.

I turned to him, too.

"We don't normally pick up people like you, so we want to know what your name is and what you are doing in the middle of nowhere."

The elder chuckled.

"You are not in the middle of nowhere, you are in Chesapeake Bay Virginia." He told us.

I was shocked. I never usually read road signs.

"Really?" I asked.

"Don't you read road signs?" Sammy asked.

"No." I answered quickly before looking at the old man,

"What's your name?"

The old man kept his eyes forward.

"I am called Red Bird. People call me Old Red."

"Old Red?" Joseph questioned.

I kicked the back of the seat.

"Old Red, you'll have to forgive my husband, he's outspoken." I apologized.

Old Red scanned me with his eyes.

"How old are you?" He asked me.

"Twenty." I answered plainly,

"Are you married?"

"I was." Old Red replied,

"I had three women."

My eyes grew,

"You've been married three times?!"

"At the same time." Old Red grumbled.

He looked at little Nemo, who was playing with his leather doll.

"Is that your son?" He asked.

"Nah. It's my nephew." I answered.

Finn joined in on the conversation.

"Is there a gas station around here?"

Old Red pointed north.

"There should be one up ahead. But I must warn you to be careful." He spoke.

"Why?" Finn asked.

"The gas station is in good condition, yet, for one reason, no one dares to take gas from there, because if they do...well...they get shot."

I cocked an eyebrow.

"Shot?"

"Shot." Old Red responded,

"Shot by my people...the Forest People."

When we all looked confused, Old Red chuckled.

"Just go North to the gas station."

Finn clicked his tongue.

"Normally, I would turn the other way, but we really need gas, so..."

He went ahead. Soon enough, we saw the gas station up ahead. It looked like it was in perfect condition. Finn grinned, driving the car forward and stopping to get gas. While we all waited, Joseph turned to me.

"Honey, do you want the front seat for a little while?"

"No, I'm okay here." I replied with a smile.

Old Red just watched out the window.

Sammy stared at him.

"So..." she broke the silence,

"What were you doing out in the cold by yourself?"

"I was praying to the Great Spirit." Old Red claimed.

My eyebrows furrowed,

"About-?"

"We need food." Was all Old Red said,

"Living in the ways of our people in the forest is very hard."

"Why are you living in the forest?" Joseph came into the conversation.

"We are the people that follow the great wolf. The creatures that capture the wicked." Red answered humbly.

"You mean Howlers?" Sammy's tone was that of utter shock.

"Yes." Old Red acknowledged.

"Why are your people sitting in the woods, with no food, following the Howlers?" I asked concernedly.

"I would not say "follow," it is more like worship, I suppose." Old Red explained.

"Why?" Joseph questioned.

"You all ask many questions." Old Red rolled his eyes.

"Well, we need to know things." I retorted.

Finn swung the car door open,

"Guys, there's gotta be food in that gas station!"

"There is only canned tuna and bottled water. It belongs to my people." Old Red told Finn firmly.

Finn rolled his eyes,

"Can't we take some? We can leave some left over."

Old Red cocked an eyebrow,

"You would?"

"Yes, I promise." Finn said truthfully.

"Promise," Old Red scoffed,

"White men make many promises, it is the main thing they destroy. They destroy promises better than any other messed-up thing they do."

"Please." Finn begged.

Finn never begged, I suppose he was just hungry and still weak from what happened to his empire.

Old Red leaned back.

"Do what you want. You can only take six cans. And I will count them when you come back."

Finn smiled.

"Thanks, old man."

"I prefer man beyond his years." Old Red told him.

I held back a snort and Finn gestured to me and Sammy.

"Come on, sisters, let's go get some tuna. Joseph, stay with the baby."

"Aye aye, captain." Joseph saluted him.

Sammy and I followed our brother into the gas station. Sure enough, there were two shelves loaded with tuna. Finn took six cans...but stuffed one more in his sock.

"Finn..." I warned.

Finn gave me a cocky grin.

"You seem to forget we are outlaws."

I slowly smiled. Finn was back to his old self again. I wanted to throw my arms around him, but I played it cool.

"Right."

With that, we headed back out.

"I'm sure the old man won't even notice." Finn pointed out.

"No, he wants to be called a "man beyond his years," remember?" I reminded him with a laugh.

The three of us laughed until Sammy stopped abruptly.

"Guys." She whispered,

"Look."

We looked to see where she was pointing.

What we saw were eight Howlers standing on a hill up ahead.

"Oh great..." I murmured,

"Look what followed us here."

Better yet, the alpha led the way.

"How could the alpha follow us if Joseph sliced his leg?" Finn exclaimed.

I was too horrified.

"He did." Was all I could say.

Not only did the alpha now have half a face...but he had only three legs. The alpha slowly limped forward while his companions charged from down the hill. Sammy abruptly grabbed our arms,

"What do we do?!"

The bitter chill of the winter winds bit our skin, but it did not match up to our fear. The Howlers barked loudly. Joseph opened the window to the car, screaming for us to get in. We tried to rush to the car, but one Howler leapt on top of it.

I searched my belt for a weapon. Nothing. The Howler on the car leapt right for me and I screamed. So, did Joseph.

"*Victoria*!" He roared.

Then, just like that, the Howler was dead at my feet. All the others in the pack, including the alpha, fled whimpering into the wilderness. I stared at the dead Howler before my feet.

An arrow had been thrusted in the side of its skull. We heard whoops and saw two men run forward with bows and arrows, along with furious looks. They aimed their next arrows for us.

"Woah, woah, woah! Hold it there!" Finn exclaimed.

"What are you doing on our land?" One man demanded.

Their looks exchanged from anger to happiness when Old Red stepped out of the car with Joseph.

Both men grinned.

"Red!" They both exclaimed and patted the old man's shoulder,

"Where have you been, man?"

"Conversing with the spirits." Old Red answered solemnly.

"Look, brother, the spirits won't do anything for us."

The other man, who had not really spoken yet, jerked his head to us.

"What's with the white people? They kidnap you?"

Old Red laughed,

"No, they were giving me a ride." He answered plainly.

"To the village?"

"Yes."

Old Red brushed his hands together,

"Let's take these kind white folks to our village. They have been in their vehicle far too long, I am sure." He turned to us,

"Does that settle well with you?"

We all smiled.

"Oh, yeah." I said.

"Get in the car with us." Finn offered, opening the door.

When the two tribal men got in the car, Old Red turned to my brother.

"Did you take only six cans of tuna?" He questioned him suspiciously.

Finn took out the six cans and smiled.

"Yep."

Old Red shook his head.

"And if I check your feet, you won't have an extra can in your socks or shoes?"

Finn gulped and tried to keep a straight voice.

"I-"

"Save it, boy." Old Red rolled his eyes and got in the car.

Finn sighed and followed behind.

—

We drove up a mountain road for about ten minutes. I became very car sick. My stomach churned and rumbled, and I thought I was about to throw up.

"The village is up ahead." Old Red told us.

The car seemed to be ten times more crowded because we let in two more people.

"Oh yeah, I see something." Finn pointed out.

Yes, he did see something. A village. A village of tents and campfires. People came towards the car. Tribal people. Some wore feathers, and some carried small children or weapons. When the car stopped, Old Red got out of the car and the weapons lowered.

The other two tribal men followed and returned to their families. I got out of the car. The air was chilly, but no snow blew. We even saw some grass. Old Red raised his arms.

"My people, I have brought with me some visitors. Treat them kindly and bring them food and water. They gave me a ride back to the village."

People came forward to shake me, Finn, Sammy, and Joseph's hands. The people were very kind. I could not help but notice that these people had walls filled with paintings. The pictures painted on the walls were pictures of wolf-like beasts. Howlers. It kind of creeped me out.

Old Red came over to me.

"The women in the tribe can bathe your baby..." he offered.

I looked at Nemo who stayed in the car, shyly peeking out the window. He was a little dirty.

"Sure. If your women don't mind." I agreed.

Old Red opened the door and outstretched his arms to baby Nemo. Nemo accepted by crawling into his arms. With that, the old man took Nemo over to a group of women. My husband walked over to me.

"They are going to offer us food. It will be a gathering of some kind." Joseph told me.

Finn and Sammy walked over too.

"They don't have much food..." Sammy told us,

"So, whatever we do...we gotta be grateful."

"Yeah with this time of year, hunting must be hard." Finn pointed out.

We all agreed and started to make ourselves comfortable.

—

The gathering began an hour after we arrived. I stared at my food. Nemo had gotten out of his bath and stared at his food.

"Daddy..." He whispered to Finn,

"This fish is staring at me..."

"It's okay, buddy. My fish is, too." I whispered back before Finn could say anything.

Joseph and Sammy were both eating their fish calmly. Women walked over with bowls of some concoction they had made. It smelled good, so I accepted a bowl.

"What is this?" I asked.

"Dog." One of the women answered.

After they left, I wanted to gag. Finn ate it as if it were SpaghettiOs.

"This is good." He remarked.

"You're gross." I spat.

"I'm grossly in love with this dog stew." Finn took a huge bite of it right in my face.

It smelled good, but dog? Really? I dipped my spoon in the bowl, taking a small bite. My eyebrows raised, and I took another bite.

"This actually isn't that bad." I grinned.

"Told ya." Finn chuckled.

Old Red stood up and raised his arms.

"My people, this is the third month we have not been affected by the great Howler. If we make offerings to the great spirit, he will keep the Howlers away from our village!"

People whooped and clapped. Old Red gestured to us.

"We have welcomed our guests, now let us tell the great story of the Howler!"

People all grinned as everyone sat down and listened. I nestled up on Joseph's shoulder and listened. Even though my group and I really knew the Howlers were constructed by the government, we still wanted to hear the story.

"Long ago," Old Red began,

"Our great spirit was having a war with the demons of the badlands. He wanted to have something to guard his land...something that would protect the great spirit's people. So, he created a wolf like creature called a Howler. Howlers fought against the demons and won every battle. Until the king of the demons possessed the Howlers into turning against the great spirit and his people."

I listened carefully with interest. Old Red gave us a smile as he waved his hand to the wall with all the paintings of Howlers.

"They killed innocent people, which is something that is not good...so, the great spirit made a deal with the Demon King. It said that he can keep the Howlers and allow the Howlers to kill guilty people followed by yearly sacrifices by our people, but he must leave the innocent be."

Old Red closed his eyes.

"Howlers are meant to kill the guilty." He whispered.

The area was so quiet...it became uncomfortable. Old Red smiled at us. Not just his people, but also me and my group.

"That is why..." he approached us carefully,

"We will be offering you..."

Joseph and I looked at each other with fear. Finn and Sammy stood up with Nemo in Finn's embrace.

"What?" We all demanded at the same time.

Old Red jerked his head at us, and Braves rushed forward to tie our wrists behind our backs.

Finn suddenly spun around before the Braves could grab his arms and he attacked them with a swift punch for both. Both Braves were knocked to the ground.

Before Finn could try anything else, he was knocked across the head with the butt of a rifle held by a warrior.

"*Hey!*" Joseph yelled, trying to attack the man that knocked my brother out.

Soon enough, he was knocked across the head too. Nemo began crying hard and Sammy held him tightly. I covered my mouth, trying to decide whether to do something.

"Tie them to the poles!" Old Red ordered.

Joseph and Finn were dragged over to one pole by one tent and Sammy and Nemo and I were brought to another pole diagonal from them.

The rope grinded against my wrists, burning the flesh. A warrior had our hands tied behind our back, plus he circled us around a pole and tied us by the waist. After we were all tied up, the Braves departed.

"Oh my God, we're gonna die, Victoria!" Sammy whispered shakily,

"They're gonna kill us!"

"Sammy, shut up!" I snapped,

"Do you really want little Nemo to hear you say that?! Shut up!"

Nemo's face turned red and tears squeezed out of his eyelids.

"Aunt Victoria, I don't wanna die..." he whimpered.

I wanted to hug the small child, but I could not due to being tied up.

"Listen to me, Nemo, are you listening?" I tried to sound as gentle as I could,

"When your daddy and Uncle Joseph wake up...we will escape...and when we do...we are going to get the heck away from Chesapeake Bay...and out of the state as fast as we can."

Nemo still cried, and I sighed desperately,

"Okay?"

"Okay." He peeped.

"You are lucky no Braves heard you say that." Sammy huffed.

I glanced at my sister.

"You know what's funny?" I asked her after a long silence passed.

"What?" She returned.

"It's funny how you used to be so nervous and shy...you shot a man instead of Joseph that one day you sought revenge for him killing our father...now you talk as if it never happened." I replied.

Sammy gave me a hard stare,

"Victoria, I know I have been cruel to your husband and you in the past...and I had a right to do that too...what he did to our father is truly unforgivable...but I realize now that you two love each other and are married...and what he did to our father was in the past. He let Finn keep Nemo instead of taking him for himself, so he could basically marry you without there being any more issues."

I took shallow breaths as she talked on.

"So yes...I was quiet. Yes, I was nervous all the time. Yes, I blamed your husband through it all...but that was in the past. This is who I am now."

I smiled at my sister from my side.

"You really did grow up, Sammy Hartley."

Sammy sucked in her cheeks.

"So did you, Victoria."

I kept trying to watch for the Braves or Old Red. We had been totally fooled. It was a real lesson. You can't trust anybody around here. At least not in these days. It was a lesson I should have learned long ago. I kept screwing it up.

—

Nighttime crept in through the mountains. The stars were glorious. No snow fell from the sky. I shivered while tied to the pole. I could hear Sammy's teeth chattering. We were nowhere near any of the campfires. Most people sat in their warm tents. Some warriors walked about, not paying attention to us. I saw a few dogs. They were cute, but they were probably meant for hunting and guarding, not meant to be house pets.

"Victoria..." Sammy whispered,

"Can we talk? Just like we used to at Black Gates and all the other facilities the government would throw us into?"

I made a face.

"We used to talk every night when it was you, me, and Shang Han...What makes this different?"

Sammy's breath came out in puffs.

"We are tied up here...almost enslaved...just like being in the facilities."

I smiled a bit.

"Yeah...let's talk..."

I could only see Sammy from the side of my face because we were all tied around the pole.

Nemo slept. His cheeks were red and rosy, and snot dribbled out of his nose. Joseph and Finn remained unconscious. Sammy glanced at me.

"What do you think life would've been like if we had a president?" She asked me.

"Terrible." I straight up answered,

"More politics and more government crap. No, thank you."

I stared at the moon and stars.

"What do you think life would've been like without Howlers?" I asked my sister.

Sammy snorted.

"We wouldn't be here."

I laughed at that. Sammy did, too.

"Well, we did live a life without Howlers once...before mother and dad died. Remember, we used to make little paper angels on Christmas and hang them up around the living room in our trailer?"

I smiled,

"Yeah, I do. Our living room only had a beaten-up yellow chair and a ratty yellow couch."

"Don't forget the old radio." Sammy reminded me,

"We had old songs...songs by people and bands named Justin Timberlake...Maroon 5, and Pink..."

"Everything we had was old." I chuckled.

"Really old." Sammy agreed.

She suddenly laughed,

"I remember when I was very little...one year we didn't have snow for winter, and I wanted to make a snowman...so you took a carrot and stuffed in Finn's nostril."

I laughed too,

"Yeah, then he ate it afterward, too." I added.

"Well, we didn't have a lot of food in the house." Sammy sighed.

"Thinking of the fact that we didn't have a lot of food always brings me back to the time dad died." I frowned,

"Remember how bad you wanted jellybeans?"

"Yeah, that was ridiculous." Sammy grumbled.

It was quiet for the next few minutes.

"I really miss them, Victoria."

I realized Sammy was crying. She sniffled,

"I miss them so much and it isn't fair that they had to die."

I tightened my jaw, staring straight ahead.

"Yeah..." I muttered,

"They would have been proud of you, Sammy."

"Really? Because sometimes I'm not so sure." She responded.

"They would have been prouder of you than they were of me." I said quickly,

"I'm married to the man that killed dad."

"We don't have to keep bringing that up." Sammy told me,

"It won't help your marriage. Just stop bringing it up."

I tried to make out constellations in the sky, but none appeared.

"What is your best memory of mother?" Sammy suddenly asked me,

"Please...tell it to me true... I want to know."

I suddenly remembered in horror: Sammy was so little when mother died. Her memory of her was not as well as mine.

I owed it to Sammy to come up with the best memory possible. I kept averting my stare to the dogs the warriors had with them.

"Well, I remember one of our neighbors that lived in the trailer next door to us had a dog that you really wanted to pet...but you were too scared because the dog was huge compared to you. Mother told you it would be okay, and she took you over to the dog. The dog was actually very friendly, and mother took your hand and laid it on the dog's soft fur."

Sammy sniffled as she listened to me finish my story,

"You were scared at first...but after a few minutes the dog was licking your face and you were laughing."

A tear rolled down my cheek.

"Awhile later, the dog got into some real pain. I remember you and I had gone next door to visit the dog and it was lying in a corner behind the neighbor's trailer. It was whimpering and whining. You and I hurried over to mother to help the dog...turns out the dog was having puppies. She gave birth to three of them that night and mother let you hold them and keep them warm."

"Then our rotten neighbors sold them..." Sammy grumbled.

"They needed money." I retorted, wanting to laugh that she could only remember that detail.

"They sold each puppy for only fifty cents." Sammy replied right back,

"*We* could even afford that."

It was quiet the next few minutes before I mumbled,

"Yeah sometimes I wonder why we didn't get one."

Sammy sighed and gazed at the sky.

"Sometimes...mother comes on my mind. I know we've spent years trying to get revenge for our dad...but our mother was killed, too. It's strange, I guess."

I shivered from the cold.

"Yeah." I said,

"Well we knew the man that killed our dad. We don't know the people that killed mother."

Another silence came before Sammy asked her final question:

"You know how people used to do super fun things back in the day?"

"Yeah." I answered.

Sammy then asked,

"What is the main thing you would want to do?"

I smiled a bit.

"I remember dad told me about something called a rollercoaster. They were super-fast and super-fun. Dad said his ancestors would do that and grandpa told him about it and now dad told his children. They pass things like roller coasters on in stories. If not a rollercoaster...then I would want to go see a movie. Not an old black-and-white film...but a real movie. Finn saw that old movie The Quiet Place because he stole the disc and watched it with a friend...I think that's what he said, anyway..."

Sammy chuckled.

"Yeah, well, I've always wanted to take a rocket and go to the moon."

My eyes grew.

"People actually did that?" I exclaimed.

"Oh yeah!" Sammy answered,

"I would go to the moon and create my own world...it would be ten times better than here."

I closed my eyes again, trying to catch a little sleep.

"Time to rest, Sammy." I whispered.

Before Sammy could reply, a few Braves gathered in a circle.

"We need to discuss the sacrifice of the prisoners."

"Sammy." I whispered almost so softly only the wind could hear me.

"What?"

"Pretend to be sleeping." I ordered in a hushed voice.

Sammy closed her eyes and so did I. I listened carefully.

"Old Red is planning to take them to the Howlers' den as an offering." A voice said.

Howlers' den? The Howlers had a den? They sure acted like wolves, alright.

"What's a Howlers' den?" A younger voice asked.

"It's where the Howlers go to breed pups. The mothers are very overprotective and will kill anyone that enters their den."

No way...we were going to be sacrificed to the Howlers' breeding grounds.

"When do we take them?"

"Tomorrow morning. Old Red is taking them."

Oh God.

I opened my left eye a little to see the Braves walking away. Sammy and I looked at one another in terror.

—

We barely got any sleep that night. My head hurt terribly, and I felt very nauseous. The sky shown an indigo color. My body finally gave me some mercy and I fell asleep. The glorious bliss of rest was interrupted around an hour and a half later when we were violently woken up by Old Red.

"Stand." He commanded.

I realized Nemo and Sammy and I were no longer tied to the pole, but our wrists remained tied behind our backs. I stood up, half stumbling. Sammy and Nemo stood up as well. Nemo glared at Old Red.

"You're mean." He mumbled,

"Wait till my daddy wakes up. He's gonna kick your butt."

Old Red scoffed,

"Your father is tied up. He won't be kicking anything."

Finn and Joseph were half-conscious when they were lifted by two warriors.

"Take them." Old Red ordered bitterly.

With that order, we were marched out of the Forest People's camp.

—

We walked on for what must have been hours. Finn was awake and being a total jerk on account of his head hurting, and he was in a crappy mood.

"Hey, I wonder why these idiots would not just take a car!" He said loudly,

"It's cuz they're too stupid!"

One warrior glared at Finn.

"The mountains are too dangerous to drive on." He said to my brother in annoyance.

Finn launched a wad of spit at the warrior's face. The warrior grunted and was about to hit him before he was stopped by Old Red.

"Don't." He told the warrior,

"He will be in enough misery when the Howlers get to him."

Finn sucked in a breath and gave a taunting smile. I wanted to tell him to knock it off. Nemo looked so tired from walking I thought he would collapse. Who would make a three-year-old kid walk for two hours? It was pure cruelty.

"Aunt Victoria...I'm tired." Nemo complained.

"It will be okay, you hear? Soon we will stop and rest." I reassured him as calmly as I could.

"Where are we going?" Nemo asked.

A warrior leaned over in the child's face with a mocking laugh.

"To get eaten by a bunch of monsters!" He said in a hoarse voice.

I wanted to viciously kick him in the face, but Nemo had a plan of his own. The small child stomped on the warrior's foot.

"Shut up!" He snapped.

The warrior outstretched a hand to slap Nemo, but Old Red spun around.

"If you lay one hand on that little boy, I will chop your hand off and feed it to the Howlers!" Old Red snapped.

The warrior sneered and walked to the back of the crowd that was escorting us to our deaths. Nemo turned to Finn.

"Daddy, that man was about to hit me!" He exclaimed.

Finn was angrier than ever.

"He will regret it...I promise."

"Time to stop and rest!" Old Red announced.

Us prisoners were brought by the edge of the mountain. The warriors built a fire and sat a little ways away from us. We all huddled together even though our wrists were tied behind our backs.

"We need to escape." Joseph whispered.

"Yeah, but how? The only way to get away is to hurl ourselves from the edge of the mountain!" I whispered back.

Joseph closed his eyes.

"All I know is that Nemo cannot and will not be fed to those Howlers." He whispered.

"Looks like you finally care about your kid." Finn observed.

"I've always cared about him!" Joseph whispered roughly,

"And that's why we all have to leap off the edge of the mountain."

"What?!" I whispered almost too loudly.

Joseph put a finger to his lips before he told us his plan.

"The mountain is not very steep. So, we will slide down. It's muddy and slippery, but it's our only choice."

"We could die!" Finn whispered harshly,

"You are an idiot!"

"We will not die!" Joseph assured us,

"We will survive. It's what we do."

I side smiled along with Sammy.

"Let's do it." Sammy said with a curt nod.

"You guys are insane." Finn shook his head.

"I wanna get out of here Finn. If it means sliding down a mountain and getting scrapes and bruises- so be it." Sammy argued.

Joseph glanced at all of us. That's when baby Nemo butted in:

"I don't like heights." He said loudly.

"Shh!" We all shushed him harshly.

Finn laid a hand on his adopted son's shoulder.

"Nemo, you need to be quiet. We're going to escape so the monsters don't eat us."

Joseph gave a small smile.

"Are we ready to slide?" He asked with determination.

"What happens when the warriors notice?" Sammy whispered.

"We run once we get to the bottom." Joseph answered casually.

"This is probably the dumbest plan I had ever heard." Finn grumbled.

"Says you, Finn." I snapped.

Joseph ignored us and held up his hand.

"On the count of three..." He whispered,

"One...two...three!"

With that, we threw ourselves down the mountain.

"*Hey!*"

We heard the warriors yell while we rolled down the steep hill of a mountain.

Joseph was right- the mountain wasn't very steep- but it was not easy to slide down either. I rolled down, my shoulder hit rocks and were scraped over sharp sticks. Mud caked my clothes. It felt like I was rolling forever. Before we knew it, we all reached the bottom.

Standing up to run, I cried out in pain.

"My ankle!" I screeched.

It felt like an icicle stabbed me in the bone. Joseph picked me up bridal-style. Finn scooped up Nemo in his arms. We all started running.

I felt like we were free until an arrow whizzed past my ear. I yelped when we saw Old Red and his men firing arrows at us from above.

"Come on!" Sammy urged us while we struggled to get away.

Arrows struck the ground like lightning bolts and hit trees like pinning the tail on a donkey. Just when I thought we made it far enough, I heard a cry of pain. Chills ran up my spine and I saw Finn clutching his shoulder. My eyes bulged out of my head when I saw that an arrow had gone right through his flesh.

"God!"

He turned to the warriors while he ran,

"Damn you!" He hollered.

Luckily, we got far enough from them that their aim was way off. We all whooped.

"We made it!" I exclaimed.

Finn groaned while Nemo was set on the ground. Blood seeped through Finn's shirt. Joseph huffed.

"Okay, Finn. You're gonna have to bear with me." He warned him.

Finn huffed in and out as Joseph snapped the arrow launched in Finn's shoulder, who yelled loudly in pain. It made me nervous that the warriors and Old Red would hear us.

"God, that hurt!" Finn shouted.

"Shut up and hold still!" Joseph rolled his eyes.

We were all freezing from the snow that covered the ground. Now that we were off the mountain and now there was no patch of ground in sight. Goosebumps covered my skin while Joseph tied a ripped off piece of his shirt around Finn's shoulder.

"It's gonna get infected." Sammy muttered.

"You're not a doctor." Finn snapped.

"Yeah well everyone can tell by that wound." Sammy sighed.

She rose to her feet.

"Look you guys, I don't know about you...but I actually kind of want to go check out that Howler's den."

I don't know about you, but I was thinking the cold was getting to my sister's brain.

"Why?" I demanded,

"We just escaped from being trapped in there! Why do you want to go back?!"

"Listen to my idea!" Sammy urged us,

"One of the warriors mentioned that is the breeding grounds for Howlers. That's why there are more and more around! If we go to their den with weapons and an idea of some kind...maybe, we can stop them from breeding!"

I was kind of understanding what she meant.

"So, you mean...we will kill the Howlers off?"

"Exactly!" Sammy declared.

"I can't believe I'm saying this...but I'm with her." Joseph said.

"You two are whack..." Finn growled.

Little Nemo trotted over by us and folded his hands- he looked adorable.

"Is my daddy going to be okay?" He asked Joseph.

Joseph smiled. So did Finn, even though he was in agony from his bleeding shoulder.

"I'll be fine, Nemo. Why don't you let Sammy carry you while we walk?"

I crossed my arms.

"You all do realize that if we go to the Howlers' Den, the warriors and Old Red might be there?"

"Why would they? They were only going to the Howlers' Den to sacrifice us." Joseph pointed out.

"True." Sammy agreed.

We contemplated Sammy's idea for a long time. The only sounds around us were the wind and the bristle of snow-covered bushes. Finally, I nodded.

"I'm in." I whispered.

Sammy smiled at me, as did Joseph.

"I'm in, too." He agreed.

"Me three!" Nemo echoed in a small voice.

Finn struggled to stand because he was sore from his shoulder, but huffed,

"This is crazy...but I'm in."

Sammy, very happy to hear that we agreed with her plan, declared,

"Alright, then. Let's go find that Howlers' den...and let those beasts meet their maker."

Part Eleven

After preparing for the moment we would enter the Howlers' Den, we made it to our destination two days after escaping from Old Red and his people. The only weapons we had were three knives, a handgun with only two bullets left, and a machete. We also had a genius named Joseph amongst us who knew how to light a fire survivor-style, so we could have torches.

Deep down, I was terrified to enter the home of the Howlers. Howlers have been a problem for me over half my life. Hopefully, we would be able to put an end to this.

We would destroy the breeding ground of those monsters and stop the spawn of those hell-raising beasts. We knew where the den was by following the direction Old Red would have taken us, and soon enough we came across paw prints.

The paw prints multiplied as we came closer to their den. Finally, it came into sight. The sight gave me shivers. Paw prints led to multiple mountains. Great. More climbing. We saw a few openings, along with a lone Howler walking out to howl.

The noise rang into the air like church bells on a Sunday. Goosebumps crawled up my skin.

Finn sighed crossly.

"Someone needs to stay with Nemo. We can't be letting a three-year-old go inside to a death sentence."

"It's not a death sentence." Sammy retorted.

"Well, he's right." Joseph pointed out.

The five of us remained silent for a while. I turned to my sister:

"Sammy, you stay with Nemo. Joseph and Finn along with myself will go inside."

That pissed Sammy off.

"No way! I'm going too!" She insisted.

"Sammy you are fourteen- fifteen, actually. That makes you the youngest besides Nemo. You're staying with him." I ordered.

Sammy closed her eyes,

"Victoria...I have been running from Howlers alongside you for years. I have a right to go on this adventure as well."

I stared into Sammy's beautiful, wide blue eyes. Her face was riddled with hopefulness.

"Please?" She pleaded.

I groaned quietly, turning to Joseph.

"Joseph...you will stay here." I told my husband.

Joseph wanted to argue but he held his tongue.

"Fine."

Finn collected the weapons that Joseph was supposed to have. With that, Finn kneeled before Nemo, the only child he had.

"Nemo, you will stay with Joseph. Be a good boy. Daddy loves you very much." Finn told his adopted son.

"Love you too, Daddy." Nemo replied, giving him a hug.

With that, my siblings and I exchanged glances,

"Let's go." I told them.

Joseph quickly kissed my head and I hugged him securely.

"I love you." I told my husband.

"I love you, too." Joseph replied,

"Please come back safe."

I touched his face with a warm smile.

"I will."

After saying our farewells, my siblings and I slowly crept for the closest opening to the Howlers' Den.

Climbing is not as easy as it seems. Of course, we climbed up cliffs with the Forest People, but these rocky hills were nothing like the mountains Old Red and our group climbed across. This was the hard way. The sneaky way. It was hard to try to stay out of the Howlers' sight when they lingered outside their den. It must be a massive den. We had to end the lives of these beasts because these were the beasts that made us more than miserable. If we killed off the breeding ground of the Howlers, it would be like slapping the government in the face.

After all, the government was responsible for creating these dogs from hell.

Sammy was the one that would carry the torch. Joseph taught us how to light fires from scratch. This was our most terrifying adventure yet. I held the machete and a switchblade, which was one of the three knives possessed by Joseph.

I felt confident I would make it out alive on the outside. On the inside, I was terrified. After making it through a thin ledge, we saw an opening with no Howlers in sight.

"This way." Finn guided us over to the entry.

The doorway to the den was just one big black hole surrounded by plants and vines dangling over it like a curtain.

I took a breath.

"Let's go."

—

Besides the torch Sammy clutched in her hand, darkness surrounded us. This place was like a mansion made of rocks. We could hear small streams of water trickling through cracks within the rocks. Sammy's torch illuminated paw prints all over the dusty ground.

The three of us had to stay alert constantly.

No Howlers in sight so far, but we knew they were up ahead.

"Come on." Finn whispered almost so quiet we couldn't hear.

We tiptoed over to a huge rock with our weapons. The three of us gazed ahead, and Sammy kept the torch light as faint as she could.

A horrific sight lay before us:

There must have been a hundred Howlers. Some were even puppies! Better yet, we saw the alpha. He stood on a sledge as if it were a throne. His mate stood next to him with two small pups.

"There are so many." Sammy breathed.

My heart pounded against my chest. My head spun like a globe. Finn pointed to where the pack was resting.

"See over there? There is a ton of dry brush."

"And there." I pointed to a spot right next to the alpha Howler.

"Also there." Finn gestured to a spot right next to us.

We both looked at the torch that Sammy held.

"We can burn this place out." I thought aloud,

"All it takes is some dry brush."

"There are several openings." Sammy shook her head,

"It wouldn't work."

"I ain't asking. I'm telling." I said sternly,

"That's how we will beat the Howlers."

"How will we block all the openings?" Finn asked with a side smile.

I thought a second.

"We will-"

I was cut off by the barking of a Howler that stood right behind us.

"Oh, God." Sammy said with wide eyes.

Finn immediately took the torch from Sammy's hand, setting the dry brush next to us ablaze. The Howler began barking, which alerted his pack that their first entry had been blocked off by flames.

The entire pack barked and howled in return, scrambling in different directions.

"Oh, crap." I huffed,

"They're going through the other entries, so they can circle back around and trap us."

The Howler behind us growled lowly. It did not last long, because Finn took the torch and thrusted it towards the beast. Sparks flew out into the snout of the Howler, who gave a loud yelp. The creature moved aside, giving us time to scurry out of the hole and past the flames as quick as we could. The Howler inside was toast.

We climbed a few more ledges and mountain sides to find another entry to block off. Finn tried hard to save the light of the torch. During our climbing, we saw a few Howlers across from where we were climbing.

Chills ran up my flesh. Especially when one of them was about to jump across the gap between both cliffs- and onto our side.

"Oh, come on!" Finn spat.

The Howler barked loudly before taking a leap for us. I screamed, as did Sammy. Finn cussed so loud that Mexico could hear him. To our luck, the Howler had plummeted down into a rushing river that was below the gap between us and the other Howlers.

"That thing almost got us!" Sammy cried.

"We have to keep climbing before another one jumps for us!" Finn demanded.

The three of us tried to edge our way across the thin ledge that we stood on as quickly as we could. The beasts that tried to kill us did not follow, only went back inside their den through another entry.

"How many entries are there, do you think?" I asked my siblings.

"I think there are three more besides the one we burnt out." Sammy answered.

"No. There's four more." Finn corrected her by pointing to a smaller opening further back.

I sighed,

"We have to light all of those entries on fire to trap the Howlers inside their den. That way they will either burn to death or die from the amount of smoke." I explained.

"Agreed." Finn declared.

When Finn held the torch in his hand, I was afraid he would burn me with it as we climbed. Luckily, the wind had not picked up, so our fire was fine.

"There's dry brush all around in the caves." Sammy pointed out,

"This will be a piece of cake!"

"Yeah, well, these robot-animals won't go down without a fight." Finn mumbled.

Sammy gasped,

"I see the alpha!" She said frantically.

Sure enough, the alpha stood outside the largest entry to the den with a menacing look on his face.

"I swear to God, that creature gave us the most crap out of all the Howlers." I huffed.

"Once I get another mansion, I want its head to hang on my wall." Finn decided.

Sammy and I snorted.

"Yeah, like that's happening." I chuckled.

Finn gave me a dirty look before we made it off our tiny ledge and onto a safer level of ground. I checked to see if the alpha Howler remained near us. He was not.

It became oddly quiet.

"Where is the pack?" I whispered.

My question was answered when we all looked up. A Howler stood on a ledge just above our heads. It barked, reaching down with its jaws and trying to sink its teeth into us. It's teeth nearly reached our heads. We all scurried forward and the Howler jumped onto the ground we stood on. It faced us with a snarl.

Its eyes locked with mine before lunging in the air towards me.

Within the few moments I had, I scrambled to grab the machete, but there was no need.

I felt myself being pushed out of the way. Instead of me being the one to receive the fangs of the vicious beast, it was Sammy.

"*Sammy!*" Finn hollered.

It took moments for me to realize what happened. The Howler sank its fangs into Sammy's leg and dragged her away. Sammy screamed in pain for us to run.

I snapped out of it. A Howler just dragged away my sister. It ran her into the den. Finn and I bolted after her like a couple of racehorses. The animal was too fast, unfortunately, and the two of them were out of sight in minutes.

My brother and I finally caught up and ran into the den without thinking twice. No Howler in sight. I quickly turned to Finn.

"Finn, we have to separate to find her!" I exclaimed,

"I know you have a torch in your hand- continue to light all the entries aflame but leave the fourth entry- the smallest entry open for us to get out. I will go find Sammy because I have the best weapon."

Finn's eyes were clouded by tears.

"She had a small knife..." he whispered,

"Maybe she'll be okay."

I did my best to stay the strongest.

"I don't know, buddy. I pray she is."

With that, we separated.

I hurried down through the den. All I wanted was to find my sister. There were no Howlers in sight even though I'd been looking for them for a while now.

The air around me grew chillier as I continued moving deeper into the den. There was a faint smell of smoke. Maybe this plan wasn't as good of an idea as I thought. I felt as though I needed to find Finn and tell him to stop lighting all the openings to the den aflame.

"Sammy!" I whispered sharply.

No response.

The smell of smoke grew a little. My heart began to thump loudly.

"Sammy!" I called.

To hell with the Howlers. I had to find my sister. Before I could call for her again, I fell through the ground. A scream erupted from me before I hit the mud. When landing on my back, all I could do was look up. I must have been eight feet down in the ground. Dry grass fell on me along with some dirt from the good size hole I fell through.

I could not move. Searing aches traveled up my back while the mud seeped through my clothes and hair.

"Help!" I called,

"Finn! Help me!"

My God. I was doomed.

—

I must have been laying here for at least thirty minutes. I'd been calling for help so much that my throat became dry. Now I really wanted water. My head spun and my heart continued to race.

Slowly, I drifted off to sleep. Even though my mind screamed for me to wake up.

—

We sat in our old metal trailer with our radio playing a song by a band called The Wren in 2203. I shaded a picture on a tiny piece of paper with a small smile and giggle. Sammy stuck her tongue out in concentration while she colored her picture. Finn was playing heads and tails by himself with a penny.

Dad sat at the table eating an orange.

"I'm hungry, daddy!" Sammy peeped,

"When's mommy coming home with groceries?"

"She'll be home soon, baby." Dad reassured her.

He seemed to be thinking.

"I told her to take the handgun with her in case if there came any trouble."

"I could protect mom!" Finn insisted.

Dad smiled,

"Oh, really? Well, just try and be as gentle of a person as you can."

"Why?" Finn asked curiously.

Dad gave us some of his orange.

"Because killing ain't the answer, son. It's peace."

We kept waiting for mother to return with the groceries. She did not come back. Daytime turned into sunset. Dad became worried.

"Should we go looking for her?" I asked dad.

"No, Victoria. I'm gonna look for her. You stay here with your brother and sister." Dad ordered.

"Yes, sir." I replied.

Dad handed me a knife.

"Protect your little brother and sister, Victoria." Dad told me.

I accepted the knife, staring at the sharp blade.

"I will." I promised.

—

My eyes opened widely. Protect your little brother and sister. That was my duty. My calling. For years and years, we had survived and fought for our lives. Sammy saved mine. Now I needed to save hers.

I slowly got to my feet. My back still ached, but I did not think it was broken. I looked up, pretty sure I was about eight feet underground. I saw roots, but nothing I could necessarily grab onto.

I dug my fingers into the wall of dirt and slowly began to climb. Unfortunately, about halfway up, the dirt broke from under my feet and I fell to the ground again.

"No!" I shouted.

I needed to get up.

"Help!" I cried,

"Help me, please!"

It was as if God heard me...because I heard a voice call back.

"*Victoria*?!"

Finn.

"*Finn*!" I screamed,

"*Finn, I'm down here*!"

Before I knew it, I saw Finn at the top of the hole.

"Victoria Hartley, what are you doing down there?!"

"Sightseeing!" I answered sarcastically,

"Help me up! Please!"

Finn looked around for something that he could grab to help me get up. It became clear that a lightbulb stood on Finn's head when a smile came to his face.

"I got it!" He exclaimed.

I did not have time to ask because Finn was already in action of his plan. He took off his shirt and began to unbutton his jeans.

"What are you doing?" I sighed.

Finn stood in his boxers and tied the legs of his jeans and his rolled-up shirt. He must be making a rope. He tried to hoist it down. It only went about halfway.

"Okay, Victoria. You're gonna have to jump!" He told me.

I took a breath.

"I can try."

I took a running start, then leaping for the air. I missed. I tried again, but that time I fell knees first into the dirt.

"Let me try climbing a little first." I suggested.

"Hurry!" Finn pleaded,

"We gotta find Sammy!"

I started climbing. This went much smoother. Before the dirt could break, I hoisted myself up fast enough to grab Finn's rope of clothes. With all his strength, Finn pulled me up.

Once I made it up, we happily embraced one another.

"Did you light all the openings to the den except the small one?" I asked.

"No. I got most of them. I still need to get a couple more." Finn answered.

"We don't have time for that right now. We need to get Sammy out of here." I said.

Finn picked up the torch from where he stuck it in the ground. A small flame survived yet. Finn gently blew on it to let the fire grow once again.

"Come on." I told him.

We both ran forward to look for Sammy. We followed the many tracks until it led us to what we were looking for.

Sammy.

She lay, pale, on the ground. The sight of her terrified me. Claw marks the size of skateboards ran up her legs, along with a bite mark in her shoulder. Her right thigh had been pretty chewed up. She lay there, shivering.

"Sammy!" I sobbed and ran to her with Finn on my heels.

I grabbed her face. Sammy shivered in a ghoulish way.

"Run..." She croaked.

Finn picked her up; blood dripped onto the ground like drops of rain.

We heard a snap of teeth and growl from in front of us. My blood boiled with anger when I saw the alpha Howler stand before us.

"He did it." Sammy whispered,

"The alpha did it."

I pulled the machete from my belt. This beast was gonna die.

I gripped my machete in anger.

"Alright, beastie. Let's settle this how we should have settled this long ago."

The alpha growled loudly and approached me slowly.

My grip on my machete seemed just as tight as my throat. I screamed loudly and ran for the alpha who leapt over my head, dodging my blade.

Finn backed away with Sammy in his arms.

Glaring into the eyes of the alpha Howler, I remembered everything:

The running, the chasing, the hiding. This was it. No more. No more running, chasing, or hiding.

I yelled madly, slashing my blade and snipping the white fur from the conniving alpha. Finn clutched our dying sister tightly.

"Do it, Victoria! Kill it!"

The hollering that erupted from me did not sound like myself. I kept slashing the blade over and over as the alpha Howler barked.

The barking and screaming continued. I felt my leg tingle with pain when the alpha slashed my leg with his claws. I cried out but whipped my sword against the Howler's flesh. It yelped in return, revealing a long scar on his side.

Finn urged me on, crying things out in the background. I roared, thrusting my blade deep into the Howler's heart. The blade impaled the mighty creature.

I pulled my machete out of the alpha Howler. It fell lifelessly to the ground. His half-face haunted me. One half was a normal wolf's face, the other was just a skull. A cold, dead skull.

I gravely stared at the robotic animal corpse for moments on end. No noise came from the others either.

More growls joined in. It was as if we had forgotten there was a whole pack that the world needed to be rid of. I reached out to take the torch Finn was managing to hold while also carrying Sammy.

I glanced at the flame of the torch and smiled when thousands of yellow eyes peered at us.

Dry brush covered the ground everywhere.

When some Howlers began to run forward, I lit the dry brush aflame and kicked it towards the beasts. They cried out, backing away quickly. I smiled a bit. Was that the last entry?

I sighed to realize I was wrong. They ran away from the flames and down another tunnel.

"They are going for another entry!" Finn huffed.

"It doesn't matter. The last entry is small. It was the one we originally planned to escape from. Remember? It's right over there!" I told him.

"Go, light it quickly!" Finn urged me.

I ran with the torch to go light the last opening to the den on fire.

After collecting some dry brush and lighting it, I grinned. All the Howlers were trapped. We could hear the shrieks and howls of all the animals burning inside.

I know there may be more Howlers out there, but we destroyed their one and only source of breeding grounds. Hopefully anyway.

As sounds of howling and cries filled the air, my siblings and I made our way down the mountain. I disposed of the torch and we hurried Sammy down as fast as we could.

The moment finally arrived when we made it back to the spot where Joseph and Nemo were waiting. To our surprise, no one was there. Joseph and Nemo were gone.

I felt confused.

"Where's my husband?" I thought out loud.

"Where's my son?" Finn echoed.

"*Stop right there, fugitives!*" We heard a recognizable voice command us.

My siblings and I spun around to see someone we would never expect to see. I felt as if I was staring into the eyes of the devil. Far worse than any beast I've laid eyes on.

"D- "I could not even stammer the words in a horrific whisper,

"Doctor Kinderman?"

The aged woman stood with a shock pen in one hand and a gun in the other.

It couldn't be.

It couldn't be Doctor Kinderman from Black Gates. I killed every worker and gov there with rat poison. She could not possibly be alive! I watched her fall to the ground dead the very night we escaped.

Finn's lips slightly parted with his eyes squinted in outrage. Sammy had her face hidden in his chest, still shaking from all the blood she had been losing.

Doctor Kinderman wickedly smiled.

"Hello, Patient 606." She greeted me lightly,

"We had been looking for you for quite some time. I suppose you managed to burn the breeding ground for our little spies. How spiteful."

"How are you alive?" I asked in a terrified voice.

Just when Doctor Kinderman was about to answer, we heard muffled voices. I gasped once my eyes fell on Joseph and Nemo. Their mouths had been shut by tape and they were trapped in chains. Dozens of government soldiers stood behind Doctor Kinderman.

Doctor Kinderman shook her head, clicking her tongue.

"Oh, Victoria Hartley...did you really think you could dispose of me? All around were flyers of you and your brother and sister wanted for robberies, escapes, murders! How could you even figure that you would survive without being brought right back into my loving arms?"

Finn spat at her, followed by horrible curses that I won't repeat.

Doctor Kinderman observed Sammy.

"It appears this one is dying. Take her." She told one of the soldiers.

Finn backed away, shouting profanities, but the policemen took her from his arms. Finn could not do a thing to fight back while the man held our suffering sister. I looked from Doctor Kinderman, to the gun and shock pen she held, and then back at her.

"You conniving snake!" I barked,

"You will suffer for what you are doing to all these outlaws!"

"Suffer?" Doctor Kinderman laughed,

"Your brother Finn here pretty much wiped out the entire wealthy population due to his little empire burning down."

She approached us,

"Not to mention the horrible scandal of you and the infamous Joseph Stonewall marrying. It's preposterous! To think, Finn adopted Nehemiah Rigby—the grandson of a deceased millionaire—is crazy. Well, I may say not...Finn has always had lust for power and what was the other one? Money!"

"Go to hell!" Finn hollered.

Doctor Kinderman now approached me,

"I knew you three would plot an escape if I put you in a room together, I knew you would plan something, Victoria, if you heard my phone call about the Howlers. If it sacrificed others, so be it. It gave me an excuse to kill you three."

"Why didn't you just kill us?" I shook with rage.

"Because I am with the government." Kinderman hissed,

"I play by the rules."

Doctor Kinderman jabbed her shock pen against Finn and stunned him roughly. That sparked terrible anger in my heart.

"Leave him alone!" I screamed, lunging forward.

Doctor Kinderman cried out. I slammed my fist into her face repeatedly, watching the blood trickle out of her nose and feeling the break of her teeth.

Everything around me went black.

Part Twelve

Dad came home late that night. His expression had been one I never seen on him before. He always seemed happy and calm. Now a look of defeat and depression clouded his face.

"Dad!" Sammy exclaimed, jumping to her feet,

"Where's mommy? Did you find her?"

Dad's eyes were bloodshot.

"Yeah, baby. I found her." He answered hoarsely.

I got to my feet along with Finn.

"Where is she?" I asked him.

Dad brushed his pants and squatted down.

"You know, kids, do you remember when grandpa left to go someplace else and that we would see him again someday?" He asked us.

I did not like where this was going.

"Yes." Finn answered.

"I told you three that he went to go live with grandma and most of your aunts, uncles, and cousins?" Dad continued his question.

"Yes!" Sammy smiled,

"But where's mommy?"

Dad let out a shaky breath.

"She uh...she went up there with grandpa and the others...in heaven..." Daddy whispered, a tear rolling down his cheek.

Now, I couldn't be entirely sure...but I was positive that a small crack formed in my heart that day. Dad couldn't stitch it back up. Nothing in the entire world could stitch it back up.

Sammy became confused.

"Will we see her again?" She asked.

"Of course." Dad promised,

"It will just be a very long time."

"How long?" Finn cried.

Dad kissed Finn's head gently.

"A long time." He answered again,

"But don't worry. It will go by quicker than you think! And we will see mom again. That's a promise."

Finn wrapped his arms around Dad in a great big bear hug and cried for a long time. Sammy joined in, still confused about the conundrum. I could only stand and stare. My whole body felt limp as if it had been beating by a million rocks. It hurt as if someone took my heart and ripped it right from my chest.

Your mother is dead! My mind kept screaming.

Dad extended his reach to let me in the group hug, I reluctantly joined.

It was better if I were left alone. I wanted to bury myself underground and hide for a thousand years. My heart ached; my bones quivered. At last, I let out a sob and fulfilled my need to cry.

After Finn and Sammy went to sleep, I made my way out of the bed the three of us shared and walked over to Dad. He sat on the porch outside our metal trailer. The stars sparkled extra bright tonight. Most likely because mother was up there. I joined him on the porch, twiddling my tiny thumbs.

"How did it happen?" I finally peeped.

Dad turned towards me as if he just realized I was there.

"Victoria! Girl, you scared me." He scolded, his cheeks tearstained and teeth clenched.

There is no disheartening sight than to see your father, the person you loved and cared for deeply, fall into despair.

"How did it happen?" I repeated,

"How did mother-?"

"That is something you don't need to know." Dad shook his head,

"You are far too young to know of such things, Victoria. I ain't gonna tell you."

"Please." I begged,

"I'm her daughter. I can be a big girl and handle it. I have a right to know...please, daddy."

My dad sat in the dark with me for a long time, staring at the night sky.

"Other outlaws." He finally answered.

My eyes froze on the stars; I would never look at anything else again. My dad clenched his teeth so hard that veins popped from his head and he tried to hold back a sob.

"They took the food she got for us...along with the only weapon she carried. They left her in the dust to die..." he said shakily.

My hands shook but my face showed no fear. I told him I could handle it. I had to live up to what I told him I would do. Dad covered his face awhile. I almost stood up to go before he grabbed my hand.

"Please." He pleaded,

"If anything ever happens to me, you need to take care of Finn and Sammy!"

"Nothing will happen to you, daddy." I protested,

"I will care for Finn and Sammy. I love them! I love them like they are the only thing I have in the world! I have you, and I... I had mother. She'll be watching over us, dad. I can tell you that. Her eyes will never be taken off of us."

Dad touched my cheek.

"She loved you so much, Victoria."

I held his hand to my small cheek.

"I miss her." I sighed, my eyes burning with tears and sadness.

"I know. I do too." Dad replied.

There was one other thing I had to know.

"Where is she now?" I was almost too afraid to ask.

"I buried her already." Dad sighed,

"The looks of her would have frightened the little ones."

My face flushed a deep red.

"Mommy..." I whimpered.

I could not bear holding my tears in anymore. I burst out crying once again, collapsing into my dad's arms. He shushed me gently and rubbed my back.

—

My eyes opened to a bright light. All I could feel was the nauseating pain from my head. Did that malicious woman's comrades knock me out?

I studied my surroundings. I saw Joseph. He crawled over to me with a smile.

"You're awake." He grinned.

I reached out to touch his face.

"Joseph?"

"Yes, my love. You're alright. I promise." My husband told me.

I clutched my head.

"Where are we?" I groaned.

Joseph closed his eyes a moment.

"We are in the last facility in the world. All the gov's came together and formed this place where all the outlaws are trapped and cannot leave, ever. Eventually they are all put to death."

I slowly sat up with his help.

"How do you know this?" I asked.

"Because other prisoners told me." Joseph answered,

"Look around!"

I turned my gaze to my surroundings once more. Hundreds of people lay on the floor. We were all trapped in some sort of room.

You could say it was as large as a gymnasium. My body twitched a bit before all my memory came back.

"Oh my God! Finn! Nemo! Sammy! Where are they, Joseph?!" I demanded.

"Finn and Nemo are asleep over there." Joseph pointed to where my brother and his son lay resting next to each other.

I was almost too afraid to ask,

"And Sammy?"

Joseph looked down.

"She's in the hospital wing." He answered quietly.

My heart fell into pieces like a shattered window.

The hospital wing? Sammy? I took a deep breath.

"Why are we locked in this room?" I stared at the barred doors.

"It is rest time now." Joseph explained,

"In about five minutes it will be time for dinner. You can ask a guard there."

I could not believe what was happening. After so many years of running from the government, we ended up caught in their web of prisoners once again.

I weakly rested my head on my hard mat. It was my pillow.

"We gotta get out of here." I whispered.

Joseph huffed.

"There is no possible way we could escape. I talked to one of the oldest prisoners that stayed here. He said there is an electric fence surrounding the premises, followed by another layer of electric fence that circled around it almost one hundred feet high, and then you would only have to walk through miles of wasteland without food and water." He told me.

I stared at him.

"So, we're never getting out of here?" I sighed.

"Most likely not." Joseph returned sadly,

"We will all be put to death here."

I did not want to believe him. All my life I was able to escape the hands of death. Would now be any different?

Suddenly, a buzzer rang loudly. All the prisoners got to their feet. Joseph stood up with me. I saw Finn pick up Nemo.

"Victoria!" He grinned,

"You're awake!"

The two both hugged me, and I faced my brother and his young son. Finn's shoulder had been stitched up from where he was shot with an arrow.

"How long have I been passed out?" I asked him.

"A couple days." Finn answered,

"I woke up one day before you did. Man, this place sucks. I gotta say, Black Gates was ten times better."

"What is this place even called?" I turned to Joseph.

"I don't know." Joseph answered, his voice tinged with uncertainty.

A guard unlocked the door with a loud bang.

"Come get dinner!" He ordered us.

Everyone got in line. One thing I noticed was that everyone wore a name tag with a patient number labeled on it. I even had one. Patient 606. I almost totally forgot I was stamped with that that Godawful name.

Some fat man with rosy cheeks was handing out these weird-looking bars. One by one, the prisoners accepted them. When I received mine, I grimaced in disgust. It smelled like dung.

"What is this?" I whispered to Finn.

"Food bars." He answered with a shake of his head.

When he saw my pinched-up face, he chuckled.

"Don't worry. It's as bad as it smells."

"You're no help." I rolled my eyes.

"Quiet!" A guard hollered at us.

We came to another room with a few tables that everyone would have to fit in. There were no chairs.

"What kind of place is this?" I asked my husband.

"It's not even a place. This is the gateway to our maker." Joseph replied darkly.

We all sat down. I opened the handmade wrapper to my "food bar." It looked like baked barf in a bar form.

"I'm worried about Sammy." I swallowed hard.

"We all are." Finn replied.

"Daddy, I hate these stupid bars!" Nemo snapped grumpily.

"I know you do, buddy. But you got to follow their rules if you wanna stay with me." Finn replied softly.

My eyebrows furrowed.

"What do you mean by that?"

Finn gave me a sad look.

"Well, Doctor Kinderman told me if Nemo can follow the rules, then we can stay together. If not, he gets sent away." He said.

Hearing that made me ten times angrier. What kind of sick person would take away someone's child? I looked at my food bar. I had to eat something. I slowly took a bite of the bar. I did not know how to describe it. It was the most disgusting, horrible, chewy thing I had ever tasted. When biting into it, it was hard at first. Once it dissolved, it became chewy and the texture was like gravel.

I flipped the wrapper over to see the ingredients. Chicken, eggs, vegetable paste, tomato paste, flour, and breadcrumbs with raisins. This was the worst—I wouldn't even call it food. It would be more accurate as just a substance.

Nemo picked at the bar, only eating some of it. Finn plugged his nose while eating. Joseph stuffed it down and drank his bottle of water.

I tried holding my breath while eating it.

"Patient 606!" Some guard announced with a clipboard.

I raised my hand slightly. The man locked eyes with me.

"You're wanted in Doctor Kinderman's quarters."

I rolled my eyes and got to my feet.

"See you all later." I waved meekly.

Finn and Joseph smiled. Nemo picked at his food bar with a pouty face. I followed the guard down several halls.

"Hurry up!" The guard snapped.

"I'm going as fast as you are, jackass." I retorted.

At that moment, I realized there was no point in insulting the guards. Some of them did not actually want to work here. Some were just doing it to survive and stay alive. The guard said nothing but brought me to a set of double glass doors. He pressed a buzzer and spoke into the intercom:

"Got the fugitive, ma'am."

"Send her in." Doctor Kinderman responded through the mic.

The guard opened the door for me but did not follow me into the room. I was left alone with the woman I despised. There was a point in insulting her. After all, this woman would be the one putting me to death. I might as well have some fun.

"Sit down, Victoria." Doctor Kinderman instructed.

"I'd rather stand." I bitterly replied.

Doctor Kinderman laughed,

"That's funny...you thought I wasn't serious?"

She snapped her fingers and some man came out of nowhere and shocked me with his shock pen. I jumped a little, only getting more pissed by the minute. Doctor Kinderman sat at her desk with nasty pride.

"Now..." her glare darkened,

"Sit down."

My lips tightened as I made my way forward. I sat in the soft chair. It reminded me of Black Gates.

"What do you want?" I huffed.

Doctor Kinderman fiddled with her necklace that she wore. She grinned.

"I wanted to tell you...you will be escorted to your death tomorrow night."

I didn't feel all that intimidated. I took it smoothly, as if I were getting a morning greeting. Doctor Kinderman frowned.

"Why aren't you reacting?"

I sat frozen like a statue for a few minutes.

"Well, I guess death does not matter to me anymore. I've been through so much. If you wanna put me to death, so be it."

Doctor Kinderman looked a little disgruntled at first but regained her composure quickly.

I swallowed hard and stood up. Doctor Kinderman stayed seated but smiled darkly.

"Let me add the fact that I'm the one doing the honors," she chuckled.

I averted my eyes down. Now I cared. I did not want this awful woman to be the person that killed me. I shoved my chair back and opened the door. I could not walk away alone; a guard had to escort me.

—

I laid awake in silence that night. My husband asked me if I was okay, and I lied by telling him that I was fine.

I was going to die tomorrow night.

Normally, I would fight it. Normally, I would run away with my brother and sister and never look back.

Now I felt done with running. This was my last rodeo. My last night alone with my thoughts.

I contemplated everything I had been through. The many events that took place in my life. From the moment my mother died, then my father. From the moment my brother and sister and I went from facility to facility.

I thought of it all. How I became one with the man that killed my dad. Men that battled for my affection in Finn's ridiculously large house. I thought I was going to die when those Howlers came to tear down Finn's Empire.

As usual, I made it. I've always made it. I may have gotten mighty close to dying plenty of times, but I always survived.

My eyes closed for some sleep.

I stood in the middle of nowhere. Everything around me was dark.

"Hello?!" My voice echoed throughout the empty space I stood in.

I looked at my feet. I stood on a small patch of grass. Weird. Just before I figured I was completely alone; I heard a voice.

"Victoria."

I spun around, and my mouth dropped open. The person that stood before me...he looked so familiar. My eyes watered when I came to realize it was my father.

"Dad?" I whimpered.

He grinned at me. Another person walked next to him. A woman. Her sweet smile caused tears of joy to escape my eyes.

"Mother?"

She laughed happily, and both my parents came to embrace me. Was I among them? Did those awful people kill me in my sleep?

"Am I dead?" I asked them.

Dad chuckled,

"No, kiddo. You ain't dead. Just asleep."

"Why are you two here?" I asked next.

"To tell you that you are wrong for giving up." Mother answered.

I closed my eyes and sighed. They still stood before me by the time I opened them.

"Look, I don't know what else you want me to do...I failed...I tried protecting Finn and Sammy. All went wrong, and I am so sorry." I apologized.

Mother kissed my cheek, calming me down.

"You did not fail, Victoria." She told me gently,

"You have succeeded in more than what I could ever have done as a wife and as a parent."

I shook my head, laughing with tears streaming down my face.

"Surely you don't mean that."

"I do." Mother guaranteed me.

I quickly turned to my dad. I'm sure he had quite a bit to say to me.

"Dad...Joseph and I... we..." I could barely say what I wanted to say.

"It's okay." Dad stopped me,

"He's a good man. He just had a bad heart, and I forgave him long ago for what he did to me. You turned him into a good man, Victoria. You did good."

At that point, I could not stop bawling. My dad was not angry with me. Nor was my mother. I felt a huge weight remove itself from my shoulders.

"I really missed you both." I whispered shakily.

"Victoria, you need to leave the past behind you. Keep surviving. You cannot give up now." Dad urged me.

"What can I do, dad? I don't know what I can do to keep surviving..." I replied desperately.

"Believe in yourself." Mother encouraged me.

"Don't give up because you think you are trapped." Dad added,

"You may be stuck in the mud now, but you will find that vine to pull yourself out. You won't sink, you will stand again."

I laughed a bit.

"You don't have to get cheesy. I got the message."

"Good." My dad chuckled,

"Now, go down there and make us proud."

I smiled at them both.

"I love you guys."

"We love you too." Mother responded,

"Now go!"

I woke up to hearing the morning buzzer. What just happened? Was that dream even real? I knew today would be the day I was to be put to death. I looked at Joseph, who stretched.

Should I tell him?

No. I wouldn't want him or my siblings to worry.

A guard opened the door.

"Alright everyone, on your feet! Let's go!"

Everyone got up. The buzzer sounded through the room again.

"PUSH-UPS." It said.

Everyone groaned and got on the ground. Finn started his pushups next to me.

"Something's wrong...I can tell. What is it, Victoria?" He asked me under his breath.

I pushed myself to do three push-ups so far. My brother knew everything about me. We always told each other stuff before I met Joseph. Sammy could not always know because she was considered the baby of the family.

I looked my brother in the eyes as we did our workout.

"Doctor Kinderman...she... she is putting me to death tonight."

The look on my brother's face could not be described as anything but horror.

"What?" He whispered.

"Victoria." I turned my head to see Joseph had heard,

"What the hell did you just say?"

I sighed.

"Guys...Doctor Kinderman is gonna kill me tonight."

"How do you know?" Joseph asked me angrily.

"She told me." I replied calmly.

"We won't let her lay a finger on you." Finn promised me.

"Guys, you can't do anything. This is my last day to live and I wanna remember it as a good day." I told them.

"Don't be stupid." My husband spat.

"Yeah, we ain't gonna let you die." Finn echoed.

Joseph kept his eyes straight ahead.

"How long do you have?" He whispered.

I jumped to my feet.

"Six to seven hours probably."

"That's how long we have to plan on saving you." Joseph directed this comment at Finn.

I shook my head,

"It's too risky."

Joseph kissed my head.

"Risky is our middle name." He said gently.

Nemo grumbled as he got to his feet as well.

"I'm tired, daddy." He said to Finn.

"I know, buddy. It will be rest time soon." He reassured him.

The door opened.

"Patient 606 and 607, you are wanted in the hall, please." A guard announced.

All the prisoners looked around. Finn and I stared at each other. That was us. We hurried out into the hall and the guard shut the door. Finn and I waited for the guard to speak, but he did not.

He jerked his head and we followed him.

"What's going on?" Finn demanded.

The guard huffed.

"Your sister Sammy wants to see you." He said lazily.

My heart burst with joy.

"Really? How is she?" I exclaimed.

The guard did not respond; he kept walking forward.

I wanted to ask a million questions. I had been so worried about my little sister. I knew Finn felt the same way.

"Why are you gov's letting us see her now?" Finn asked suspiciously.

The guard finally turned around to look us straight in the eyes.

"Because she's dying." He almost whispered.

I stood in my tracks. I could not even look to see Finn's reaction. My whole world crashed before my feet. My death would not even matter now. I could not even burst into tears. Did I hear him right? Did he say my sister was going to die? Sammy? The little, innocent girl who got her life ruined because of a mistake that had not been her fault?

Sammy, the girl we dragged along on all our journeys? She couldn't be dying! Finn and I solemnly followed the guard the rest of the way until we made it to the room where Sammy lay in her bed.

The sight of her filled my eyes with tears. Her entire body was pale like white frosting on a cake. Her thickly framed glasses had been removed and her wide blue eyes looked almost lifeless. She looked like a total stranger.

Finn and I quietly approached her. She smiled through her cracked lips.

"Hi, guys." She croaked.

The scars from the alpha Howler formed dark purple stripes all over her skin where they patched her up.

Finn and I said nothing. Our throats swelled like a tight knot. Sammy could tell. Sammy knew us very well.

"The doctors are letting me be alone with you for a few minutes." She told us in a choppy voice,

"I really missed you."

I forced myself to speak.

"We missed you, too."

I sat with her at the edge of her bed. Finn stayed put. Sammy locked eyes with me. I always loved her huge blue eyes. They were so beautiful.

"I know what's gonna happen with you tonight." She said to me.

"I won't allow it, either. Victoria, you cannot allow yourself to die."

I became defensive.

"Oh, but you can?" I cried.

"Victoria...I am sorry. I tried." Sammy apologized,

"I tried."

I began to sob a little.

"I know." I whimpered.

Finn still said nothing. All he did was stand there. Why was he just standing there? Sammy took my hand. Her cold skin touched the warmth of mine. Almost like fire and ice.

"Survive, Victoria." She whispered to me,

"You and Finn gotta go on."

Finn slowly walked forward and sat on the bed.

"We will, Sammy." He promised before I could say anything,

"I swear to you, we will."

There had been a silence that came after that. Sammy stared up at the ceiling.

"What do you think it's like up there?" She asked suddenly.

I wrapped my arm around her.

"I'm sure it's wonderful."

I couldn't take my eyes off all the scars. Anybody could tell that she was in horrible pain.

"Does it hurt?" I asked mildly.

"Yes." Sammy breathed.

I glanced at Finn who was taking short breaths to contain his weeping.

"Victoria." Sammy could hardly gasp,

"Hold me."

Tears squeezed from my cheeks as I took my only sister into my arms, holding her frail body tightly. Sammy inhaled and exhaled quickly. We sat with her for an hour. Guards and doctors checked on us every so often.

Sammy suddenly sat up in alarm,

"Victoria! I can't breathe!" She gasped.

I held her as she kicked and coughed for air. Finn took her hand, holding it and shaking horribly.

"I can't breathe!" She repeated, dazing at the ceiling.

"Go to the light!" I urged her;

"Go to the light, Sammy!"

Sammy coughed and hiccupped for any source of breath.

"It hurts!" She cried hoarsely.

"Sammy! Go to the light!"

Sammy sucked in as much air as she could for what seemed to be forever. She finally stopped, her eyes became wide and a smile edged across her lips.

"I..." a small laugh of joy escaped from her,

"I see it! I see a light!" She cried.

I closed my eyes and sniffled. Finn's face was red, and tears escaped his eyes. Sammy had a single tear roll down her cheek.

"Victoria...Finn...I can see mom and dad."

She closed her eyes after that. She did not open them again. Sammy Hartley had died. I let out a horrified breath.

"She's gone." I whimpered,

"Oh, Sammy."

Finn kissed our dead sister's hand as some people entered the room. I began to sob over her.

"Oh God, why?" I cried.

"Come on now." One guard brought Finn out of the room.

Finn did not even fight back. I did, on the other hand. Some man lightly took my arm and I screamed bloody murder. I tried gripping onto Sammy, but the stupid guard pried my hands off. He carried me over his shoulder while I kicked and screamed like a two-year-old.

—

Finn and I entered the room where all the prisoners were. My eyes locked with Joseph's, and he knew what happened.

I let out a sob and ran into his arms. We embraced each other in tears and sadness for what seemed to be an eternity.

—

I stood before all the prisoners. It was supposed to be rest time, but I had to say something for my sister. I had to speak for Sammy since we couldn't attend a funeral or anything. I folded my hands and took a breath;

"I am Victoria Hartley. Some of you know me as Patient 606. I am the sister of the fugitive that died today..."

I took a few steps forward;

"I watched my parents die, and now I had to watch my sister die."

The room stayed dead silent. My lips tightened.

"She did not deserve to die in vain! The Howlers that the government created are responsible for her death! Those gov's created those animals... they-" My throat swelled in hate and tears,

"Those beasts murdered Sammy!"

Commotion broke out between all the prisoners; however, Finn remained silent. I began to feel the burn of the fire that sparked in my heart.

"Are we gonna let the government kill us off like we are cockroaches in the sun?!" I shouted.

"No!" A few prisoners yelled.

Their enthusiasm was not good enough.

"*Will we allow them to end our lives*?!" I screamed with all my might.

"No!" More people joined in.

"*Can we fight for our lives or not*?!" I raised my fist in the air.

When I did, I felt Sammy's spirit among us, she cheered us on. She wanted us to fight for our freedom.

"*Yes!*" People's voices echoed throughout the room.

We chanted the words "we will fight!" over and over until our throats became scratchy.

Guards busted into the room with guns in their hands.

"Alright, that's enough!" They ordered.

Some screams filled the room when they saw the guns. I hurried forward, staring at them with wide eyes. One guard turned to me.

"Patient 606 come with us."

I stood before the men that would take me away. My time had come. Joseph ran for me.

"You will not take my wife!" He screeched at the guards.

I laid a hand tenderly on his cheek,

"Joseph Stonewall. My time to die is now. I ain't sad or scared. You have to go on."

I gave him a willful look.

"Do it for me."

I moved onto Finn and grasped his shoulders.

"Take care of Nemo." I ordered,

"Take care of yourself. I love you."

Before I could bid farewell to little Nemo, Finn grabbed my arm.

"Victoria." He said with clenched teeth,

"I will never be hungry for power or money again. I promise I will survive and focus on what matters most: my family."

At that moment, I looked at my brother differently. I was proud of him. My brother had changed into a better young man.

"I'm so glad to hear that, Finn." I told him, my eyes sparkling with tears.

I moved on to Nemo, his small face became red and he threw his arms around my neck.

"I love you, Aunt Victoria." He peeped.

I kissed his squishy cheek, wetted by salty tears.

"I love you too, Nehemiah Rigby Hartley. Take care of your daddy." I told him gently.

Finn picked up his son, kissing his hair. Three of the closest people in my life all gave me a nod. I then turned to the guards, bitterly following them. My dramatic act had worked. When the guards weren't looking, I quick turned back to Finn, Joseph, and Nemo.

I winked.

They all winked back and smiled. Did you think I was gonna just lay down and die? No. I wouldn't. I am Patient 606. I am a survivor.

I kept my head up high while I walked with the guards. No one would cause me to bow my head in shame and fear again. I thought of Nemo, such a blessed little boy. I thought of Joseph Stonewall, a man that had once been evil but became a better man and my husband. I thought of Finn. He was my little brother and always a money-loving, car-obsessed fool with no brain for what really mattered until today. He became a much better person. Lastly, I thought of Sammy. Quiet and shy at first, but after this adventure, she turned into a brave, headstrong girl with so much fight all of Troy would lose a battle to her.

I entered the room where I would be put to death. Doctor Kinderman awaited me there.

"Hello, Patient 606." Doctor Kinderman greeted me.

I opened my mouth in a wide smile.

"Hello, Doctor Kinderman." I replied nicely while I sat in the chair.

Doctor Kinderman cocked an eyebrow with curiosity.

"How are you feeling?" She asked.

I rolled up my sleeves.

"Ready to get this over with." I replied.

I heard a loud bang outside. Doctor Kinderman looked up in alarm. I side smiled. Finn and Joseph were coming for my rescue. She looked at me with wide eyes.

"What did you do?" She demanded.

I shrugged casually.

"Nothing." I answered plainly,

"The real question is what did you do? Locking us all in here like we were animals? Why?"

Doctor Kinderman got out a shot with a long needle.

"To dispose of people like you." She answered darkly.

My eyes widened in a small amount of fear. I blinked once before a bullet whizzed through the window, breaking the glass and hitting Doctor Kinderman right between the eyes. She fell to the ground. One second, she was alive, one second, she was dead.

The man who shot her was Joseph. He and Finn entered the room. I saw the gun in my husband's hand.

That sly man must have fought a guard off to get to it. Finn held onto Nemo, who hid his face. I stood there, marveling at how well we knocked this place down. More sounds of yells and victory shouts sounded throughout the halls. Outlaws were escaping.

Joseph shrugged with a laugh.

"Ready to go?" He asked with determination.

I faced them with the same answer I had given Sammy and Finn long ago when we escaped Black Gates:

"Let's get outta here."

Made in the USA
Monee, IL
25 October 2023

45154525R00171